RIP TIDE

KAT FALLS

SCHOLASTIC INC.
NEW YORK TORONTO LONDON AUCKLAND
SYDNEY MEXICO CITY NEW DELHI HONG KONG

ISBN 978-0-545-43175-0

Copyright © 2011 by Kat Falls. All rights reserved. Published by Scholastic Inc. SCHOLASTIC and associated logos are trademarks and/or registered trademarks of Scholastic Inc.

12 11 10 9 8 7 6 5 4 3 2 1   12 13 14 15 16 17/0

Printed in the U.S.A.   40

First Scholastic paperback printing, January 2012

The text type was set in Sabon.

Book design by Christopher Stengel

To my dear friend Merle,
for turning her home into
a writer's getaway. And
to my family, for being so
understanding and supportive
while I got away.

Easing back on the throttle, I slowed the submarine's speed. The light-streaked ocean around us seemed vast and empty, but I knew better. We were heading into the biggest trash vortex in the Atlantic. A piece of history could broadside us at any time.

Sure enough, a shape swirled out of the darkness, glimmering in the sub's head beams. Gemma leaned into the viewport. "A bicycle," she said with amazement. "Just like in old photos."

"That means we're almost there," I told her.

"We're hiding a wagon full of crops in the open ocean?"

"In the middle of the trash gyre," I explained. "Genius, right?" I checked the rear monitor to make sure the sealed wagon was still hitched to the back of our sub. "No one ever comes in here."

She shot me a knowing look. "For good reason, I'll bet."

"Divers worry about getting crushed—"

"Do they?" she asked, a smile hovering on her lips.

"—but I've explored the vortex plenty and I'm still alive."

"Ty, please don't take this the wrong way. . . ." Flipping back her long hair, she tugged a life preserver out from under her seat.

While she fastened the vest, I tilted the cruiser into a steep descent. With its barrel-shaped body mounted on twin thermal engines, the sub had enough heft to plow through the floating debris. I, however, was not so hardy; the sight of so much trash always hollowed out my gut.

At fifty feet down, it was just small objects gliding by—a headless doll, plastic bags, soda cans, and fishermen's nets. Though abandoned, the nets were as effective as ever at trapping creatures, and I had to look away when we passed a tangled dolphin, long drowned. We pushed deeper, and larger items tumbled by—a TV trailing wires, a mannequin, a sparkling chandelier—as if caught in a slow underwater hurricane. It seemed like all the junk from past centuries had found its way here, to drift in an enormous circle forever.

"Where did this stuff come from?" Gemma shifted onto her knees to look up through the sub's flexiglass canopy.

"Winds and currents picked it up from all over the Atlantic." I swerved to avoid hitting a stroller.

Flipping on the exterior spotlight, I moved the beam across the drifting objects, not knowing what many were. A powerful upwelling kept them afloat while wreckfish, longer than me, lurked in the nooks, with their lower jaws thrust out as if anticipating a fight.

When the gyre's rotation slowed to a standstill, I knew that we'd reached the center. Here, the debris simply turned in place.

"This is probably a stupid question," Gemma said, shifting her gaze to me, "but if we leave the wagon here, what's to stop it from floating away?"

"I'm going to hitch it on to something big."

"Okay. What's to stop both things from floating away?"

"We're in the eye of the vortex. None of this scrap is going anywhere. Besides, I'll be back at dawn to get it. Pa didn't want the wagon to sit in the field overnight, all loaded up, looking like easy pickings. Just 'cause we're the only settlers willing to sell to the surfs doesn't mean we trust them."

"Still, I can't hear your father saying, 'Go hide the wagon in the *giant trash vortex*.'"

"He doesn't care where I stash it as long as it's safe."

She smiled. "Uh-huh."

"Now, that's an anchor." Dead ahead, a fragment of an airplane pivoted on end with all the speed of a starfish.

Flipping the sub into idle, I grabbed my helmet from the seat behind me.

Gemma's blue eyes widened. "You're not going out there?"

"How else am I going to hitch the wagon on to that chunk of aluminum?"

"With those pincher-arm things."

"That'll take forever." I headed down the aisle between the seats.

"You said that sea creatures have been migrating everywhere. If ocean currents carried all this trash here, then something could have hitched a ride."

She was right, of course. Fishermen were constantly pulling marine life out of the Atlantic that used to live only in the Pacific or off the coast of Australia. So much land had flooded during the Rising that new channels had formed between the oceans.

"I'll be fine," I said, hoping it was true. Biting down on a tube in the base of my helmet, I inhaled a lungful of oxygen-infused liquid and then dropped out of the hatch in the cruiser's floor.

"You better be," she said through the receiver in my helmet. "Because if I have to come out there to rescue you, it's going to ruin my day."

That was putting it mildly. She hadn't dipped so much as a toe into the ocean in over a month. A fact that pained me. But she'd agreed to come out in the cruiser today —

4

for the first time in weeks—so maybe someday she would try diving again.

I shot her a thumbs-up since I couldn't talk with Liquigen in my lungs. With three kicks, I was at the cruiser's stern, though the upwelling was so strong that it took effort to stay level. After attaching the wagon's line to my dive belt, I stroked toward the piece of algae-covered airplane, only to stop short as dozens of large shadows streaked past me. Using my Dark Gift, I shot sonar at them and saw in my mind that they were piked dogfish—sharks, yes, but not a threat to humans. Still, I didn't like the frenzied way they were swimming—as if fleeing.

I sent a series of clicks into the black depths. Tense seconds went by, and when the echo finally bounced back, the mental image was too cluttered to be of use. Far below lay a graveyard of derelict vessels that had been swept there by the currents. Within the pileup were cavities and crannies galore, which meant that *anything* could be lurking down there, hidden from my view—Dark Gift or not. A chilling thought.

Still, I was glad for my biosonar. So what if Topside doctors attributed subsea kids' Dark Gifts to intense water pressure messing with our brains? I felt fine. Healthy. And was relieved that my parents had stopped worrying so much about me. Of course, it had only been four months since they'd learned that Dark Gifts weren't a myth. And that both of their children had one.

Since I couldn't get a read on the mountain of wreckage below, I turned my attention back to finding a place to hitch the wagon. I'd spotted a pair of portholes that would work when Gemma's shout filled my helmet. I spun toward the cruiser. Then my brain caught up with my retinas, and I realized that I had glimpsed a huge shape hanging motionless beside me.

With a half turn, I found myself facing an enormous squid. Floating upright, it stood at least six feet tall, its purplish red body so thick I couldn't have put my arms around it if I'd wanted to. The squid hovered, watching me. When its skin flashed to neon white and then blood-red, a name came to me—*diablo rojo*. Red devil. A creature with a reputation even more terrifying than its looks.

Edging back, I tried to suppress all the stories of these particular squid dragging swimmers into the depths and eating them alive. Not tall tales, but real accounts with witnesses. Of all the predators of the deep, squid got my heart pounding like nothing else. Sharks were fearsome, but just beasts. Whereas, in this creature's eyes I saw an intelligence that scared me to the core.

Again its skin rippled from luminous white to dark red, and I knew that couldn't be good. No doubt the squid was trying to confuse its prey. Me.

CHAPTER
TWO

Escaping the diablo rojo would be impossible with the wagon's towline attached to my belt. Slowly, I reached for the clip, but that triggered a reaction. Flinging out a tentacle, the squid walloped me across the shoulders with such force, my head snapped back.

Stunned, I straightened to see the creature flip itself horizontal with all eight tentacles and both feeder arms extended forward—pointing at me. I thrashed away, but the squid jetted in so fast I didn't have time to escape. It slammed into my chest and sent me flying, but not out of reach.

Forcing my eyes open, I found myself enveloped within the umbrella of the creature's body. I tried to unholster my dive knife, but the squid had my arms pinned to my sides. Tightening its grip, it pulled me against its razor-sharp beak and tried to crack open my helmet like it was a tuna's skull. Thankfully the flexiglass held.

Gemma yelled something in my ear, but all I could focus on was the squid's spike-covered tongue, inches from my eyes. I struggled to get free but the suckers on the squid's tentacles were lined with tiny teeth. Like thorns, they dug into my diveskin — probably not ripping through its iron nanoparticle coating, but even a snag could foul up the computer sensors that were woven between the layers. If that happened, I'd end up with a lot worse than torn skin. At this depth, I'd freeze.

The thought electrified me. I forced my knife upward, despite the squid's stranglehold of a hug, and jabbed blindly. A ribbon of blue blood drifted up. At most I'd nicked a tentacle, but it was enough to send the squid flapping into the depths, carried away by its head fins.

Slumping, I glanced at the cruiser and saw Gemma's stark face pressed to the viewport. The whole attack had lasted less than a minute. She hadn't had time to react.

"What was that thing?" she shrieked in my ear. Probably had been the whole time, but now her voice penetrated my consciousness. "I told you to use the pincher-arm things. But no. You have to swim with monsters." She sounded terrified and furious all at once.

I waved to let her know I was okay, though I wasn't going to reholster my knife anytime soon.

"Great. So glad you're fine," she snapped. "Now get back in the sub."

I held up a finger and sent a series of clicks into the depths. But with so much piled wreckage below me, it was impossible to tell where the squid had gone. Moving quickly, I looped the wagon's towline through the plane's empty portholes and fastened the clip.

Had my shine attracted the squid? I wondered.

Having faintly glowing skin could sometimes be a liability subsea. Yet most of the Benthic Territory settlers ate bioluminescent fish, and so we were all luminous to some degree. But I hadn't immigrated to the deep like most settlers. I'd spent my whole life in the ocean, so my shine was a little brighter than the average.

"Can you please hurry—" Gemma's words cut off on a gasp. "On the sonar screen. Something is rising fast."

I flipped around, knife up, figuring the squid was back. But it was worse than that. One series of sonar clicks told me the creature wasn't alone. Something I should have seen coming, since I knew that red devils were the only squid to hunt as a pack.

I kicked for the cruiser as they shot out of the deep—three of them, equally huge. They slowed to hover between the sub and me with their skin rippling from white to red then back again, which now I knew for sure was pre-attack behavior.

"Ty, hide!" Gemma shouted as she plowed the cruiser into the squid from behind. Instead of scattering, they whipped around to attack the sub.

"Oh!" she cried with disgust. "Get off, you slimy freaks." She banged on the viewport and then turned on the wipers.

Knowing she'd be fine, I grabbed the moment to dart inside the hunk of airplane.

"Hey, can these things climb through the hatch?" Gemma demanded suddenly. "They can, can't they? I'm shutting the hatch."

I stayed put, and a moment later she returned to the microphone. "Okay, they took off. They're mugging some poor fish."

As she said it, I peered through the porthole and saw the squid in the distance, dragging a thrashing tarpon into the depths. Over eight feet long, it should keep them busy for a while. At least, I hoped so. Just then, the ocean filled with what sounded like dozens of diveskins being torn open simultaneously, followed by brutal chops. I shivered, knowing the bone and tissue being ripped apart could have been mine.

"Ty, where are you?" Gemma asked.

Unable to reply because of the Liquigen in my lungs, I started to swim out from under the airplane fragment, but then noticed a thick chain nearby, descending into the depths. I ducked out the opposite side instead, only to freeze at the sight before me.

Seemed I wasn't the only one who thought the trash gyre made a good hiding spot.

"Come out," Gemma demanded through the speaker in my helmet. "I can't see you."

I rounded the chunk of plane and beckoned her forward, indicating with my arms that she had plenty of room. Her exasperated sigh filled my helmet, but she put the cruiser in gear.

After checking with my sonar that the squid really had taken off, I turned back to the thing anchored nearby — a shaggy seamount, floating in the still, dark water. An illusion, of course, since seamounts don't float. But the structure before me was so enormous, I couldn't capture its shape with my sonar. I kicked in for a closer look, feeling like a minnow next to it.

"What is *that*?"

Even through the crackly receiver, I could hear the awe in Gemma's voice.

I spelled out the letters slowly since sign language was still new to her: *township*.

At least that was my best guess. Rounded and several stories high, it was definitely big enough to provide living quarters for four to five hundred people as well as the other facilities a community needed — filtration tanks for fresh water, kitchens and food storage, oxygen and heat generators. And the vessel sure was old and dinged up like every township I'd ever seen.

"A wreck?" she asked.

I shrugged. Seemed like the reasonable explanation.

Why else would it be submerged in the trash gyre? Townships could travel subsea, but from what I knew, most stayed on the ocean's surface with their roofs retracted—fully or partially, depending on the shape of the vessel. So, yes, this probably was a wreck. But what a waste, sinking it here, when it could have been sold off for parts.

I didn't see any glowing viewports or movement or any other signs of life on the inside, though the outside teemed with it. In fact, the exterior had its own mini-ecosystem going on. Barnacles encrusted the vertical windows; crabs frittered through the mangy seaweed that had started to sprout on the side panels; clouds of fish hovered all around.

Using my dive knife, I scraped away the algae on one window but could only see my own glowing reflection. Tapping on the wrist screen built into my diveskin, I intensified my helmet's crown lights. After focusing them into one beam, I aimed it through the window, only to jerk back in surprise. A teenage boy lay slumped against the sill, with a blanket draped over his shoulders. His head rested on the crook of his arm as if he'd fallen asleep while peering outside.

If he lived on a township, he was a surf—short for "surfeit population." I couldn't remember seeing one like him, with his shaved head and the geometric tattoos edging his face. But then, I'd never gotten such a close view of a surf before.

"What is it?" Gemma asked. "What do you see?"

I motioned for her to wait, then banged against the flexiglass with the butt of my knife. The kid didn't wake up. Didn't even twitch.

Unease rolled through me like cold fog as I treaded water in front of the window. Nothing indicated the township's engines were working. No hum of a turbine. No lights. No streams of bubbles. That meant no oxygen. No heat.

I shivered with the realization that I'd just tried to wake a corpse. Making it eerier, the boy looked to be exactly my age. Fifteen.

"Is there someone dead in there?" Gemma asked suddenly. "That's what you're looking at, isn't it? A dead person?"

When I nodded, she jammed the cruiser into reverse and backed up a boat's length.

Still, I hovered with my chest aching as though I'd inhaled too much Liquigen. Whoever he was, he could have been dead for a while. Maybe even years. He was so perfectly preserved, who could tell? The lack of air and frigid water temperature had to have turned the township into one giant walk-in freezer.

"Ty," Gemma's voice said softly inside my ear. "Come back. We'll radio for help."

Sounded good to me. I sure wasn't itching to go poking around a ghost town, but a single thought kept me from stroking away. What if someone inside was still alive and needed help?

Doubtful, yes, considering that seaweed had put down roots on the exterior. But a stationary township wasn't necessarily a broken one. What if this township had been sitting here awhile but the engines had conked out only days ago? I had to check for survivors, no matter how unsettling the thought was.

I motioned to Gemma that I was heading inside. When she said, "Be careful," I realized part of me had been hoping she'd talk me out of it.

Dropping under the immense structure gave me the uneasy sense of swimming beneath an island. The bottom was flat, so finding the entry port was easy enough. But one glance told me where the problem lay.

I swam out and circled the township's perimeter. But with each hatch that I passed my stroke slowed. By the time I made it all the way around, my arms felt too heavy to lift—not because I was tired but because of what I'd seen.

Every single hatch door had been chained shut . . . from the outside.

THREE

"Are you sure we shouldn't wait for your parents to get here?" Gemma asked as I used the cruiser's extendable metal clippers to cut through the township's anchor chains.

"Why?" I replied. "I'm doing exactly what they'd do."

I shattered the last link, and as the final chain fell away, the township pulled free and began a lazy ascent to the surface. "I could tell it was built to float," I explained. "The hydro-turbines under the ship are just for propulsion."

We watched the township's progress as it knocked into debris. Satisfied that nothing would stop its rise completely, I zoomed the cruiser toward the surface, passing the township, to crash through the waves.

The setting sun cast a pink glow over the wide-open expanse of ocean. There wasn't a hint of land or a ship in sight. When Gemma threw open the hatch in the sub's canopy roof, I braced myself for the blast of hot air. She hopped right out and slid down the hull onto one of the narrow runners along the cockpit.

I stayed put, needing longer to adjust. Even at this late hour, the light seared into me while the heat boiled my body into overcooked seaweed. Whenever I surfaced, all I could think about was diving back into the ocean. But after another deep breath, I forced myself up and out of the hatch.

Gemma leaned back on the sub's canopy, one leg bent. She'd put on a diveskin to come out with me, even though she had no intention of getting in the water. With all the time she'd been spending at the Trade Station lately, her face had a permanent flush and her long brown hair was streakier than ever. The effects of UV exposure looked pretty on her, but I shifted my gaze to the patch of churning water where the township would surface. I knew that living subsea didn't come naturally to some people. They couldn't get past their terror of drowning or the wildlife or the black depths. I wasn't sure which fear ended up being too much for Gemma after just three months of living with us. All she would say was that the ocean scared her and that she missed the sunlight and air. Still, I kept hoping that she'd give living subsea another chance.

Gulls screeched overhead and waves smacked against the hull, but we remained silent as the township emerged from the ocean, growing wider as it rose.

"It's a spiral," she said finally.

"A nautilus," I agreed, spotting the pattern under the barnacles. "The windows are the stripes of the shell. The flexiglass dome in front"—I pointed to the sloping section that ended in a point—"makes up the tentacles."

"How do you see tentacles?"

"They're bunched together." I dropped back into the pilot seat. "Ready?"

Her nod was hesitant at best, but I went ahead and steered the cruiser alongside the township's bumper. Then I turned on the autopilot and climbed out of the sub. The computer would keep her alongside the township. "I'm just going in for a moment. And I won't touch anything. The Seaguard will want to see it as is."

Gemma nodded. "I'll help you open the hatch."

It didn't take long to cut through the chain that was strung from the wheel to a handgrip on the hull. But as I pulled open the hatch, I had the distinct feeling we were opening a tomb. Cold air hissed out of the air lock. Under other circumstances, I'd have welcomed the relief from the heat, but this chill settled into my gut. With one breath, I knew the oxygen was thin. Rather than risk getting dizzy, I inhaled Liquigen into my lungs.

Gemma scrambled back, her face pale under her freckles. "You're sure about this?"

With a nod, I ventured into the air lock.

"I'll be right here, guarding the cruiser," she called after me.

The rear door of the air lock stood ajar, and I stepped through to find myself in a big open area. Probably the town square. With the algae and sea life coating the flexidome, the sunlight that filtered through had a greenish tinge, which gave the space an eerie feel. Or maybe the twitchy sensation inside me wasn't caused by the dim light, but by the sight of people curled up on the floor and bundled in blankets. I was glad for the Liquigen in my lungs that kept me from calling out "hello," knowing that the reply would be icy silence.

Moving closer, I saw that under the blankets, they were wearing life preservers—had been waiting for a rescue that never came. I swallowed, trying to lose the feeling of something wedged in my windpipe, and turned away, wanting to leave before I got a look at any one person. I didn't want to see that some were little kids, even though the logical part of my brain already knew it.

Shifting my gaze upward, I noticed that the flexidome folded down in layers, like a series of tentacles, which would open the town square to the sky. Not that the control panel would be working.

Careful to disturb nothing, I circled to the shallow pool that dominated the middle of the square. There was no water in it, only gleaming white crystals that encrusted the sides and bottom. Too chunky to be ice. I broke off a single crystal and tasted it. Salt.

A narrow channel fed into the pool, which I followed to where it spiraled up the township's center, running alongside curving stairs. Most of the doors to the living quarters on the next level stood open, but I didn't climb the staircase. I didn't need to look further. No one could have survived the deep freeze that had gripped this town and choked the life out of it.

I made my way back to the town square and found Gemma studying the empty pool in the center. She met my eyes. "No one?"

With both of the air lock's hatches open, enough oxygen must have seeped in from outside. I inhaled to make the Liquigen in my lungs evaporate. "I don't think so."

She shivered slightly. After a moment she bent and touched the crystals in the pool. She seemed surprised at how easily a chunk broke off in her hand. When she held it up to catch the light, I realized the crystal reminded me of the shapes tattooed on the dead boy's face.

"What is it?" Gemma asked.

"Nomad was a salt farm." *The thin air must be dulling my senses,* I thought. Instead of horror or outrage, I felt only a creeping numbness.

"Nomad?"

I pointed to the word painted above the square. "The township's name."

"Why would someone do this to them?"

I shook my head, having no answer as to why. Nor did I have one for the question that had floated through my mind ever since seeing the chains across the hatches: *Who* would do it?

*   *   *

Within an hour, Pa, Ma, and I and a few of our neighbors had managed to tow the township to the Trade Station. We left it bobbing next to the Surface Deck, which was an enormous two-level ring floating on top of the ocean. The lower station lay hidden one hundred feet subsea, with an elevator cable connecting the two.

Given the late hour, the Surface Deck was deserted. The fish market that circled the promenade, fifteen feet above the waves, had closed hours ago. And only a few boats were hitched to the docking-ring at water level, illuminated by the lights of the promenade above.

"Heck of a find," Raj said as he stood back, eyeing the township. Broad, bearded, and loud, he came off more like an outlaw than a pioneer. "Them being all dead"—he waved his seaweed cigar—"makes it your salvage, no debate."

"Wonder why I'm not throwing a party?" I replied as I waited for Pa and Lars. They were inside, trying to figure out what had gone wrong with Nomad's engines.

"'Cause you're not counting up the subload of money you'll make," Raj said. As if I'd missed his point.

"It's a chum deal for them, all right," Jibby acknowledged, tipping his shaggy blond head toward the township. "But you do stand to make a small fortune off this."

"Gemma and I found it together," I corrected, since she'd ducked into the lounge to shed her diveskin the moment we'd docked.

"Even if the engines are fried, you can bust up this sucker and sell it for parts," Jibby went on, ignoring my mention of Gemma. At twenty-three, he was too old for her—at least as far as I was concerned. She was only fifteen. But she was also the only girl in Benthic Territory anywhere near his age, and a pretty one at that, so Jibby had already proposed marriage twice. And though he'd been turned down both times, he wasn't about to give up hope, which I found both funny and annoying.

Soon enough, Pa and Lars stumbled out of the township. Lars was big and pale on any given day, but now he'd out-blanch a spookfish as he leaned against the ladder that led up to the promenade. Slamming the hatch closed, Pa wedged a crowbar into the handle as extra measure. Then he dropped to a knee at the edge of the docking-ring and splashed seawater on his face. No one spoke, letting them regain their composure.

"The engine's been disabled. Definitely sabotage," Pa said in a hoarse voice. "But it looks like they got a backup generator going for a while at least. It put out enough power to get the blowers running, but not the heat. Those poor surfs died of hypothermia long before their air gave out."

"Most of the equipment is close to fifty years old," Lars added, still leaning against the ladder. "They were lucky to get the backup generator running at all."

"Not lucky enough," I muttered.

"They probably hoped someone would find them in time," Jibby said sadly.

Lars grimaced. "But had no way to send out a distress signal."

I couldn't imagine how awful it would be, watching the people you love freeze to death.

"Who would do such a thing?" my mother asked. Arms crossed, she seemed to be holding her distress in check. "Anchor an entire township and chain the hatches?"

"No idea," Pa said. He sounded riled, which was rare for him. "But since we've got no ranger, I'm calling the Seaguard."

"Sure that's smart?" Lars pushed off from the wall, his legs steadier now. "You're meeting with the surfs from Drift tomorrow."

"What does that have to do with it?" Ma asked. "Selling our crops isn't illegal anymore."

Representative Tupper had seemed so proud of himself when he'd passed on that nugget. The Assembly had denied our bid for statehood—said Benthic Territory wasn't old enough, established enough, and didn't have enough citizens. But as a small concession, they would allow us to pay our property taxes in cash instead of produce from then on. A step forward, for sure, but the government wanted to buy our goods for next to nothing. And we discovered that selling our produce leaf by leaf, fish by fish, at the market was taking more time than any settler had to spare.

"You make this public knowledge"—Lars nodded at the derelict township—"by bringing in the Seaguard, the Drift surfs will hear about it."

"So?" I asked as Gemma slipped past Raj to stand by me. She looked every bit the Topsider in a loose-falling green caftan, cinched at her waist with a tasseled rope. Remnants from her life in a stack-city.

"What if they blame you for what happened to Nomad?" Lars demanded. "Surfs are unreasonable on a good day. Just look at 'em wrong, and they turn savage. Which is why this plan of yours, John, selling in bulk to surf townships . . . Well, you know I think you're crazy." He paused as if he still couldn't believe Pa was considering it. "I'm just saying, we should keep quiet about Nomad until after your deal is done."

"Drift's sachem isn't looking for a onetime sale," Pa said. "He wants to buy our greens every month. He's not going to fly off the handle."

"What's a sachem?" Gemma whispered to me.

"A township's leader."

"You're talking about *surfs*," Raj said, prying his seaweed cigar from his mouth. "Lars is right. Their sun-baked brains could interpret this all manners of wrong. Leaving you facing the killing end of a trident."

"Look," Pa said, "we can't depend on the Commonwealth anymore. They haven't even sent us a new ranger. And if we try to go it alone, this settlement will never be anything but an isolated backwater town. To thrive, we need to make alliances out here on the ocean. So I'm calling the Seaguard now, because if they were settlers" — he pointed at Nomad — "we wouldn't even be talking about this." With that, he headed into the lounge to make the call.

"Because settlers don't go around killing folk and turning their innards into clothes," Raj shouted after him.

Gemma's eyes grew wide. "Surfs do that?"

"No," Ma said, glaring at Raj. "It's a rumor passed on by people who should know better."

"Hey, we've all seen them in their gut-skin raincoats," he said, indicating the rest of us with a sweep of his cigar.

"Those see-through coats are made of human guts?" Jibby looked astounded. "I thought it was seal intestine."

"It is," Ma said firmly.

"How can you be sure?" Raj challenged.

Ma threw up a hand in exasperation.

"What's the big deal?" Gemma asked me once the adults had dispersed. "So you're selling some seaweed to a township."

"It's a first. That makes people nervous. Well, that and the fact the surfs raid each other and floaters for stuff like freshwater. And they've been known to set sickly babies and old people adrift."

"And you want to be friends with them?"

" 'Friends' would be overstating it. We just want to do business."

As I faced the lounge and she the ocean, I noticed that in the moonlight her freckled skin was glowing softly. She'd told me that she wanted a shine like mine, and she'd certainly eaten a lot of bioluminescent fish in the three months that she'd lived with us. But it usually took a new settler at least a year before his skin started to reflect his diet. Yet hers was luminous tonight.

"Are you getting a shine?" I asked, smashing down the impulse to touch her cheek.

"What? I don't think—Ty, look at the water!"

Turning, I saw the adults had stopped in their tracks to stare at the ocean. With good reason—the water around Nomad was glowing with white light. The eerie light's reflection had given Gemma's skin the look of a shine.

She stumbled back. "It's them, isn't it?"

"Who?"

She pointed at the derelict township, now little more than a hulking silhouette against the night sky. "The ghosts we let out," she whispered.

CHAPTER
FOUR

"There's no such thing as ghosts," I assured her.

Still Gemma stared at the phosphorescent water as if it were going to well up and suck her under. "You also said there was no such thing as Dark Gifts," she reminded me.

"Yeah, but this time I don't have anything to hide. Look at that!"

The eerie light spread across the ocean in every direction, like molten metal of the purest white, all the way to the horizon. Shaken by the sight, Gemma backed into the wall of the lounge.

"That's one heck of a big ghost," I teased.

She shot me an evil look. "Ghosts are as real as Dark Gifts. I've seen them."

"Them?" I asked with a straight face. "You mean different ghosts on different days or a whole bunch at once, darting around like a school of mackerel?"

She crossed her arms. At least she didn't look scared anymore, just annoyed.

"Okay, you've seen ghosts. Plural," I conceded as I settled on the edge of the docking-ring. "But this"—

I skimmed my dive boot across the water, producing silvery gleams and bluish spangles — "is totally natural. Sailors call it a milky sea." I glanced back and saw that she'd relaxed a smidge. "We're lucky to see it," I continued. "Doesn't happen very often."

She slipped off her sandals. "When it does happen, is there usually a ship of dead people nearby?" she asked, settling in next to me.

"Not usually," I replied, glad that her sense of humor was back.

We sat in silence for a while. Between the radiant water and soft breeze, it would have been a perfect moment to kiss her . . . if the last time hadn't gone so badly. In fact, despite what she said, I suspected that our second kiss ever had brought on her first subsea panic attack. Or at least contributed to it. We'd been preparing to drop out of the cruiser with our spearguns to hunt for dinner when I'd stopped her from putting on her helmet. It hadn't even been much of a kiss. Just a quick press of lips to gauge her reaction since I hadn't so much as hugged her since she'd moved in with us. She'd smiled afterward — had even taken my hand as we slipped into the ocean. But two minutes later, she'd turned scary pale and shoved me away. Then came the sweating and shaking, which ended with her frenzied retreat back into the sub. By the time I'd climbed in, she'd drawn herself into a tight ball, and she refused to talk the whole way back to the homestead. At first, it didn't occur to me that my kiss might have unsettled her. That qualm came later, after I'd waited for some signal from her, encouragement to try again, and it never came. Within the month, she'd moved out.

I missed having her in our house. Missed exploring the ocean together. Missed *her*. Not that I'd ever said so out loud. The thought of saying it now sent a flame up my neck and roasted my cheeks. I ducked my face before Gemma noticed. She'd been the one to point out that instead of blushing like other people, I "glow"—which was an exaggeration. My skin just brightens a little; that's all.

"Glacial," she said, admiring the water. "It's like the whole ocean has a shine."

"Yeah. It's bacteria."

She wrinkled her nose as if I'd just ruined the view.

"It's rare to see so much clumped together," I said, trying to bring back her enjoyment of it. "Takes the right mix of oily surface scum for the bacteria to grow."

"Can we just look at the pretty water without explaining it?"

I nodded, realizing that it *would* have been a good moment to tell her how much I missed her. . . . Except that now I didn't want to talk, not when I knew for sure that I'd end up saying something stupid.

I was almost grateful when Pa called me over then to help secure the township.

When we finally got Nomad tied off, my parents headed home in one sub, while I was to return in the cruiser. But I couldn't leave without saying good-bye to Gemma. I found her by the door to the lounge, which wasn't much of a lounge; really, it was just an empty locker room inside the Surface Deck.

She'd been out in the sub with me for a good portion of the day and hadn't seemed nervous at all. Okay, subs weren't the problem. Diving was. But still, I had hope. "Want to come back with me tonight?" I asked, trying to sound like it would be no big deal.

The question flustered her. "I do. Really. But it's better if I stay here."

"Why?" I asked. "Because you don't want to swim in the ocean anymore? That doesn't mean you have to stop living with us."

"Your home is *in* the ocean. Makes it kind of hard."

"And bunking under the promenade is easy?" I made no effort to hide my skepticism. "On a bench."

"Come here." She pulled me into the lounge. "I haven't slept on a bench in weeks." She lifted a chain from around her neck—one I hadn't even noticed that she was wearing. A key dangled from it, which she used to unlock a door in the back of the lounge that I'd never noticed, either. "Remember Mel, the bartender in the Saloon? She kept trying to get me to use one of the empty rooms on the Quarters Deck, where the staff lives. But that's in the lower station and, well, I'd rather stay up here. So she found me a bed and gave me the key to this. . . ." She pulled open the door as if unveiling a prize.

A storage closet. She was excited about a closet with a cot wedged inside, which took up most of the space. Her duffel bag ate up the rest.

I did remember Mel, the bartender with a shaved head. As tough as her exterior was, she'd certainly come to my defense when I'd gotten in over my head with the Seablite Gang. Of course she was looking out for Gemma now.

"I didn't show you before," she explained, "because I didn't know if I was going to stay."

"And now you know," I managed to say, though my mouth had gone dry.

"Mel said no one uses this closet. That I can consider it my space."

It didn't surprise me that Gemma seemed to relish that phrase: "my space." As an orphan, she'd grown up on the mainland as a ward of the Commonwealth in a boarding home. She'd moved constantly into whatever dormitory happened to have an empty bed, whether the other girls were her age or not. She'd never been allotted so much as a corner to call her own, never mind a whole closet.

She pointed to a small porthole that looked onto the docking-ring. "It's even got a window."

All along she'd told me that living at the Trade Station wasn't so bad. That she enjoyed working in the fish market on weekdays. Running errands for the merchants. I thought she'd been putting a good spin on it so that my parents wouldn't worry. Now I realized that I'd read her wrong. Utterly and completely wrong. She liked living in a storage closet. Liked working for the fish vendors in the scalding sun. Probably even liked being surrounded by the hordes of shoppers. Crowds didn't bother her. Not even when they were haggling and yelling and stank like hot, dead fish. She was never coming back to live with us. Not even if she completely conquered her fear of swimming in the ocean.

She watched me, surely catching every thought that passed through my head. That was another thing about her. She could read people with uncanny accuracy. A gift I didn't possess.

"Guess you have everything you need," I said.

"Not everything."

She paused, but I said nothing. What was there to say?

"I miss being a part of your family," she finished.

I nodded, not trusting my voice. She hadn't said she missed being with *me*. "You're always part of our family," I finally managed to mumble. "No matter where you bunk."

She flashed me a smile, wide and warm, but it just made me feel worse.

"Okay." I headed for the door. "I should get going."

"Ty, wait," she called after me.

But I'd already stepped out. I saw that the ocean had lost its glow, which seemed fitting. She joined me on the docking-ring.

At that moment, Jibby clambered down a ladder from the promenade. "Oh, good," he said, spotting Gemma. "I thought you'd left with John and Carolyn."

"No," she said, but didn't mention that she was living here full-time now.

"I just wondered . . ." He shot me a guilty look.

"Ask her whatever you want," I told him. "Has nothing to do with me."

Relief swept over his features, though hers seemed to tighten.

"You want to see your brother?" Jibby asked her.

Of all the things I expected him to say — including proposing marriage again — that was not one of them. Gemma looked as surprised as I felt.

"I got two tickets to the bare-knuckle boxing match

at Rip Tide tomorrow night." He held up a synthetic paper flyer. "Won them in a poker game. Then I saw who was fighting."

"Richard?" she asked in amazement.

"Yeah, well, Shade," Jibby said. Which was the name her brother went by ever since he'd become an outlaw and the leader of the notorious Seablite Gang.

"How do you know it's the same Shade?" I asked.

He waved us under one of the lights that circled the edge of the promenade. "There can't be two that look like that," he said, handing her the flyer.

Standing in the pool of light, Gemma studied the flyer and smiled. Then she showed me the drawing of the two boxers. One of the men pictured was her brother, no question. The dark-skinned, tattooed version of him anyway. What the flyer didn't mention was that Shade had a Dark Gift that let him change the color of his skin at whim like a squid.

"What's Rip Tide?" Gemma asked as she read the flyer.

"An off-coast city south of here," Jibby said. "Kinda like our Trade Station but for surfs."

"Sounds great," she said absently, her eyes on Shade's picture. "Can I keep this?"

Her apparent longing for her brother had me worried. She hadn't heard from him at all in the past four months.

Not since he took off with his gang after locking a group of us—her included—in the lower station when it disengaged from the Surface Deck and sank. To be fair, Shade hadn't known the lower station had sprung a leak. But still, trapping us subsea without vehicles or Liquigen was just another item on a long list of his dangerous activities, which included deflating our neighbors' house. Reckless, menacing, and vengeful—why would anyone miss him? But clearly, she did.

"Sure, keep it," Jibby said. "So, does that mean you want to go?" When she didn't answer him right off, he added, "We can get a note to Shade. Tell him that you're ringside."

Since she'd lit up at the mention of her brother, I didn't understand her hesitation. Then I noticed her gaze had drifted to me. Did she think I'd judge her for wanting to see Shade? Just because I didn't like him or his gang didn't mean —

"I'd love to, Jibby," she said abruptly. "I do want to see Richard. Shade," she corrected.

I headed for the cruiser, desperate to submerge and let the ocean close over me. As I unhitched the tether line, they made their plans. A minute later Jibby strode toward his sub, and I couldn't help but notice the extra bounce in his step.

Gemma joined me by the hitching post. It was time to say good night, but the thought of leaving her here all alone stung like a cut rinsed in salt water. "Are you sure you don't want to come back with me for the night? Zoe misses you more than you can imagine."

When she hesitated, I saw my chance and grabbed it. I pointed at the derelict township that banged against the docking-ring with every swell. "It's just that I worry about you, sleeping here, with a ghost town hitched right outside your window. . . ."

FIVE

"Lots of people have bad diving experiences," I said as we zoomed toward the shimmering bubble fence that surrounded my family's ocean-floor homestead. "But then they try again and—"

"I did try again," Gemma said. "And again. Anyway, it's not about one bad experience."

The cruiser hit the dense stream of bubbles and burst into the pale golden light on the other side. The boundary lamps around our property had begun to dim to simulate nightfall.

"Then what is it?" I couldn't shake the feeling that there was something she wasn't telling me. I steered the cruiser toward my house, which floated like an enormous jellyfish over our fields of seaweed and kelp.

"I just . . ." She lifted a hand and dropped it as if words were useless—as if I'd never understand. "The ocean is filled with terrifying things," she said finally.

"Like red devil squid."

If I'd just stayed in the sub today, she wouldn't have

seen them and wouldn't have had another "terrifying thing" to add to her list. And to tell her the ocean was safe would be like asking her to believe in mermaids. The ocean was a wilderness filled with beasts that viewed man as prey and plenty of creatures that could kill a human with a single bite, prick, or sting.

"Squid qualify," she agreed with a shiver. "But they're not the worst."

I nodded, knowing that she was afraid of being eaten by a shark, even though I'd assured her that it didn't happen very often. She'd said that my response was "less than comforting."

"But all of this . . ." she said, gazing at the acres of green and the schooling fish, whirling like jewel-colored cyclones or gliding in coordinated precision. "I miss being here."

Good, I thought.

As pleased as I was that Gemma had agreed to come home with me for the night, it wasn't like I got much out of the deal. We spent the evening playing cards with my parents and my nine-year-old sister, Zoe. I figured that was more than enough time spent in our "quality-time room," as Gemma loved to call the living room. But then Gemma had to help Zoe feed her pets, which took awhile because my sister's room was crammed with dozens of aquariums filled to the rims with sea life. When Ma started braiding Gemma's hair in some intricate style as Pa read aloud to Zoe, I gave up hope of getting any time alone with her.

I retreated to my bedroom, wishing my parents would disappear for a while. Take a trip to the Topside. Something. But Gemma popped in my room soon enough.

"Polishing your treasure, Captain Bluebeard?"

Embarrassed, I put the cutlass I had been restoring back on its shelf alongside the other artifacts that I'd dug out of the seafloor. Dirks and china, chalices and jewelry. All stored neatly on shelves that lined my room.

"I can't stop thinking about that township," she said while pausing by a stone deity that I used as a stand for whatever necklace or medallion I had yet to research and tag. She lifted a rope of pearls from the statue's neck and draped it around hers. "I think the 'wealth did it."

"Killed off a whole township? Why?"

"Why force boys to live in a reformatory on the seafloor?" she replied, referring to the reform home her brother had once been sent to—Seablite.

I couldn't argue with her. From the little I'd heard, the experience would have scarred any kid—emotionally and physically. The doctor who'd been in charge of Seablite Reformatory, Doc Kunze, had discovered that the incarcerated boys were gaining new abilities on account of living subsea. He'd made it his mission to find out why . . . only he'd gone about his investigation with a scalpel.

"Know how Representative Tupper explains what happened in Seablite?" I asked her as I settled back on my bed. "*Lack of oversight.*"

She stopped poking through the stuff on my shelves long enough to shoot me a look. "Oh, really?"

"According to him, the Commonwealth is not an evil government—just overextended, and sometimes things fall through the cracks. Lack of oversight is what let Doc get away with experimenting on the boys in Seablite."

Gemma frowned. "A lot more than lack of oversight anchored that township and left those people to die."

"I'll say."

When she took a seat at the foot of my bed like she used to—facing me, tucking up her legs—a thousand sea anemones bloomed inside me, tentacles fluttering and firing. As thrilled as I was to have her to myself, suddenly I could think of nothing to say.

After a moment she asked, "Are you nervous about tomorrow?"

"Selling crops to Drift? No." Which was true, even though Drift's sachem was straight out of a nightmare, with his face and scalp erupting with skin cancer. "What can go wrong? They need our greens. We want to sell them. Simple deal."

"What about the rations the 'wealth sends them? That was part of the Surf Treaty, right? If people agreed to move on to the townships, the government would supply anything they couldn't grow or make."

"Drift's sachem said the 'wealth is sending them half of what they got five years ago."

"Must be a lack of oversight," Gemma said dryly.

Even when piqued, she was pretty. With her sun-streaked braids pinned up like a crown and her sea green caftan tucked around her legs, she could pass for a mermaid. Though I'd never seen one pictured with freckles. . . .

"You know it's cruel to lead Jibby on," I said, broaching the subject that kept hijacking my thoughts. "Unless you've changed your mind about him."

She smiled. "Nope. Still not ready to get married."

"Then why'd you say yes to the boxing match? To see Shade?"

"Yes," she said quickly. "That's why."

I'd suspected as much. He was her brother and it made sense that she'd want to see him. But I couldn't forget that living with Shade on the *Specter*, his gang's submarine, had been her first choice four months ago. She'd only agreed to live with us after he'd refused her.

"Your parents are going to say it's getting too late for talking any minute now."

"Probably," I agreed. "We're rendezvousing with Drift at dawn, and I have to fetch the wagon before that. You want to come?"

"Sure," she said, sounding deliberately casual.

"You don't have to get out of the sub."

"It's not that." She paused. "Well, it is that. But I was just thinking, I don't want to find another township in the trash gyre. Though I suppose now you'll be able to stake a claim down here with your half of the money."

"Yeah. When I'm of age." There was no doubt that finding Nomad had gotten me a lot closer to realizing my dream, which had seemed unattainable ever since the 'wealth stopped subsidizing new homesteads. Because of the terrible thing done to the surfs on Nomad — the cold-blooded murder of an entire town — I hadn't let myself take any pleasure in finding such a valuable salvage. But now, without the derelict township bobbing nearby, dark and silent, a giddy warmth spread through me. My own land. One hundred acres of subsea frontier — gorgeous and teeming with wildlife.

"Must be nice to know exactly what you want," she mused.

"Need," I corrected. "I wouldn't survive living Topside, crammed into a stack-city with a million other people and no nature."

"And no monsters trying to eat you. You're right, you'd die of boredom." As she got to her feet, her smile turned rueful. "I'll go with you tomorrow, though I'll probably regret it." Leaning in, she gave me a quick hug.

"'Night," I said, purposely casual, so she wouldn't know that her touch had sent my pulse into overdrive.

"Oh, and by the way," she called over her shoulder as she headed for Zoe's room, "you're glowing."

The fog surrounded us, giving the surface of the ocean a ghostly feel. Until the sun rose and burned it off, I didn't dare drive the cruiser any faster for fear of scraping the rim of the submerged atoll. Even the shipwreck posed a threat in vapor this dense—we had to be almost on top of it.

Popping the hatch, I stood on the pilot seat to get a better vantage. "Drift looks like a giant Portuguese man-of-war with a blue-and-purple flexiglass dome," I told Gemma, who amazingly enough was wearing her dive-skin for the second time in two days.

"I can't see anything in this fog," she said.

I sent a series of clicks into the haze—pitched too high for Gemma to hear—then considered the picture that the echoes formed in my brain. I could make out the grounded transport ship ahead, creaking with each wave, but no township, which was strange. We weren't late. I'd chosen to hide the wagon in the trash vortex in part because it was close to the rendezvous point.

"Maybe it's submerged." Gemma joined me in the open hatch.

"Doubtful." I knew that the surfs aboard Drift were fishermen and seal hunters. The township could travel subsea, but mostly it kept to the ocean's surface while dragging electrified nets below.

"Maybe your parents changed the meeting place because of the fog."

"No, I'll bet they're inside the wreck, still waiting for Drift to show." Dropping back into the pilot seat, I steered the cruiser alongside the wreck and turned on the auto-pilot. "I'm going in to see what Pa wants to do with the wagon." I hoisted myself out of the cruiser. "Grab a spear-gun from the back."

"You've got one in your holster."

"I mean for you. A precaution in case surfs show up and try to take the crop without paying." Catching her look of alarm, I asked, "Remember how to load it?" When she nodded, I slid onto the cruiser's narrow side deck. "Give a shout if you see anything."

I eyed the shadowy outline of the shipwreck within the fog. The bow and stern towers rose over the waves but the flat deck in the middle was under the waterline. At one time this ship had been a luxury transport vessel that took people up and down the East Coast on a regu-lar schedule. But a storm had pushed the ship off course, and a rogue wave had dumped it on top of a submerged atoll. Since then, it had been stripped of its velvet seats and leather paneling, but the Seaguard left the hull in place to keep other ships from running aground as well.

Gingerly, I leapt from the cruiser's bumper onto a balcony in the bow tower, splashing down in water up to my waist. Wanting a better vantage point, I climbed up to the next balcony, using the holes in the rusted hull as toeholds. The railing was long gone and the floor looked anything but solid. I stepped through the opening that had once been a sliding glass door, moved quickly through the private cabin and into the hall beyond.

The corridor opened onto a large atrium in the center of the tower. Leaning over the low wall, I looked for the gaping hole in the floor one story down, where the boiler had exploded when the ship crashed. Now ocean waves lapped in the pit. If the wagon hadn't been attached to the cruiser, I would have surfaced there. As it was, I expected to see the Slicky bobbing in the char-rimmed hole, but there was no sign of our minisub. Strange, since my parents were right where I thought they'd be — off to one side of the atrium.

They were talking with a wiry, leather-skinned man, whom I recognized as Drift's sachem, Hadal. As always, his gnarled appearance stopped me cold. The half ear Hadal had lost to skin cancer wasn't even his most alarming feature. That distinction belonged to the two small horns, sprouting on the left side of his hairless head. Cutaneous horns — shriveled and yellow like old fingernails. Another horrible effect of too much sun over too many years. Shoving down my disgust, I noticed that Hadal was alone, which seemed even weirder than our missing minisub.

Before calling down, I scanned the atrium. Broken panes in the filthy skylight created a few scattered patches of light below. Enough that I could make out figures moving silently around the perimeter. My Dark Gift didn't work nearly as well in air as it did subsea, but I sent out a series of clicks and waited for its echo to bounce back to me. The picture it formed sent an icy shiver down my spine. Those were surfs slipping along the walls, surrounding my parents. I doubted that Ma and Pa even knew they were there.

The lurkers were bare chested, which rebounded as a much sharper echo than clothing did, and gripping tridents of all sizes — some short and clubbed on one end, others long and wickedly spiked. Tridents were a common surf tool, but these men were wielding them like weapons. Looked primed for bloodshed. Would Pa be shaking hands with Hadal now if he knew? Not a chance.

Not daring to breathe, I unholstered my speargun and edged forward. As I lifted the tip, movement in the hole below caught my eye—a rising sub, which must have entered through the breached hull. Too big to be the Slicky.

"Pa!" I hollered as I took aim at Hadal. "They've got you surrounded!"

As my parents whirled, looking for me, the surfs dashed into the light. The shock on my parents' faces confirmed my suspicion: They hadn't known there were more surfs in the atrium. Before they could react, Hadal leapt behind my mother and twisted her arm up her back. A move that turned my panic into rage.

Loping forward, a sun-fried surf hurled his trident at me. I dropped into a crouch just as the weapon whistled past my head and smashed into the wall. I popped up again in time to see another surf sprint for the stairs, while the rest closed in on my parents. Would skewering a couple of them make things worse? My trigger finger itched to let a spear fly. I wouldn't aim to kill. Still, I nixed the idea. There was no way to disable them all before one did serious damage to my parents.

"Ty!" Pa yelled. "Take off!"

Behind him, the submarine surfaced in the break in the floor. Green and wicked looking, with a prow that ended in a spiraled drill bit.

"Ty, go!" Ma shouted as Hadal hauled her toward the waiting sub.

I followed the crust-skinned savages with the tip of

my speargun as they forced my parents aboard. Footsteps pounded up the stairs beside me. Trying to fight off the horde by myself was sure failure. But if I followed their submarine in the cruiser, I could radio their coordinates to the Seaguard and get my parents back that way.

Just as the footsteps reached the top of the stairs, I took off.

CHAPTER
SIX

Feeling sick and fighting back paralyzing fear, I raced back to the cabin and locked the door. It wouldn't keep the surf out forever, only slow him down. The sun was up now and from the balcony, I spotted Gemma in the thinning fog. When she waved, I shouted, "It's a trap!" and hoped my words weren't lost in the wind.

The door banged open behind me as I studied the churning sea below. Climbing down would take longer than I had, but the two-story jump was a risk. Aside from the undertow, who knew if rocks or wreckage lay hidden beneath the waves? Wishing I hadn't left my helmet in the sub, I felt for a handhold in the rusted hull.

"Move and I'll spill your guts," said a harsh voice behind me. I turned to see a surf with blisters erupting across his bare chest. "Inside." When he jerked his trident toward the door, sunlight gleamed off its dagger-sharp tines.

Watching Gemma drop into the cockpit, I considered my options. She had the cruiser primed to go. The jump might be worth the risk now.

"Inside!" the surf repeated. "Or I'll—" His threat ended in a yelp that turned into a scream, while his trident clattered to the floor.

Baffled, I watched him sink until he lay sprawled in the doorway, howling and clutching at his naked back. Behind him stood a messy-haired little girl in a diveskin. Zoe.

"What did you do?!"

She held up a slender spike. "Rockfish spine," she said. No doubt plucked off one of her pets. Tossing it aside, she stepped over the crying man. "He won't die."

No, but the pain from the fish toxin would make him wish he had. I knew, having stuck my hand in the wrong crevice once. "Why didn't you just shock him?" I asked.

She shot me a look and I knew. She couldn't control her Dark Gift. Always worried that she might cause permanent damage or even kill someone.

"Come on," she said. She grabbed my arm and pulled me away from the surf, who was now curled up in pain. "Pa told me to leave in the Slicky. And that was before the scary guys showed up. Are we going to follow them?"

"Where's the Slicky?"

She pointed across the water where waves swirled around the aft tower. Zoe had been piloting subs since she was six. If I could get her over there safely, she could zip out of here.

Looking around, I spotted a cable hanging from

the deck above. Following it with my eyes, I saw that it ended under water at the other end of the ship, not far from the minisub. Unfastening her dive belt, I tossed one end over the cable and tugged it closer to the balcony, taking out the slack. It seemed sturdy enough. Knowing what to do without being told, she flipped her helmet into place, sealed it, and took the ends of the belt from me.

"Get in the Slicky and go to the Trade Station," I told her. "Call the Seaguard."

"What about you?"

"I'm going after that sub."

"Me, too!"

"No! The Slicky can't outpace anything." Not that that was the point. But telling her it was too dangerous would guarantee she'd try to follow them. "If you don't tell the Seaguard that surfs took Ma and Pa, how are we going to get them back?"

Zoe paled. Nodding, she launched herself into the air. I scrambled to the edge to watch her. Holding fast to the ends of the dive belt, she flew down the makeshift zip line as it bucked in the high winds. Within seconds, she sluiced into the waves and disappeared in the spray. A moment later she appeared inside the Slicky's cockpit.

Quickly, I bent over the writhing man. The wound was just a prick. His pain would last a week at most. Not that I should care. Drift's cancer-riddled sachem had just kidnapped my parents. Yet the words tumbled out of my mouth. "Put a hot compress on it. Heat breaks down the venom."

I started to unfasten my own belt, but a flash of green caught my eye. My heart quickened. The sub had torn out of the wreck and was now closing in on the cruiser. "Gemma!" I pointed to the vehicle headed her way and motioned for her to submerge. But then I realized that even if she could escape, she wouldn't know to follow the green sub, didn't know that Drift's sachem had forced Ma and Pa aboard.

Footsteps echoed through the corridor, heading my way. I studied the waves, aimed for the one wink of blue amidst the geysers of spray, and dove off the balcony.

The second I knifed into the water, relief swept through me. No debris or rocks broke my fall. I slowed my descent and flipped over. Once I located the cruiser bobbing above, I blasted high-pitched clicks upward. The cruiser's control panel would pick up the sound and, I hoped, Gemma would guess the source.

I swam for the wagon. As soon as I got a grip on its back rail, I clicked again loudly and the cruiser took off, tilting as it went. Shooting sonar over my shoulder, I sensed the green sub coming for us. After our crops or me? I didn't know. But we couldn't exactly follow the surfs if they were chasing us. An even more pressing question: How much longer could I hold my breath? Not much. I had to get Gemma to surface, and soon.

The cruiser lurched and bucked. Clearly, Gemma hadn't had much practice driving the family sub—and none with a wagon of crops hitched to the back. I tried clicking at her again, but moving this fast, my sounds weren't reaching her.

Grasping the rubber straps that enclosed the wagon, one after the other, I pulled myself to the middle of the lid. Then I held on and tried to kneel, but I couldn't fight the slipstream. If I didn't get my head above water in the next thirty seconds, I'd have to drop off. In a last-ditch effort, I waved frantically at the cruiser's rearview camera.

Gemma must have gotten the message. The cruiser charged for the surface so fast that it rocketed past the waves with the wagon flying behind. Both were too heavy to arc and so smacked down with enough force to knock the wind out of me. But I didn't have time to curl up in pain. The green sub surfaced right behind us. With its long drilling ram and cigar-shaped body, it could be mistaken for a sickly green narwhal. The two green windows at the waterline were the beast's eyes.

Where had surfs gotten such a state-of-the-art submarine?

I didn't have time to ponder that mystery. If they took us hostage, too, we'd be no use to Ma and Pa. If it was the wagon they were after, better to let them have it.

Again using the straps, I pulled myself across the lid to the front of the wagon, which was no easy task. The wagon weighed so much less than the sub, it skipped over the swells and smacked down in the valleys. Knowing my grip would break on the next drop, I lunged for the back of the cruiser, only to zip across the slick fiberglass, grappling for a hold until finally I snagged the splash rail — just before flying past it.

Without stopping to catch my breath, I unclipped the towline and looked back to see the wagon bob in our wake for an instant and then disappear under the waves. Valuable seaweed and two days' worth of sweat were packed in that wagon, but I didn't care. So long as sinking it got the surfs off our tail.

Sure enough, their sub circled back. Through the twin green windows, I saw several shadows but could make out no faces. I wished I could see if my parents were all right. Then as fast as it had appeared, the craft submerged once more.

I crawled along the cruiser's narrow deck, and Gemma opened the hatch for me. She scrambled aside so that I could drop into the pilot seat. Then, though I was soaked in sweat and shaking with fatigue, I shoved the joystick forward and took us into a near-vertical hydroplane. Something brushed my hand, and I looked down to see Gemma slip her fingers through mine. Any other day, I would have been thrilled. But now, I felt numb with despair.

"What happened to your parents?" she asked.

"The surfs took them." Ma and Pa had given Hadal the benefit of the doubt, but Drift's sachem had proved that surfs were as savage as everyone said. Slowing, I leveled off the cruiser. "I don't know what to do." My voice cracked as I spoke, which shamed me as much as my indecision did. "I don't know whether to follow them or go get help."

"Ty." She jabbed a finger at the monitor.

One glance had me sharing her alarm. The green sub was zooming upward, heading right for us. Jerking the joystick toward me, I altered our course. But so did the sub—and it slammed into the cruiser's belly. The sharpened spar punctured the hull and jammed in so hard, its point drilled through the floor between our seats. Then the sub retracted its spar, leaving what I could only imagine was a gaping hole in the cruiser's underside.

"Get your helmet on," I yelled, flipping mine into place.

As Gemma sealed her helmet, I saw that her hands were shaking, and that added worry to the jumble of feelings inside me. Would she be able to handle the plunge into the ocean? Or would she freeze up like last time?

Water spurted through the hole in the floor. "Don't worry," I told her. "We've got a raft." It was in the drawer under her seat, but before bending down to get it, I took one more look outside. Good thing, because the green sub had circled back and was zooming straight for us, clearly intending to crack our viewport.

I red-lined the cruiser's throttle. The engine was slow to respond but not dead. I aimed for the seafloor, dipping just as the green sub rocketed over us. I stayed on course. If the surfs thought we were sunk, maybe it would buy us enough time to escape.

Nudging Gemma to one side, I located the drawer under her seat. Though the water was now up to our knees, I managed to yank out the raft. Thrusting the folded square into her arms, I took control of the cruiser again, pulling up its nose just as we hit the seafloor. We plowed through half an acre of ooze before coming to a stop. Now we had a new problem: With the viewport buried in muck, I couldn't see if it was safe to get out. And the sludge was too thick for the wipers. The only good part: Water had stopped leaking in through the hole.

"We have to get out now," I told Gemma as I switched on the cruiser's pulse so that I could find it later. "Fill up your lungs with Liquigen." Plunging my hands beneath the water on the floor, I slid back the hatch cover. The cruiser's body was mounted on top of its two engines, so there was space to crawl out from underneath. I shoved a foot through the hatch, into the ooze. It was plenty soft. We'd be able to burrow our way out easily enough. I just hoped the green sub wasn't hovering nearby, waiting for us.

"I'll go first and clear a path. Follow me as quickly as you can." Taking the folded raft from her, I met her eyes. "We won't be outside long. Just stay close to me. As soon as I get the raft inflated, it'll take us to the surface."

She nodded, though her expression was bleak.

I wished I had something more comforting to tell her. I unspooled a short length of cord from my belt and clipped the end to the raft in case I needed two hands to dig out. After sucking Liquigen into my lungs, I pushed out of the hatch arms first. Even for me, being buried in muck underneath the cruiser was a scary sensation. But I wiggled forward, burrowing like a hagfish through the ooze until I reached the end of the cruiser's body.

Getting to my feet, I rubbed the mud from my helmet and used my Dark Gift to look around. About half a mile back, I saw the narwhal sub hovering over the seafloor as two divers attached the wagon to the back. We had to get out of here before they finished the job. Working quickly,

I located the cruiser's tank of compressed air and attached the raft's nozzle.

As the raft began to inflate, Gemma crawled out. She stood, only to then keel to one side and grab for the splash rail. Clearly, our skid of a landing had shaken her up.

I gripped one of the raft's looped handles with my left hand. With my right, I freed the cord from Gemma's belt and clipped it to mine. As the raft inflated, it was harder to hold in place, and I didn't want it pulling me to the surface without her.

Gemma looked over her shoulder and then whipped around as if she'd seen something. I tried to get her attention, but now I needed both hands to keep the raft by the air tank. I nudged her with my foot, but she didn't seem to remember that I was there. She turned again, peering into the darkness. Even with her crown lights on high, there was no way she could see very far. But using sonar, I knew there was nothing nearby but a shoal of eagle rays.

The real threat was from the green sub, and one series of clicks told me that the divers had finished attaching the wagon. Luckily the raft was nearly inflated.

When I faced Gemma again, I cringed. Her whole body trembling, she crumpled and curled into a ball in the ooze. With the raft pulling me off my feet, I braced myself against the cruiser and reached for Gemma but could only graze her thigh with my fingertips. She didn't notice. I yanked at the cord that joined us, finally getting her attention. She extended her hand, and I caught it. With a tug, I pulled her to her feet and held her close.

Just then, the nozzle popped out of the air tank and the raft burst upward, nearly jerking my arm from its socket as I held on. Our combined weight slowed the raft's ascent but didn't stop it. Eyes closed, Gemma looped her arms around my neck. With her helmet pressed to mine, I could see her eyes fluttering under the lids, as if she were in the midst of a nightmare. She didn't even open them when we crashed through a school of tuna. I tightened my grip on her as the fish—each weighing at least four hundred pounds—buffeted us about in a flurry of blue bodies and yellow fins. Finally the tuna whirled away and I spotted the first shafts of sunlight penetrating the darkness. "*Hold on*," I told her silently. "*We're almost there.*"

As soon as the raft burst through the waves, I rolled her aboard. By the time I hoisted myself in, she was curled up again.

"Gemma," I said as soon as my lungs cleared. "We're out of the water."

With her helmet still sealed, she shook her head. Not in answer to me, but as if to get rid of some awful vision. Pulling her hands from the flexiglass, I struggled to unsnap the seal. She erupted into choked sobs.

"Breathe!" I said, though I knew it wasn't the Liquigen

that kept the air from entering her lungs. I threw aside her helmet and held her face between my hands. "You're all right. We're in the raft."

She blinked at me and then scrambled to lean over the side and vomit. I held her hair back, wishing I could do more. When the heaving finally stopped, she rinsed out her mouth with seawater over and over, then sat up and pushed me back with a shaky hand.

"I am never going in the ocean again," she said between gasps.

"It was as bad as last time?"

Without answering, she crawled away to sit in a corner with her arms around her knees.

"Gemma, I don't think you're crazy. I don't."

"It doesn't matter," she said. "I won't see you anymore."

"What are you talking about?"

"I'll be living at the Trade Station forever."

"Even if that's true, I'll visit you there."

She looked at me, desperately unhappy, and finally said, "Sure. It's a plan."

Why did I get the sense that she was patronizing me? Like I was too stupid to see that this was impossible. "I'm sorry. I shouldn't have brought you today."

"It's not your fault." She straightened her legs, suddenly all business. "How do we get out of here?"

"Our diveskins have radio beacons."

She nodded and seemed to relax.

I didn't want to panic her with the whole truth just yet: that no one would know to look for the beacon. Once Zoe reached the Trade Station and told people about the kidnapping, their concern would be for my parents. A chunk of time would have to pass — hours at least — before someone would think to search for us in the open ocean.

SEVEN

Ten minutes after our dip in the ocean, Gemma had recovered her poise as the raft rocked with the waves and we roasted in the sun.

"Can't you call a couple of dolphins to come give us a ride?" she asked. "Like you did when the lower station sank?"

"I don't have any control over dolphins," I explained. "I can send out a distress signal like theirs, and if they're in the area, they'll usually come check it out. But I can't give them directions on how to tow us back to the Trade Station."

"It can't hurt to try," she said. "You're the one who says that dolphins are really smart."

With a shrug, I slipped over the side and into the ocean. She was right: It couldn't hurt to try. Once I'd submerged, I imitated the agitated clicks of a dolphin in distress.

No reply. No pod of dolphins had heard. I tried several more times. Still nothing. Before climbing back into the raft, I threw out clicks that would travel far and fast to see what was in the area. And when the echo bounced back and formed a picture in my mind, I inhaled seawater. *Oh, no no no.* I scrambled back into the raft. I should have known better. Should have known that yes, it *could* hurt to try.

"What's wrong?" Gemma asked, seeing my expression.

"A pod of orcas is headed this way."

"Great. Can you get them to tow us back to the Trade Station?"

"Know why orcas are called killer whales?" I asked, while unholstering my speargun. "Because they eat their own species—as in, anything in the dolphin family. Especially a wounded dolphin, which is why they're hurrying this way. My distress call . . . that was their dinner bell."

"Okay, the distress call, bad idea," Gemma said, clearly trying to remain calm. "But you told me that orcas don't eat people."

"Right." I scanned the water around us. "But I never said that they don't *kill* people. The only sure thing about orcas is that they're unpredictable. Every group is different. Like humans. Some pods are playful. Others ruthless."

"Let's hope we get one of those playful pods."

"There." I pointed to where a six-foot dorsal fin broke the waves.

"Oh! That's big," she gasped.

I'd seen three with my biosonar. The typical number for a transient pod. A good hunting number. And orcas were, without a doubt, the smartest hunters in the ocean. They knew how to gang up on a whale four times their size and force its mouth open so that one of them could dart inside and rip out the whale's tongue — an orca delicacy.

Now two of them made a wide circle of the raft. I kept the speargun across my knees in case either had experience with a harpoon. I didn't want to trigger any bad memories. But where was the third orca?

I got my answer when the ocean exploded next to us and the black-and-white orca propelled itself out of the water. I froze, transfixed by its ascending body. For a timeless moment, the massive animal seemed to hang in the air, and then, as if snapped back to normal speed, it dropped broadside down. Amidst a curtain of spray, the orca sank beneath the waves, leaving us soaked.

I released the breath I'd been holding. "He was taking a look at us. To see if it was worth tipping the raft over."

Gemma pushed her sopping bangs out of her eyes. "And what did he decide?"

I saw no sign of any of the orcas now. "They submerged."

"Is that good or bad?"

"I don't know. We'll find out."

After a minute, Gemma said, "Actually, if we're both going to die" — she lay back in the raft — "I'd rather not watch." Her expression turned puzzled. "Do orcas thrum?"

"What?"

"Hear that? Definitely a thrum."

I froze, listening, but heard only the lap of waves.

"Like a sub."

"You're hearing something under the water?" I lay down with my ear pressed to the bottom of the raft.

"I'm not totally hearing it," she admitted. "It's more like a vibration."

I have exceptional hearing, according to the doctors who tested me when my Dark Gift first emerged. Better hearing than is considered normal for a human, and yet I didn't hear or feel any vibration.

I sat up, deciding to slip into the ocean to take a quick look around. If there was a sub nearby, I'd see it with my sonar. But just as I was about to climb out, a flexiglass dome broke the waves, not twenty feet away from us.

Water sluiced from the sub's dome, and I caught sight of blond curls as the driver gave a hearty wave. Zoe. She must have tried to follow the green sub anyway, even though the Slicky could never keep up. It had taken her this long to get this far.

Moments later, as I hauled myself into the Slicky behind Gemma, Zoe grinned from the pilot seat. She didn't even wait for me to catch my breath before asking, "Aren't you glad I never listen to you?"

As I powered the Slicky over the waves, closing in on the Trade Station, I sensed something was wrong. But I put it down to my churning thoughts about what the surfs might have done to my parents.

"It's too quiet," Gemma said, sounding spooked.

Right. That's what was missing — the noise. It was a weekday, yet only the gulls screeched overhead. Where were the market sounds? For that matter, where was the market? The Surface Deck was barren. No colorful stalls circling the promenade. No fish vendors hollering, no buyers haggling. And only a scattering of boats bobbed along the outer docking-ring. A chill swept over me.

"Go around," Zoe said, leaning over the pilot bench between us. "Maybe everyone is on the other side."

As I started to circle the Surface Deck, three skimmers shot out of the waves ahead of us. With their two pods linked by a slender joint, they looked like wasps.

"What are those?" Zoe cried.

"Seaguard skimmers," I told her.

"Probably here for Nomad," Gemma guessed.

As the skimmers rounded the curve of the docking-ring, the larger pods in back of all three tipped on their sides.

"Glacial," Zoe said.

I knew that not only could a skimmer submerge entirely, but also when cruising atop the waves the back pod could flip over to let the strapped-in trooper scan the ocean below. Yet I didn't share that information. I was too sick and shaken about my parents to care about fast vehicles.

I followed the skimmers around to the opposite side of the Surface Deck and nearly plowed into a long line of hitched Seaguard vessels. But that wasn't as alarming as what the uniformed troopers were doing. Like a bucket brigade, they were carrying corpses out of the derelict township.

The Seaguard captain stepped over the bodies laid out along the promenade as if looking for something, though what, I couldn't guess because—thankfully—tarps covered the dead. When I'd come aboard, I'd told Captain Revas about Drift taking my parents. Now as I waited for her to say that the Seaguard was on the case, I stayed down by the corpses' feet, some of which poked out—bare, callused, and crusted with salt.

The line of dead circled the whole Surface Deck and was more than a little tough to look at. Gemma had done me the favor of taking Zoe below, promising to get her a scoop of whale-milk ice cream in the dining hall. After letting me out at the docking-ring, they took the Slicky down to the lower station, to enter at the access level. If they'd docked up here, they would have had to waltz past the dead surfs to reach the elevator shaft.

Zoe was a fierce little girl, but she was only nine. Why put an image like this into her brain? I knew it would haunt me forever.

Squatting by a body, Captain Revas pulled the tarp back and frowned. Clearly not the person she was looking for. She flipped the tarp back into place and stood. Like her troopers, she wore a trim jumpsuit of windproof material with mesh strips running down the sides for ventilation. Finally, she faced me. Her eyes were barely visible under the brim of her patrol cap. "What were your parents doing anywhere near Drift?"

I stiffened at the question. "We were selling them seaweed and kelp."

Revas was probably in her late twenties—younger than I'd expected a Seaguard captain to be, but it didn't make her any less intimidating, with her hard expression and her dark hair lashed back tight.

"We weren't doing anything illegal," I added, trying not to fidget under her stare. "The 'wealth said we can sell our crops."

"To townships?" Her tone was both incredulous and insulting. As if my parents were idiots.

"To anyone we want," I snapped.

Stepping over corpses, Captain Revas strode to me. "And your parents thought it was a good idea to do business with desperate people who *hate* subsea pioneers?"

"What are you talking about? They don't hate us."

"Really?" she scoffed. "You know that ordinance that keeps townships from crossing into Benthic Territory . . . ?"

"What about it?"

"The surfs are holding on to some resentment about it. At least, that's what I've heard."

I bristled at the judgment in her voice. "Those townships would drag their nets through our farms, scooping up our livestock and plowing through our plankton fields."

Revas squatted by another corpse and lifted the tarp to study the man's face. *Was she even listening to me?*

"We had to do something about it," I added. "The 'wealth backed us up."

"Yes, I know." Looking dissatisfied, she replaced the tarp and rose. "You passed an ordinance that covers most of the eastern continental shelf, which happened to be the townships' primary fishing grounds since they launched eighty years ago."

"They have the rest of the Atlantic to fish in."

"Kid, you know better than most that there are more fish on the shelf than off. And finding and catching them is a heck of a lot easier there."

That brought me up short. The fish on the abyssal plain were few and far between and not particularly good eating. Mostly there was mud and a smattering of sea cucumbers.

"See why it might rub the surfs the wrong way to buy seaweed from settlers?" she asked.

I shook my head. How had I missed that? How had everyone missed that? A disquieting thought struck me. Maybe the settlers hadn't missed it. Maybe they just hadn't cared.

No. That couldn't be it. The settlers were the good guys. Well, except for the time a group of my neighbors tried to lynch Shade. That hadn't been a pretty moment. But Ma and Pa had known nothing about it. Came running to stop it when they heard.

"My parents must not have realized the consequences of the ordinance," I said aloud.

"Of course not." Her expression said the opposite. Looking across the promenade, Revas studied her troopers—all in ocean blue jumpsuits with low-slung gun belts. Her gaze stopped on a woman carrying a child-sized bundle. "Hatorah," she called out.

"Even if they did have some idea," I went on in my parents' defense, "I can guarantee they didn't know that the surfs hate us."

"Possible." Revas glanced at me. "You settlers do keep to yourselves."

My parents had been kidnapped and this captain acted as if it was their own fault. "We're not keeping to ourselves; we're putting in long days on our farms because the 'wealth doesn't give *us* monthly handouts. Not like the townships get. We have to work hard for what we have."

"Want me to pass that on to the surfs who took your parents?" she asked evenly. "Or would you like me to try to resolve this in a way that won't incite violence?"

I shut my mouth. She had a point. If the surfs did hate the settlers, then my parents were in even more danger than I'd realized—a notion as cold and buffeting as a current surging toward the abyss.

EIGHT

"First, Nomad's sachem is not among the dead," Captain Revas told the trooper named Hatorah. "Get someone to find out if he's been spotted alive since Nomad disappeared—maybe at Rip Tide or the black market. After you've assigned that, get his story." She gestured to me. "Significant details, everything. Then take out three skimmers to comb the area for Drift. Pull up pictures and its dimensions so you don't investigate every sonar blip."

"That's it?" I demanded. "Three skimmers?"

The trooper's brows shot up at my disrespectful tone.

As if I cared. "That's all you're sending out to look for my parents?"

"Even if I had vehicles to spare, which I don't"— Revas's voice held a warning—"the situation calls for diplomacy, not a show of might. The surfs on Drift took your parents for a reason."

"They had *no* reason. We were selling them crops."

"Go home, kid, or you'll just make things worse. I will do what I can to find your parents and negotiate their release. But they're not the reason I'm here." She pointed at the line of corpses. "They are. Three townships have disappeared in the past nine months. That's over a thousand people who got shuffled to the bottom of too many priority lists. But not mine."

Missing townships? That was news to me. Not that anyone in the 'wealth ever heard much about the surfs except whenever a township attacked some poor floater family, stole their supplies, and set fire to their houseboat. "Disappeared how?"

"Now that's the question, isn't it? Nomad is the first one to turn up. And when you tell me you found it anchored in the trash gyre, it makes me think the others didn't sink in a storm."

"Which one o' you is Captain Revas?" A stocky man climbed up the ladder from the docking-ring. He was overdressed for the heat in a shirt with a cascading collar and a purple frock coat. He stopped short upon seeing the corpses, then flipped up the lenses on his sun-goggles to squint at Revas's cap badge. "Guess it's you. Mayor Fife sent me to see if it's true—someone found Nomad?"

"Who are you?" Captain Revas asked.

"Ratter," he said simply, and then tacked on "ma'am," along with a smile that revealed his green teeth and a wad of chewing-weed crammed inside his cheek.

"Well, Ratter, you can tell your boss there are no survivors."

"That's a terrible shame."

"Did one of Fife's prizefighters live on Nomad?" Revas asked pointedly. "Is that why he's so interested?"

"No, ma'am. Mayor Fife cares about them surfs. Been worried sick since Nomad went missing." Ratter spit the chunk of seaweed onto the deck, where it glistened like a lump of algae between two tarp-covered bodies.

"Wipe it up," Captain Revas ordered.

I straightened at the intensity underlying her words. Had it been me, I would have scrambled to comply. But Ratter gave her a peevish look.

"I ain't going to touch chewed chew."

With icy calm, Revas unholstered her harpistol and aimed between Ratter's eyes. "Wipe. It. Up."

I eased back a step, not trusting Ratter to be smart enough to realize that, though she might not shoot to kill, Captain Revas *would* pull the trigger if he didn't obey.

Scowling, he bent and scooped up the wet hunk of chew.

The exchange tripped a wire in me, setting off my anger. Captain Revas cared more about someone disrespecting a dead surf than my parents' abduction. Maybe surfs weren't the only ones who hated the pioneers. Though if Revas was biased, I'd bet on the glaciers refreezing before her admission of it.

With the wad of wet seaweed clenched in his fist,

Ratter said, "Fife also wants you to know that if everybody aboard is dead, he gets to decide what to do with the township, being as he's the Commonwealth's surfeit agent."

Captain Revas holstered her pistol. "Inform the mayor that Nomad is part of an investigation and that the Seaguard will be holding on to it indefinitely."

"But after that?" Ratter pressed.

"It's my salvage," I cut in. "I found it. There are no survivors. So when the Seaguard is done checking it out, Nomad belongs to me."

Ratter glared at me.

I didn't care if I sounded like a jerk, interrupting their conversation. Or callous because of the bodies at our feet. It felt good to show up Captain Revas. I knew the salvage laws as well as any ocean dweller.

Jaw clenched, Revas peeled her eyes from me like I was a bucket of fish guts and turned to her trooper. "Get this backwater brat out of my sight."

My neighbors, Shurl and Lars Peavey, came as soon as I called them and agreed to take Zoe while I searched for my parents. Zoe had to be forced, kicking and screaming, into their sub.

"What if she shocks one of them?" Gemma asked worriedly.

"She won't," I said, as their sub disappeared under the waves. "She's too scared to shock people she hates. She sure isn't going to shoot electricity at someone she loves."

"So what do we do now?" Gemma asked.

After everything she'd been through that day, the fact that she could still say "we" amazed me. "I can't rely on three skimmers to find my parents. I'm going to Rip Tide," I told her.

"Where the boxing match is?"

"Yeah. It's about half a day's sail south of here. The townships pick up their rations there. I know the chance of Drift showing up is slim, but I want to talk to the surfeit agent. Maybe he's heard something—knows what Drift's sachem wants with my parents. Or what it will take to get them back. And if he doesn't, maybe he can tell me the coordinates of Drift's fishing grounds. At least that would give me somewhere to start looking."

"I'll go with you."

"Thanks. But I've put you in enough danger for one day."

"I don't care about that. I care about getting your parents back." Her attention jumped to someone behind me. "Hey, that's my stuff!"

I turned to see a Seaguard trooper emerging from the lounge with a duffel bag in his arms.

"Good. You can take it with you." He dropped the

duffel at Gemma's feet. "I think I got everything. But take a final look-see."

"Final look?"

"You have to clear out. Captain's orders."

"But—" Gemma stopped herself. "Who's your captain?"

"Don't waste your breath," I told her.

Ignoring me, she looked expectantly at the trooper.

"The kid's right. No way Captain Revas is going to let a teenage girl hang around a Seaguard fort."

"Since when is our Trade Station a fort?" I demanded.

"Since the Assembly said so," he replied evenly. "It's a good central location."

"For what?" I asked.

"To bring stability and justice to the ocean frontier," he said, clearly quoting someone. A superior probably. Or an Assembly representative.

Just what the settlers needed—a garrison right in the middle of the territory so the 'wealth could keep tabs on us and meddle in our business. Already the Trade Station felt different. Like all the life had been sucked out of it.

Looking close to tears, Gemma picked up her duffel bag and hugged it to her body. "So," she said, clearing her throat. "Do you want to ask Jibby for his tickets to the boxing match or should I?"

*　*　*

"Of course they took your storage closet," I told Gemma. "The 'wealth doesn't care about people's families or homes. And the Seaguard is nothing but the government's fist."

Shoving the Slicky's joystick forward, I laid on the speed even though the boxing match didn't start for hours. Jibby had handed over his tickets willingly once he'd heard why I wanted to go to Rip Tide.

Next to me on the pilot bench, Gemma remained silent. She'd changed out of her diveskin before we'd left the Trade Station. No surprise there. But I was taken aback when she'd returned to the docking-ring in a sheer turquoise sari. I'd seen her in Topsider dresses before, but never anything so fancy. Maybe it was an everyday outfit by stack-city standards, but out on the ocean, only rich tourists wore such frippery. The sort of people who dropped by the Trade Station to gawk at the crazy pioneers who'd settled on the ocean floor. And when those tourists spotted me, out came the cameras, accompanied by stares and exclamations over my skin. Or worse, they'd comment on what reckless parents I must have to raise me in the subsea wilderness.

Pretty much all my experiences with Topsiders had left me feeling wary and embarrassed, which had to be why unease slid through me when Gemma had stepped from the lounge in a fluttery piece of nothing. Or maybe it was because wrapped in a sari she seemed older. More sophisticated. And that unsettling combination made me want to dive into the ocean and get lost in a school of silversides. Instead, I'd busied myself unhitching the Slicky while hoping that she didn't expect a compliment. Anything out of my mouth would've sounded insincere since really I wanted her back in a diveskin or at least a nondescript dress from her boarding-home days.

I glanced at her, sitting so close to me on the pilot bench, yet seeming so far away. She stared out the viewport with a faint pucker between her brows.

"You're not homeless," I said, guessing at her thoughts. "You can always live with us."

She shot me a pained look. "Stay inside your house all day while you and your family work outside? I can't."

"Why not? None of us mind."

"Because I'd feel useless and trapped."

"What are your other options, though? It's not like you can move in with Shade."

Her lips tightened and she went back to looking at the passing ocean.

"You're not seriously considering it?" But she was. I could tell she was.

"He's going to be at Rip Tide while we're there. I may as well talk to him," she said as if it was no big deal.

"If you think Shade has changed his mind about letting

you live with outlaws, you *are* crazy." When her brother had told her no last time, he'd been firm to the point of cruelty. And I sincerely hoped he'd stick to his guns.

She threw up a hand in frustration. "Fine. I'll move to a township."

How could she even joke about it, knowing that a bunch of crust-skinned savages had just kidnapped my parents? "You'd become a surf?"

"I already am. Surfeit population. May as well admit it."

"No, you're not. Not to us." *Not to me.* "You'd be better off moving back to the mainland."

"And live where? Stack-cities are restricted communities. Even the really awful ones—so dirty and old, you'd never want to visit—even they will only let you in if you have an access pass." She folded her arms across her body as if trying to stay warm. "Before, I dreamed about finding a home. Now I'll be lucky to find a place to live."

"I don't see how living on the *Specter* would be any different than living with us. You—"

"Can we concentrate on rescuing your parents? That's going to be hard enough. We can worry about me later," she said firmly. "After we've put your family back together."

Being a pioneer, I knew *stubborn* could be a useful trait. Most of the settlers in the territory were stubborn to the point of being intractable. But Gemma dove into *stubborn* the way I slipped into the deep, as a way to escape tension and noise. At least my way came with a view.

I knew we were nearing Rip Tide when we passed under a township that had dropped anchor off the rocky coast.

"Townships aren't allowed to come this close to the mainland anywhere but by Rip Tide," I told Gemma.

"Why not?"

"They're big and don't maneuver well. The coastal states passed laws to keep them away from the marinas and smaller vehicles."

We spotted more townships bobbing above us. I'd never seen so many gathered in one place. I scanned the bunch, looking for Drift. But judging from their undersides, none resembled an enormous Portuguese man-of-war.

"Let's surface," Gemma said. "I want to see what they look like." The moment we broke through the waves, her interest evaporated. "They're just mountains of metal and flexiglass."

"The older ones, yeah. It took awhile for the government to realize that the surfs would be better off if they had some way to support themselves. That's when they started designing townships for specific trades. Like Nomad, which was built to be a salt farm."

"Look, an airship." Gemma pointed at a brightly striped dirigible hovering far off in the sky. "It's tethered," she said with some surprise, "like they are on top of stack-cities."

"It's probably hitched to Rip Tide. We're getting close."

I took the Slicky subsea, where we could speed along much faster, until the town's steel legs popped onto the sonar screen. I got us as close to the hulking structure as I dared and headed for the surface to crash through ten-foot swells.

The ancient offshore drilling platform towered over us — seven stories tall. Before the Rising, the oil rig would have hovered above the water with room for boats to cruise underneath. Now the waves lapped at the town's underside, which probably meant that come high tide the first level would flood completely.

These derelict platforms off the Commonwealth's coasts had been converted into lots of things, like prisons. And wind and tide turbine islands, all with thick cables on the seafloor for sending the produced energy back to the mainland. But most became ramshackle towns, offering shelter to thousands of displaced people. Frankly, I would have preferred living on a converted drilling platform to being shut up in a stack-city. At least the platform was surrounded by sea and sky, not hemmed in by other concrete towers.

Cruising the Slicky alongside Rip Tide, I looked for a place to hitch her but couldn't find a single boat cleat or even an entryway. The rusting metal walls bore only a thick crust of barnacles, mussels, limpets, and snails. Rip Tide might have been an impressive drilling platform in its day, with its seven decks and enormous center tower, but it sure didn't make for a very welcoming town. Giving up, I rounded a corner and steered for the rocky coast.

"There," Gemma said, pointing up. "That's how we get on."

Thick cables swung overhead, stretched between Rip Tide and the cliff, with two steel towers in between. The cliff was quite a ways off. But then a cable car came into view, and I realized it covered the distance fast. Packed with people, the car zipped over us and banged through an opening on a middle deck.

"Did that look safe to you?" Gemma asked. "That didn't look safe."

"See another way to get aboard?"

"No," she said, sounding grumpy.

I sped the Slicky toward the coast, where I spotted clusters of vehicles moored at the base of the cliff. The docks were no more than long iron girders jutting into the waves. After locking down the Slicky's control panel, I cracked the hatch in her side and winced. All of Rip Tide probably felt like this—like the inside of a space heater cranked to the max. I hitched the Slicky to a cleat, put on a low-brim hat for coverage, and tied a bandana around my neck like the people who lived on houseboats did. Of course, the floaters were trying to block the UV rays. Me, I just wanted to keep people from staring at my skin.

Gemma hiked up her sari and we walked the length of the narrow girder with our arms out for balance. We passed a wide assortment of vehicles: a sub with a chain of living-pods bobbing behind it, houseboats piled high with the floaters' possessions, and plenty of multilevel barges. The odd part was that people were sitting atop the glass-domed living-pods and flopped on the jerry-rigged barges as if staking out claims, all vying for the best view of the oil rig. Clearly settling in for a chunk of time, which I didn't understand since it had to be 110 degrees out.

From behind us came the rolling whip of an unfurling sail. I turned to see men on a trimaran tie off the center sail so that it faced the crowd. Then the crew dropped not one but three anchors — serious overkill for such a light-weight racer. They must've really wanted the boat to hold its position.

"They're going to broadcast the match," Gemma guessed, pointing at the sail where a glowing square appeared, projected from the trimaran's deck. Applause erupted from the crowd lounging on the docked boats. "I hope that doesn't mean there's no more room on the town."

I didn't know what it meant because I'd never seen anything like it. But now that we were onshore I spotted the airship again, pulling at its mooring line at the top of old drilling tower. A banner hung from its passenger compartment, advertising the boxing match.

Ahead of me, Gemma mounted the stairs cut into the cliff, maneuvering past the often ripe-smelling people sprawled on the steps. More floaters, I guessed, going by their faded plain tunics and loose-fitting pants. A few glanced up as I passed and did double takes upon spotting my shine. But considering how many people were packed onto the steps, I was getting off easy. The bandana and hat were working.

At the top of the cliff, we joined the long line of people waiting to board the cable car. They were mostly Topsiders from the stack-cities wearing windblown layers of gauze. Had I thought Gemma's sari was fancy? Clearly I hadn't grasped the heights to which fancy could soar. Every item on their bodies was embroidered with silver and gold or decorated with doodads such as tassels, crystals, mirrors, and metal studs. All the sparkling and glinting reminded me of the light shows put on by deep-sea creatures, though those were far more beautiful.

I met Gemma's gaze and saw how the turquoise fabric draped over her shoulder, unadorned, turned her blue eyes into tide pools.

"You look nice."

The words were out before I'd thought them through. I tensed. "Nice" was bland. I should have come up with something better. But then the smile she gave me in return was so dazzling that I couldn't remember why I hadn't told her she looked nice back at the docking-ring.

As another group of people packed into the cable car, I recognized Benton Tupper at the front of the line. I pointed him out to Gemma. "He's Benthic Territory's representative," I said, noting that he was not wearing his official blue Assembly robes but some sort of striped muumuu, which made him look like a market stall. "He should be too busy for boxing matches—busy getting us statehood. Or at least a vote in the Assembly."

Gemma was less interested in Tupper than the cable car itself. On our side of the barrier rope, a guy with a padlocked box sold tickets. On the other, a man with an iron hook at the end of a pole had snagged the cable car by its doorframe and was now struggling to hold it steady.

"Do you think inspectors come out regularly to test this setup?" She eyed the open cable car warily. "Because it looks like it was built by a monkey with heatstroke."

"Oh, chum," I muttered—not because of the unsafe cable car. Now that we'd made it to the front of the line, I recognized the burly, snub-nosed man selling tickets. Ratter—still in his purple frock coat and goggles with the lenses flipped up. The man who'd offended Captain

Revas with his chewing-weed. I hadn't forgotten his reaction when I'd announced that Nomad was my salvage: He'd glared at me with bloodshot eyes. But in case I needed reminding, he gave me a repeat performance now with extra malice—enough to make my skin crawl.

NINE

With his beady eyes fixed on me, Ratter spat out a hunk of chewing-weed, leaving a line of green spittle down his unshaven chin. "You're that pioneer kid that thinks he's got a claim to Nomad."

"Good to see you, too." I held up the tickets. No way was I going to let him intimidate me. Nor would I take the time to set him straight about salvage rights.

Ignoring the tickets, he looked me over. "What's wrong with you?"

"What?"

"Your skin don't look right," he pronounced. "We don't let sick folk on Rip Tide. Mayor Fife's orders." With that, he pulled a hunk of dried seaweed from a pocket of his frock coat.

"He's fine." Gemma snatched the tickets from my hand and shoved them at Ratter. "Healthier than you by a long shot."

After picking off the lint, Ratter popped the weed into his mouth and chewed like he was thinking hard. Finally he said, "No minors allowed without an adult." He must have really taxed his brain to come up with that one.

"We're with two adults," Gemma countered. She hooked her thumb at the two men behind us in line. Bare chested and streaked with orange zinc-paste from their faces on down, they could only be fishermen off the same boat. "We're even taking them to lunch before the match."

It sounded like a fair trade to me, but one of the fishermen said, "Don't know 'em from a codfish."

"What's the holdup, Ratter?" yelled the guy with the gaff hook as he slipped a few feet toward the edge of the cliff. "I can take two more!"

"I got Dark Life here that's giving me trouble."

Well, that sure clarified the issue. "You have a problem with pioneers?" I demanded.

"I have a problem with you," he spat. "Now step outta line. 'Cause you're not getting onto Rip Tide."

I started to argue, but Gemma dragged me to one side.

"Girl, *you* can go if you want," he offered with a smile that showed off his moldy-looking teeth.

"Maybe," she told him, and then turned to me. "What's your representative's name?"

"Benton Tupper." Guessing her plan, I looked for him. At the Trade Station, Tupper's yellow and purple striped muumuu would have stood out like a beacon among the settlers' sleek diveskins and the simply clothed floaters, but not on a cable car filled with Topsiders. "There," I said, finally spying Tupper's wispy head above the rest.

"Representative Benton Tupper!" she shouted at the top of her lungs.

He whirled, spotted us, and ducked behind a large woman trailing about twenty veils.

Gemma cupped her hands around her mouth. "We have important Assembly business to discuss with you!"

Tupper stayed down, and I couldn't blame him since I found myself backing away from her as people turned to look.

"Benton Tupper," she hollered, "Commonwealth of States representative for Benthic Territory, please show yourself!"

That did the trick. Tupper popped up, making shushing gestures at her. Then he saw that absolutely everyone in line and on the cable car was staring at him. Realizing that it was a lost cause, he waved feebly at us.

Gemma traipsed over to Ratter, who glared at me like I was a plague-carrying rodent. "That's Ty's Uncle Benton," she said in her cheeriest voice. "He's in the Assembly. He's very important."

Scowling, Ratter jerked his head to indicate that we could board.

The guy with the gaff slid forward another foot;

now there was a gap between the cliff and the cable car. Gemma hesitated, eyeing that gap, only to have him shove her aboard. The instant I followed, he slammed the door, freed his hook, and launched the cable car with a kick of a lever.

We sailed into the air, whizzing along the steel cable at breakneck speed. Tupper shot me a reproachful look, which wrung not one drop of guilt from me. "Thanks," I said to Gemma as she leaned over the side to look down. She straightened instantly, clearly not liking what she saw.

"You're John Townson's boy," Tupper said. "First child born in the territory, yes?"

I nodded, though I wasn't only the first kid born in the territory, but the first person ever born subsea. "My name is Ty," I told him. "I won't tell anyone that I saw you here."

Relaxing, Tupper waved aside my assurance. "So what if I enjoy the occasional bare-knuckle match? My fellow reps are too uptight to know what they're missing. A couple of surfs going at it, no rules. It's a thrill like nothing else. Not even dogfighting comes close."

My brows rose in surprise. I'd never seen this side of our representative.

"I heard about your parents," Tupper said abruptly.

"You did?" News traveled fast. I wondered if Captain Revas had been the one to report it.

"Yes, bad business that—taking people captive." He shook his head as if dismayed by the surfs' lack of manners.

"Can you help me get them back?"

"Me?"

"Yes. Order the Seaguard to send out more skimmers to search for them."

Tupper's smile was wry. "Spoken like a true frontier boy."

"What's that supposed to mean?"

"That I don't expect you to know where I fall in the Commonwealth's chain of command. The answer is nowhere. But don't worry. The Seaguard will get them back. They always do."

Always do? Before I could ask what he meant, Gemma grabbed my hand so tightly I winced. Leaning out, I saw the oil platform ahead, coming up fast. The original drilling tower now served as a lighthouse and was flanked by a crane nearly as tall. People bustled along on every level, visible because a half wall enclosed each deck. All except for the fifth level, where a wide section of the wall had been knocked out to serve as a landing dock, and we were zooming right for it.

"Oh, relax," Tupper told Gemma. "Even if the cable does snap, the fall won't kill you. Well," he amended, "being dashed against the rocks might, but there's no point in focusing on that, now is there?"

She didn't reply. Maybe she didn't know he was speaking to her since she'd pulled the veil from her head and was using it to cover her eyes.

With a muffled bang, the cable car slammed into the padded opening of the oil rig. As we lurched in unison, another man with a gaff caught the car, only to get dragged several feet before it finally stopped.

"Hop down," he ordered. "And don't stumble or you'll cushion the next guy's fall." I glanced over the side to see that the car hung several feet above the steel deck. "Jump!" he yelled. "I can't hold her for more'n a minute."

The doors on the far end of the car burst open and people clattered out. From the laughter and chatter, it seemed that the ride and jump were part of the pleasure for the mainlanders. Guess their moving walkways and shuttle trains didn't require much from them.

We were the last off. The man with the hook swung the car around a support girder and held it still on the other side. There, another crowd waited—a few surfs, but mostly locals, looking truculent.

"If you don't have a ticket for the match, you must vacate Rip Tide before the next gong," the gaff man yelled. "Or you will be making your exit with a splash."

There was grumbling as the crowd stepped onto the mounting block and pulled themselves into the cable car. But none protested outright at being forced from the town.

One surf, not much older than me, was hoisted up by his friends, crutches and all. He was wearing pants with one leg cut off above the knee—only he didn't have a knee or any part of his left leg from there on down. And he hadn't been born that way. Clearly his leg had been amputated . . . by something with teeth.

I learned from the gaff man that I should look on the sundeck for Fife, who was both mayor of Rip Tide and the Commonwealth's surfeit agent in charge of distributing government rations to the surf population. Fife had probably gotten the job as surf agent because Rip Tide was off coast, which meant the townships could be kept away from the mainland harbors.

Gemma and I left the landing bay and entered the stream of fluttering caftans and veils. I checked that my hat was pulled low and bandana tugged high on my neck. It was nerve-wracking—knowing that I was headed into a town filled with surfs who disliked subsea settlers, maybe even hated us. I'd have to keep up my guard.

An enormous hole took up the center of the town, cut through all seven decks, which made sense since it had once been the drill well. Now a bustling walkway circled it on each level. Rip Tide was certainly no hermetically sealed stack-city. Stores, saloons, gambling halls, and family dwellings had been constructed between the decks. But with both the interior and exterior walkways open to the elements, every inch of the ancient oil rig was slimed, rusted, rotted, and wet.

Not counting my stay in a stack-city when I was nine, Rip Tide was the biggest town I'd ever strolled through. There was so much to see, I was both overwhelmed and curious. But I didn't have time to give in to either feeling. Finding Fife was going to be no easy task. Not when Rip Tide was bursting at the bolts with loud, pushy boxing fans. Hundreds of feet tromped across the metal decks above, while shouts and laughter rebounded off the hard surfaces. And the stifling heat just made it all worse.

"What's the matter?" Gemma asked, stopping in the middle of the human river with a look of concern.

She could talk here? With all the jostling and chattering, I couldn't even breathe. I tugged her off the walkway and into the wide opening of a livery stable that rented mantaboards, Jet Skis, and other small vehicles by the hour. "Give me a minute."

"Oh, right," she said with sudden understanding. "The crowd."

I felt foolish needing time to acclimate, but breathing was kind of a necessity. I took off my bandana and used it to wipe the sweat from my face. Cold seawater would have felt better.

"When we get away from the landing dock, it should thin out," she assured me.

Wishing I was standing at the edge of Coldsleep Canyon with nothing but whale song in my ears, I gestured her forward. "Okay. You lead."

Smiling, she said, "Just give a shout if you want to stop again," and took off, elbowing her way through the throng effortlessly, forcing me to keep up or risk losing her. I trailed in her wake, trying to ignore the press of bodies, only to do a double take as a tough-looking girl cut past us. Her clothes left her torso exposed and revealed a long semicircle of scars.

Gemma dropped back to walk beside me. "That was from a bite, wasn't it?"

"No question," I confirmed. I wanted to speed up and get a better look at the girl's skin but figured that would come off as rude. It was just that I had seen my share of shark bites on fish, dolphins, humans. Dead and alive. From the tooth marks and width of the chomp, I could usually tell not only what kind of shark took the bite, but estimate the beast's size. Yet, in the glimpse that I'd gotten, something about the girl's scar seemed odd.

Gemma jabbed my arm. "You said sharks don't attack people very often."

"I didn't say *never*."

"Okay. But have you noticed that several people here are missing big chunks of their bodies? That's more than 'not very often.'"

"Yeah," I admitted. "I noticed."

"Know what else is strange? They're showing off the damage. As if getting bitten by a shark is something to be proud of."

That part surprised me. But now that she mentioned it, I figured she was right. The surfs did seem to dress in ways that drew attention to their scars.

I shrugged, as baffled as she was.

Ahead of us, a sign posted above the stairwell read: TODAY: SURFS ALLOWED USE OF SUNDECK ONLY.

"What does that mean?" I asked Gemma. "They can't walk around anywhere else on Rip Tide?"

"Don't know." She waved me toward the stairs. "You go ahead. I'm going to find out where the boxers hang out before the match."

"I don't think we should separate," I said, trying to keep a lid on my panic. "I'll never find you in this—"

"Go look for Mayor Fife on the sundeck. I'll find you," she promised, then spun on her heel and shot out of sight.

I felt a stab of resentment toward Shade for taking her away from me already. Having little choice, I headed for the stairwell, but my nerves were frayed from the noise and heat. The thought of strolling onto the top deck and adding glaring sunlight into the mix made me feel shaky and sick. I slipped into the shady nook under the stairs to get a grip on myself. If I came off like some crazed nervous wreck, no way would Mayor Fife tell me how to find Drift.

TEN

Standing in the shadows beneath the stairs, I tried to catch my breath. I kept my back to the wall and looked out at the bustling walkway. Steady dripping from the deck above splashed onto everyone equally, though the Topsiders hid under their parasols. After a moment, I realized that from this vantage point, the crowd didn't seem like such an indistinguishable mass. In fact, it was interesting to see how many different sorts of people went by — from fancy stack-city dwellers to seafloor ooze-diggers. And I'd thought the Trade Station attracted a wide variety. I'd been kidding myself.

Once I felt calmer, the sound of so many people talking at once didn't seem like such an assault on my eardrums. And if I concentrated, I could even hear individual voices as people passed. Snippets of conversation — mostly side betting on the upcoming match. I found that I could tell the swabbies and tide-runners by their slang. Even easier to identify: the mainlanders. With their elaborate sentences stuffed with extra words, I didn't even need to see the speakers. Though I had to admit people-watching was more interesting than I would have ever guessed. Especially because the mainlanders with their filmy clothes and zinc-painted faces — some made up to look like animals and birds, others more fantastical — gave me the feeling of being awake in a dream.

And then there were the surfs. Their sun-baked skin was easy to spot, though none who passed were as leathery as the surfs on Drift. Their clothing came in a wide variety and apparently depended on their township's trade. I saw salmon-skin ponchos, woven seaweed hats, and dresses of burlap and old fishing nets. But I didn't know enough about surf culture to pick out the mollusk farmers from the biofuel harvesters. Several stared at me as they headed up the stairs to the sundeck. Probably because my skin stood out in the shadows. Still, with their sun blisters, elaborate tattoos, and missing limbs — a shine should be no big deal.

Now that I had my nerves under control again, it was time to find Mayor Fife. But when I stepped from my nook, I saw a familiar striped muumuu disappear into the next shop. The sign in front read: SHAVES, SLATHER, AND ART.

Upon pushing through the swinging doors, I was relieved to see that the place wasn't too crowded. A few customers reclined in the chairs while attendants in white jackets painted their exposed skin using brushes and putty knives. Dozens of photographs on the wall displayed a variety of painted body parts—each design more intricate than the last.

I spotted Tupper in the back, seated next to a woman who was having yellow flowers painstakingly dabbed onto her bare arms. Heading for him, I passed another customer who was lying facedown on a padded table. His back glistened with a freshly painted seascape that was about as beautiful as I'd ever seen.

"Will that last?" I asked the attendant as he studied his artist's pallet.

"I'll spray it with a sweat-proof coating, but it's ephemeral beauty. Long lived as a rose."

Right. And ten times more expensive. Though when I heard Tupper tell his attendant, "Just a slather of white," I felt a twinge of disappointment. With so many colors and designs to choose from, solid white seemed a little dull.

The attendant seemed disappointed as well. "Only white?"

"I'm a traditionalist." As Tupper settled back in the chair, he spotted me and waved me closer. "Looking for me, I assume."

I glanced at the attendant and lowered my voice. "You said something before. . . . Have other people been kidnapped by surfs?"

"Oh, yes. Seems like more every year. Even happened to the Pennsylvania rep." Chuckling, Tupper closed his eyes. "I think it was Rawscale. Surfs snatched him right off his yacht. Demanded an unbelievable amount in ransom. Wouldn't even negotiate with his family."

"But they got him back eventually."

"Well, no, actually that one ended badly," Tupper said as the attendant smeared white zinc-paste over his balding pate. "But I'm sure nothing so gruesome will happen to your parents. They know better than to get huffy with savages."

"Drift hasn't asked for a ransom. At least I don't think so."

"No?" He frowned without opening his eyes. "Well, I'm sure they'll get around to it."

I shot a look at the attendant, who was now brushing goop across Tupper's lids and down his nose. The man seemed like he couldn't care less about our discussion. "What if ransom isn't the point?" I asked Tupper.

He snorted. "With surfs, money is always the point. Especially now."

"What's different about now?"

Though only a portion of his face was covered in zinc-paste, Tupper shooed the attendant aside and sat up. "Listen, Ty," he said, emphasizing my first name as if to prove he remembered it. "You have nothing to worry about. I heard that Captain Selene Revas is on the case, and she's the one Seaguard officer the surfs will deal with."

"Why's that?"

"They like her perfume." His tone may as well have been an eye roll. "Who knows? Who cares? As long as they'll negotiate with someone on our side."

Before today, I would have bristled at "our side." We were all Commonwealth citizens, after all. But now, the surfs on Drift had sunk so low in my estimation, they didn't even rank as human.

A bell gonged in the distance.

"Finish up, will you?" Tupper snapped at the attendant while lying back on the chair. "I haven't placed my bet yet."

"That was the one-hour bell, sir. You have plenty of time. The bookies don't close until the match starts."

"Thank you for your help," I told Tupper.

"Anytime," he called out. "Always happy to assist my constituents. . . ."

When I stepped out of the slather shop, sunlight flooded my eyes, coming from the town's open center. I crossed the walkway and looked over the railing. The drill well was filled with ocean, and a heavy-duty raft bobbed in the middle of the pool. Three floors up, the tower's girders did nothing to block the UV rays.

"The poor child looks lost," said a familiar voice behind me.

I turned to see a guy not much older than me sitting on the railing with his back to the four-story drop. His dark hair looked as if it rarely met up with a comb, and two gold teeth glistened among his pearly whites as he grinned at me. Eel. One of the outlaws in Shade's gang.

"Good," his companion said coldly. "Let's leave him lost, since he wasn't on the sundeck like he was supposed to be." There was no missing Pretty, who never seemed particularly pretty to me. He just looked cruel with his sharp cheekbones and ice blue eyes. His hair was as long as ever. Loose, it hung over his shoulder like an infirmary curtain he could slip behind when needed.

"Now, you know we can't," Eel said to Pretty as if I weren't within earshot. "Not when we promised Gem o' the ocean that we'd see if he was still down here."

I hated the casual way Eel said it. Like he used that phrase for Gemma all the time. Which he probably did since that's how Shade had addressed letters to her when she was younger. I knuckled down my resentment. I didn't have time to let outlaws get me riled.

"Dark Life"—Pretty swung a leg over the rail to the open side with the pool far below—"keep up or stay lost, 'cause we're not coming back for you." With that he grasped the rungs of a ladder that ran up the length of the drill well and climbed out of sight.

Eel shot me a grin. "Ain't he a charmer?" He, too, swung his legs to the other side of the rail. "Come on."

"No," I said, which made him glance back in surprise. "I'm not here to visit Shade or see his boxing match. I need to find Mayor Fife."

"We *know*. Probably why Shade sent for him. But if you don't want to come . . ."

I was at his side in a flash. "Gemma told you what happened?"

"What do you think?"

Now I saw that several ladders were mounted on the interior walls of the drill well, all climbing to the top of the tower. "Where are we going?"

"The meat locker." Eel leapt onto the ladder as easily as a floater stringing rigging between masts. It made me wonder where he had lived before he was sent to Seablite.

Avoiding the workers setting up three-tiered bleachers for the match, I swung my legs over the railing and stepped onto the ladder with a smidge more caution. I didn't share Gemma's fear of heights, but I had no intention of amusing a pair of outlaws by taking a long spill into the pool below.

When we reached the top deck, Eel jumped off. The sunlight beat down so hard, it took me a moment to see where he had gone. Especially since the bleachers were already in position on this deck and starting to fill up. Finally, I spotted him by a large fuel tank near the base of the crane. He waved and then disappeared through a door in its side. As I approached, I saw that someone had retrofitted the fuel tank with a hatch, probably taken from an old submarine. With a spin of the wheel, I opened it and peered into the shadowy interior. Cold air greeted me and I entered with a sense of relief. It was the closest I'd come all afternoon to the feel of the deep.

I waited for my eyes to adjust to the dim light and narrowly avoided slamming into a carcass hanging from a hook. Stepping around it, I cut a path through several more. From the white-striped flippers, I knew that I was walking past pieces of a minke whale. As sickened as I was by the sight, it wasn't the greasy smell of blubber making me dizzy. The fuel tank may have been empty for over a century, but I could swear the air still carried oil fumes.

I followed the sound of meaty punches and rounded another hunk of whale—to see a great white shark sailing toward me, jaws wide. My heart jerked, and I spun out of the way. But when the massive blue-gray body swung back the way it came, I realized that it was just another carcass on a hook. One that was standing in for a punching bag.

A couple of sledgehammer blows sent the great white flying again. Its gaping mouth, spilling over with teeth, arced even higher this time, forcing me to dart aside or get knocked off my feet.

"See, he found his way," I heard Eel say as I stumbled into an area where there were no carcasses, only searing light.

Squinting, I retreated back into the shadows. Sunlight streamed through a windowed hatch in the ceiling, also retrofitted, creating a tight circle of illumination in the center of the fuel tank. I spotted Gemma off to one side by a table loaded with food. Behind it, Eel busied himself heaping charred tentacles onto a plate. Gemma beckoned me over but another volley of punches drew my attention to Shade.

Head shaved and tattoos writhing, he was as menacing as ever, pounding away at the shark. When he finally straightened, his eyes found me in the dimness beyond the circle's edge. "Knew we'd meet up again."

I'd forgotten how low his voice was and the chilling way it reverberated down my spine.

Dust motes shimmered in the air around him. Or maybe they were denticles from the shark's skin. A grin spread over Shade's face. "Just never thought you'd be stupid enough to set foot on Rip Tide."

ELEVEN

On the far side of the fuel tank, someone clapped loudly. "Talk about showmanship!" said a dark-skinned man as he strolled into the open area. The buttons on his long linen cassock gleamed in the sunlight while the fringed sash around his waist made me think he was someone official. Hopefully Mayor Fife.

Taking off his flat, wide-brimmed hat, the man used it to gesture at the swinging shark. "Deliver that in the ring," he told Shade, "and I'll make you a star."

"I agreed to one fight." Shade's reply sounded more like a warning than a reminder. "Even that might not be worth the risk."

The man waved aside Shade's concern. "When you hear the cheers, you'll forget you're taking a gamble. Win, and you can make a bargeload of money doing the circuit. With your unique talents, you'll have followers in no time—fans who will travel to any off-coast town to see you fight."

"Just what I need," Shade scoffed as he unwrapped shredded strips of cloth from his hands. "A spotlight on me. May as well paint a bull's-eye on my back." His knuckles were bloody from contact with the shark's sandpaper skin. Scowling, he turned to Pretty. "Who thought this was a good idea?"

"You." Pretty thunked a bucket down on a metal drum. "And Fife," he added, shooting a droll look at the other man.

So Eel hadn't been lying. Shade really had sent for Mayor Fife. I never would have predicted that a day would come when I'd be grateful to have outlaws as allies.

Settling on top of a different drum, Pretty tied back his long hair. "I still don't see how this is a better life."

"It's honest work," protested Mayor Fife.

Eel laughed, despite having food in his mouth. "Is that supposed to be a sales pitch, Fife?"

"Brine," Pretty told Shade, pointing at the bucket.

Throwing aside the last of his hand wrappings, Shade plunged his fists into the bucket and winced. I knew that sailors soaked their hands in seawater to toughen them up. I supposed it made sense for a boxer to do the same.

From the corner of my eye, I saw Gemma gesturing me forward. She was right. I wasn't going to find answers among the dangling carcasses. I moved into the light but clearly not fast enough for her. She cut across the open area to join me.

"Well, now. Aren't *you* something?" Mayor Fife exclaimed. "You've been holding out on me, Shade."

I glanced at the outlaw, wondering how he'd react to a middle-aged man fawning over Gemma. But Shade remained impassive as he shook the seawater off his hands.

"What's your name, son?"

With a start, I realized that Fife had been talking about *me*, not Gemma. A rush of heat swept up my neck and into my face. "Ty," I said, suddenly wary.

"Would you look at that? He's glowing," Fife crowed. "And good-looking to boot. Why haven't we met?" he demanded jovially, thrusting out his hand. "Gideon Fife. Mayor to the residents of Rip Tide. Surf agent to the townships. And impresario extraordinaire when an opportunity presents itself."

Was I supposed to know what that meant? I shook his hand while hating the calculating gleam in his eyes.

"And I thought these boys had shines." Fife shook his head in mock amazement. "They dim in comparison. I know. Let's make him your cornerman," he called back to Shade.

With a stretch, Shade cracked each shoulder. "Eel and Pretty have it covered."

"You think people who came to see a fight care about a shine?" Pretty asked skeptically.

"Might be as common as cod where you're from," Fife

replied, "but I guarantee these trifling tower folk have never seen the likes of him. No offense," he said to me. "I'm just trying to do right by my boxers. And that means whatever draws the tourists and their money. Bare-knuckle, no rules . . . a little local color . . . or, in this case, local *shine*." His eyes gleamed. "How about water boy?"

"Wasting your time," Shade told Fife. "Just tell him what you know about Drift."

The mayor's good humor vanished in a blink. "You're the boy whose parents were kidnapped?"

I nodded.

"You didn't tell me he was pioneer," Fife said to Shade, sounding appalled. "Well, this changes things."

"Because surfs hate the subsea pioneers," I said. "I heard."

"It means that I don't know how to help you," he explained. "No point in offering to act as go-between or making Rip Tide the exchange location if these surfs aren't after ransom money."

"Why else take Ty's parents?" Gemma asked.

"Could be political," Fife said. "Could be revenge."

"Well, I'm not waiting around for them to explain themselves to me," I said. "They pick up their rations from Rip Tide, right?" At his nod, I went on, "So, when are they coming next?"

"Not for another two weeks. All the townships collect their rations at the start of the month."

My heart sank. "Do you know where Drift could be now? Where they fish?"

"No idea," he said, sounding genuinely sorry. "This is as far off coast as I go."

"What about other surfs?" Gemma asked him. "Can't you ask if any of them passed Drift on their way here?"

"They aren't going to tell me chum," Fife said. "I'm the man who gives them less than they need each month. They don't understand that I don't fill the orders, I just distribute what I'm sent." Sighing deeply, he glanced at Shade. "You should start getting oiled up."

"Already?" Eel complained. "The stink is going to kill my appetite."

"Nothing kills your appetite." Pretty picked up a second bucket. Tipping it, he drizzled oil across Shade's broad shoulders, which Shade then smeared down his arms and over his bare chest. Fish oil. The stench filled the fuel tank as fast as Pretty poured.

I wasn't ready to let the last topic drop. "Representative Tupper says the surfs will talk to Captain Revas. Is that true?" I asked Fife.

He snorted. "The Assembly likes to think they have a point person in the Seaguard. A happy delusion. Frankly, *you'd* have a better chance getting answers out of them. And with that shine of yours broadcasting that you're a subsea pioneer, that's saying something."

I had a sinking feeling that he was right. I'd had a sample of Captain Revas's charm that afternoon and couldn't see any reason why the surfs would want to deal with her, despite what Tupper thought.

Just then Ratter pushed past the hanging carcasses. "Sorry to interrupt, boss." Then he caught sight of me and scowled.

Tipping up her chin, Gemma glared back at him.

"What's up, Ratter?" Fife prompted.

"Couple of peeved surfs outside want to talk to you. Should I take care of them?"

"No," Fife said. "They have the right to complain. And I get paid to listen. Tell them I'll be right out."

I wondered if Mayor Fife's answer would have been different if we weren't here.

Ratter sent one more evil look my way and left. He was burly and no doubt violent, but I just didn't care that he hated me. All my worry was going toward getting my family reunited.

"That man didn't want to let Ty onto Rip Tide," Gemma told Fife angrily. "Does he have a problem with the pioneers, too?"

"Ratter has a problem with anyone who isn't like him," Fife replied. "Lucky for us, that's everybody. The world only needs one Ratter."

"If that," I muttered.

"Don't like him much, huh?" Fife asked. "Excellent. That's what I pay him for. To be nasty, so I don't have to."

"He's very good at it," Gemma said tartly, which made Fife laugh.

"Know what a ratter is?" he asked her.

When she shook her head, he explained, "A dog bred to kill vermin. The kind you can throw into a rat pit and he won't jump out until every last rodent is dead. Shakes them till their necks break. You can make money off a dog like that. When I became mayor, I made it my job to keep this town free of vermin—the two-legged kind. Ratter is the dog that helps me do that." Fife's grin was broad and sparkling. "He takes pride in his name."

Outside, a gong sounded. "Half an hour till showtime," he told Shade. "See you all ringside." He paused by me. "Sorry I wasn't more help. But stick around with your ears open. If a surf knows anything about Drift kidnapping a couple of pioneers, it'll be the talk of Rip Tide before the match is over. You might overhear something useful."

"Thanks," I said. "I'll do that."

"Being that you're Dark Life, I expect you know what a real riptide is."

"Yeah. I do."

"Good. Then you'll be careful out there." After putting on his wide-brimmed hat, Fife looked back at Shade and frowned. "Don't forget his head," he called to Pretty. "Gabion is known for ripping off ears."

As the others made their way down to the drill well, Gemma and I paused by the outside railing. The sun was starting to sink in the sky, which worried me. If the surfs on Drift hadn't demanded a ransom by now, I doubted they ever would, despite what Tupper had said.

"What is a riptide?" Gemma asked me.

Fife probably used that line a lot. Not that it wasn't fitting. "A patch of water where different currents meet up. It's turbulent. Hard to navigate. Treacherous, even."

"Hard to navigate" sure described my situation. I turned to look across the open sundeck, with its scattering of café tables. Unlike Rip Tide's other levels, this one had only a few enclosed buildings and the drill tower in the center, so I had an unobstructed view of the surfs crowding along the railing that overlooked the drill well.

"One of them must know something," I said, frustrated. "But they're not going to talk to me."

"You haven't even tried," Gemma pointed out. "Maybe they don't all hate settlers."

"That's the only thing I've heard today that I don't doubt." I glanced at her. "What about you? Did you ask Shade if you can live on the *Specter*?"

"I couldn't tell him that I'm homeless right before

his match," she said lightly. "It might have messed up his concentration."

I nodded, though who knew what kind of shape Shade would be in after the match. Hopefully he'd still have both his ears.

Suddenly the image of Shade smearing fish oil over his skin put an idea in my head. "You're right. I have to at least try talking to the surfs. But not as a pioneer."

"How—"

"I have to cover up my shine so I can pass as something else . . . like a fisherman."

She smiled, understanding my plan. "Pick a pretty color."

Fishing boats bought zinc-paste by the barrel, usually in the color of their company logo. I just picked the color I liked best: the blue of the ocean on a sunny day at twenty feet down. With that, I stripped off my shirt and got the fastest zinc-paste body job on the ocean.

The slather shop attendant had agreed to hold on to my shirt and bandana until the end of the match. Now, smeared from hairline to hip bone in blue, I crossed the sundeck, confident that I looked like the fishermen forming blocks of color in the bleachers.

Holding my breath, I hurried past the food carts. On the fifth level, I'd passed many a Topsider clutching a paper cone of crispy fried seaweed. But up here, I didn't see a single surf nibbling on samphire, the salty tangle of fried greens. Unlike most Topsiders, the surfs were meat eaters. Raw, cooked, or smoked—and often washed down with liquid whale blubber.

I liked eating fish, no question, but the big seller on the sundeck was fermented seal flipper, which smelled even fouler than it looked. Worse, the flipper came with dipping sauce, which was made from the contents of the seal's intestines—partly digested clams and greens. At one point Ma had explained that the surfs didn't have enough room on their townships to grow vegetables, so this was their solution—eating the seaweed out of sea mammals' stomachs. Made mine turn over just thinking about it.

I passed the bleachers and felt the hair on my body prickle under the zinc-paste as I noticed all the gut-skin garments—ponchos, rain shirts, and sleeveless hooded coats—and thought of Raj's charming theory: that the surfs made their waterproof outerwear out of human guts. I angled toward the nearest surf for a better look at the strips of translucent material that had been stitched together to make his anorak. Definitely an organic membrane of some sort, as sheer as a Topsider's veil. Probably scraped-out intestines or maybe a stomach lining, though who knew from what?

I decided to push aside the unsettling thought, because

it was now or never. Once the boxing match began, no one would be talking about Drift. Even if they were, I'd never hear it over the cheers and yells. Mustering my courage, I slipped into the crowd.

As soon as I'd gone two feet, the throng closed behind me and suddenly I felt like I'd plunged into the deep without inhaling Liquigen first. The water pressure in Coldsleep Canyon couldn't have squeezed the air out of my lungs any faster. I forced myself to think of Gemma—how she navigated through packed-tight bodies—and did the same. Elbowing my way to the railing, I leaned over it to breathe in air that someone else hadn't just exhaled.

If I stayed next to the drill well, I wasn't completely immersed and I could manage it. Then I noticed that the surfs around me were all armed with tridents, daggers, bows, and sheaths of arrows tipped with shark teeth and sharpened spiral shells. Clearly prepared for trouble. Their primitive weapons made me wonder again how Hadal had acquired a state-of-the-art submarine.

Speakers around Rip Tide crackled and then blared the Commonwealth national anthem. On the decks below, voices rose, singing along with gusto. But surrounding me—silence. I stole a look at the surfs along the railing. If I hadn't had an urgent reason to stay on the sundeck, I would have made a hasty exit. The surfs' expressions were nothing short of murderous, with their jaws clenched shut. Considering that they had no representative in the Assembly to speak or vote on their behalf, I could understand why they might not feel very patriotic.

When the anthem finished, talk on the sundeck started up again immediately, so I inched along the railing with my ears open. Long minutes went by and all I overheard were people making side bets on "first blood" and "first splash."

To my left, a male voice said, "Hey, Levee, who'd ya bet on? I don't know which one to go with."

I was just maneuvering by a surf in a wheelchair when a man behind me replied in a low voice, "I can tell you who not to bet on. Drift."

I froze, not daring to turn and reveal that I was listening.

"What's going on?" the other man asked quietly.

"Can't say here. Too big a crowd."

"Bad?"

I didn't hear the other's reply. Maybe he did it with a nod.

"Know anything about the contender?" the first guy said loudly as if they'd been talking about the match all along. "Twenty-to-one odds makes him mighty tempting."

"Bet there's a reason for those odds and it ain't good. These boxers pad their wins. But this surf's write-up is a total blank."

Chum, they weren't going to say anything more about Drift. Not here anyway. And I'd learned nothing. Sucking in my breath, I turned and found myself facing a man whose sun-bleached dreadlocks were piled on his head like a turban. "I can tell you about the contender," I said.

His tunic was sleeveless, and tattoos of the sun blazed on his biceps. He crossed his arms so that his hand rested on the hilt of the cleaver he had tucked into his belt. "Why would a fisherman tell me anything?"

"Because you have information I want."

The surf grew very still as if he knew exactly what I was talking about. "Listening in, were you?" he asked softly. Suddenly he yanked the cleaver from his belt and thrust it toward my face. "Where I come from, nosy people lose their noses."

TWELVE

Boxed in by the crowd, with the surf's cleaver hovering an inch from my nose, I had no way to escape. I shot a look at the man beside the furious surf. With his eel-skin pants and boots, I guessed he was a whale-hand from one of the marine dairy townships. His shirt hung open to reveal bloody bandages wrapped around his torso. At least he didn't look offended, too.

"The challenger is a friend of mine," I said, trying to keep my voice steady, though my heart was pounding in my ears. "And here's a tip: You'd be a fool not to play those odds."

The first surf said nothing, clearly still deciding whether to let me live.

But the second man spoke up. "You must be real buddies," he scoffed with a wave of his arm, "if you're stuck up here in the nosebleed section with the rest of us scum."

"I wanted to see how it looked from up here. I can go down anytime I want."

The guy laughed, clearly amused by me, only to stop short and touch his bandaged stomach with a grimace.

Rivulets of sweat were streaking the zinc on my forehead. The last thing I needed was for these two to see my shine and realize that I was a settler. I willed myself to stay calm. "You'll see. I'll head down in a minute and when I get ringside, I'll take off my hat and give you a wave."

The first man, still serious as a corpse, said, "Here's a deal. You tell me about the challenger and I don't throw you off Rip Tide."

When I didn't reply, the second guy spoke up. "Take the deal, fisherman. We're on the seventh deck. If Levee tosses you off, I'd put your survival at about twenty to one." He pressed a hand to his bandages as fresh blood soaked through them. Given the amount of blood and the size of the area bandaged, the pain had to be fierce. The fact the guy could carry on a conversation at all shocked me.

"Start with his township," the one named Levee ordered as he thrust his cleaver back into his belt.

"He's not a surf."

Neither of them believed me. "There's a reason why it's called the surf boxing circuit," the second one said.

"Does it say in the rules you have to be a surf?"

"What rules?" Levee scoffed. "But only surfs are tough enough and desperate enough to end up in that ring."

"He's both. Tough and desperate." I lowered my voice so that only they could hear me. "He's the leader of the Seablite Gang."

Whatever they'd expected me to come out with, that wasn't it. I'd actually taken them aback. So I drove my point home. "He's got a Dark Gift. Those tattoos on his back and arms? They're not tattoos. He can change the color of his skin. All in the blink of an eye. He can blend into the background so well the other guy won't even see him." I didn't feel too bad about revealing this since Shade was the one who had told me to flaunt my Dark Gift. No way he kept a lid on his. I had no doubt he was going to use it to win today.

"That's a heck of a story," the second guy said, impressed though disbelieving.

"I don't think he's lying, Krait," Levee said while eyeing me.

"I'm not. You'll know it soon enough. And if you didn't put money on those odds, you're going to choke on your regret."

He nodded. "Okay, fisherboy. I'm a gambling man. I'm going to take the chance that you're telling the truth."

"That information has got to be worth something," I said, stepping into Levee's path. With my family rapidly coming apart, what did I have to lose? "Please tell me about Drift," I said in a low voice. "I have a personal reason for asking. I won't repeat what you say."

Fear skittered over his face, shocking me. He seemed like a different man from the one who'd threatened me just a minute ago.

As Krait unwrapped his bandage partway, he said casually, "How 'bout this: If the challenger wins, Levee will talk to you." He looked at his friend. "What do you say?"

Levee straightened, regaining his bravado, and nodded. "If I make money on this match, lots of money, I'll tell you what I heard an hour ago."

"You *will* make money," I said firmly. "Where will I find you?"

Krait smiled bitterly. "Right here. The only deck we're allowed on." The loose bandage fell away from his torso and I saw the stitched wounds. Unconcerned, he began to rewrap it.

"What happened?" The words were out before I could stop myself.

He glanced up, looking mildly surprised. Then seemed to remember that he wasn't talking to another surf. "Accident," he said curtly.

I nodded, not willing to push my luck by asking more.

Heck of an accident. From what I could tell, his midsection had "accidentally" met up with some wickedly sharp teeth, set in a huge, powerful jaw. That much, I knew for sure.

I also knew that no shark took that bite. Though what did, I couldn't guess.

As I headed down to join Gemma and the outlaws, I noticed that thuggish-looking men had taken up positions on every level by the stairwell. To keep the peace or to keep surfs from wandering?

When I reached the stairwell for the second deck, the man on duty blocked my way. "Invite only for ringside," he snapped. "And I know no fishermen were invited."

Luckily, Eel came by just then, with a stuffed sack thrown over his shoulder. "Blue boy is with me," he said. Seeming to recognize Eel, the man stepped aside and we hustled down the stairs.

Eel smirked. "Worried about your pretty skin?"

I ignored the jibe. "What's in the bag?"

"It's a tablecloth," he corrected. "Would have been a crime to let that feast go to waste."

When we reached the second deck, I glanced down to see water lapping at the bottom of the last set of stairs. The tide was coming in.

This level was less crowded and easier to navigate. We headed toward the core in the middle of the town, where Gemma stood by the railing. Other members of the Seablite Gang milled around her—not as dangerous looking as I'd remembered, but then I'd only seen them briefly when they'd come for Shade at the Trade Station. I spotted Shade tipped back on a stool, eyes closed as he rubbed a block of chalk between his hands.

At the railing, I took off my hat to wave up at Levee and Krait on the sundeck and saw them wave back.

Behind me, Eel spread out the tablecloth with its

jumble of food. When he straightened, he looked over at Gemma and me and snickered. "Aren't you two sweet enough to spread on toast?"

"What?" I demanded.

Gemma turned, curious. Then, upon giving me a once-over, she said, "We match!" and broke into a smile. "Did you do it on purpose?"

In the time it took me to realize that she was talking about my zinc slather and her sari—which I had to admit were close in color—Eel answered her question. "Course he did, sweeting. Who wouldn't want to be matched with you?"

She beamed at me, which meant I couldn't admit that it hadn't even crossed my mind. Not consciously anyway. "Sure . . ." I mumbled, then noticed the outlaws' varying expressions of amusement and disgust. At least the attendant had slathered the zinc-paste on thick. Even if the blue had me coming off like a sentimental moron, the density hid my shine, which right now felt as hot and bright as the setting sun.

"That's Ty," Eel told the outlaws, and then he gestured toward the one I could have picked out in a lineup—the big guy with sharpened teeth. Not that he was smiling now to show them off.

"Hatchet," Eel said, introducing us.

Hatchet's faint shine made his tan skin glow like ambergris—though I doubted he smelled as sweet. As he looked me over, his black eyes narrowed in recognition. I'd been the reason he'd gotten his arm caught in a closing hatch a few months back. Judging from the way his fingers curled into a fist, he'd made a full recovery.

Pointing at the two outlaws by the railing, Eel said, "Trilo, short for trilobite, and Kale."

If he'd said their names in order, Trilo was the wiry one who was so focused on the water in the drill well, he didn't seem to have heard Eel. Out of all of them, he was probably closest to my age. The others had at least two years on me. The tall guy beside Trilo, Kale, didn't come off as much like an outlaw as the rest. Aside from the scar on his cheek, Kale could've passed for a Topside apprentice with his combed brown hair, steady gaze, and knee-length buttoned vest. He was even civilized enough to lift his bottle of bladder wrack ale in greeting.

Next to me, Gemma inhaled sharply. "What's in the pool?"

Only then did I notice that the water's surface was churning with activity.

Trilo pivoted to look at us with eyes like radioactive algae. An eerie color on anyone, but against his dark skin with its faint shine, the acid green seemed to glow. "Eels," he said, fingering the many charms that hung from his neck.

So that's what he'd been staring at . . . with concern, no less.

Gemma made a face. "No wonder no one wants to fall in."

Eel and Kale exchanged a look, which nudged my suspicion up another notch. "What kind of eels?" I asked.

"Lamprey," Kale replied, studiously casual.

My gaze whipped to Shade. He must have known what he was getting into. But what sane person would agree to even boarding a raft that floated on a pool of lampreys? Forget boxing on one.

"Is there a net around Rip Tide?" I asked. "Is that how they keep them in?"

Eel nodded. "Wrapped around the town's legs."

Gemma looked from him to me, trying to gauge our expressions. "Are lamprey eels the electric kind?"

"No," I said simply. No sense in freaking her out any more than she already was.

"Not even a spark," Eel added, clearly with the same intent.

Hatchet grinned, revealing his transparent, jagged teeth. "They're the suck-you-dry kind."

I could have slugged him—even if he *was* a head taller than me.

"Meaning what?" Gemma demanded.

Eel shrugged like it was no big deal. "They latch on to a person. Kinda like a leech."

"If leeches came four feet long with teeth all the way down their throats," Hatchet chortled.

Seeing Gemma's horrified expression confirmed it. Hatchet was officially my least favorite gang member.

Shade tossed the block of chalk to Pretty and stood. He seemed unfazed by the entire event. With that kind of confidence, the prize was as good as his, I told myself. There might be a few men out there bigger than him — though I hadn't met them — but I couldn't imagine anyone tougher.

I forced myself to approach him. "Thank you for getting Fife to talk to me."

"You gave her a home," he said with a nod toward Gemma.

I caught her eye. Clearly she hadn't told Shade that she'd been living at the Trade Station for the past month. With a quick shake of her head, she let me know that I wasn't to mention it now.

"Is that a pill bug?" she demanded, pointing at the broiled critter Eel was attempting to crack open.

I knew she was just trying to change the subject. Still, I couldn't help but smile at Eel's efforts. Holding the giant isopod by a hind leg, he banged it on the railing until its head popped off.

"You're not going to eat that!" Gemma gasped.

After dunking the creature into a cup of salted oil, Eel offered her one of its insectlike legs. "Want a taste?"

She crinkled her nose in revulsion, so he put the end of the leg into his own mouth and slurped loudly.

She whirled on Shade. "Haven't you taught them any manners?"

When he laughed, I was surprised at the warmth in it. And there was nothing sardonic in his response. "You're welcome to try."

Cheers broke out and echoed off the town's steel decks. We all turned to look at the far side of the platform, where the champion now stood at the edge of the pool. Dark haired and mustached, the surf threw off his towel. His muscles gleamed with oil.

Several young men on an upper deck began chanting, "Speech! Speech!" The boxer raised his fists to them and snarled with rage.

"What's that about?" I asked the outlaws.

"Gabion is mute," Kale explained.

"And they're teasing him about it?" Gemma asked, indignant. "That's just mean."

Kale hid his smile by swigging his ale, but Hatchet openly guffawed. "That's just mean," he mimicked, and cracked up all over again.

"Well, it is," she snapped. "In fact, I can't think of anything worse than making fun of someone's handicap. Maybe he acts tough"—she jabbed a finger at Gabion—"but I'm sure it hurts his feelings."

The others lost it then, including Shade, whose rumbling

laugh was as loud as it was deep. Only Pretty remained impassive, except for rolling his eyes when Eel started to choke because he'd cracked up while chewing.

I suppressed my own smile. "Making fun of Gabion," I told her in a low voice, "is probably the nicest thing that's going to happen in that ring."

As Shade went to take his place, he paused by Gemma long enough to say, "I promise not to hurt his feelings. Can't say the same for the rest of him." He gave her braid an affectionate tug and stepped up to the gap in the railing. The cheers diminished noticeably.

Just as I started to feel bad for him, the crowd reacted with shouts of excitement and a wild burst of applause. Shade's tattoos were sliding across his skin in a wanton display of his Dark Gift. The audience ate it up. No wonder Fife liked to show off the "local color."

On the other side of the drill well, Gabion scowled at Shade's newfound popularity.

Eel joined Gemma and me at the rail. "Now all Shade has to do is dump that ugly lug in the water."

"All of him," Kale clarified. "If Gabion has even one finger on the raft, the match isn't over."

"Well, that sounds easy enough," Gemma said hopefully.

Eel raised a brow. "Sure, easy. Except that anything goes. Biting, spiking, head butting . . ."

"Gouging," Trilo put in.

"Strangling," Hatchet added.

"Stop that," Gemma commanded.

I thought she didn't want to hear any more gruesome techniques, but then she added, "Use a napkin," and I realized that she was talking to Eel, who was wiping his greasy hands down the front of his shirt.

Grinning at her, he pulled the bandana from his head and daintily dabbed at his mouth.

On either side of the pool, Shade and Gabion climbed into small boats.

As the two boxers were rowed toward the raft, Eel pointed at the spectators. "They're hoping for blood and gore. Betting on it. And as you heard, Fife likes to give the tourists what they want."

Shade and Gabion stepped onto the raft in unison, yet it still tipped wildly. Clearly the barrels that kept it afloat were positioned under the middle of the raft, leaving the sides seesawing. This would be less of a boxing match, I decided, than a contest of balance.

With their eyes pinned on each other, Shade and Gabion found their footing. As soon as their movements stilled, a gong signaled the start of the match.

THIRTEEN

"Here we go," Hatchet said with a grin that exposed his disturbing-looking teeth.

Shade and his opponent squared off while trying to stay balanced. It looked hard, and I'd have bet doing it was even harder.

Gabion took the first swing, which Shade dodged easily while rippling with intense color—red to neon white, just like a diablo rojo squid. The crowd went wild over his trick. Even Gabion seemed surprised, and he dropped his fists for a moment. That's when I noticed his hands. Leaning over the railing, I tried to get a better look.

"What's wrong with his knuckles?" I asked, which had the outlaws' attention instantly. Gabion's knuckles weren't just enlarged; they bulged as if he'd pushed five small rocks under his skin.

"Would you look at that," Eel said with disgust. "He's injected them."

"With what?" Gemma asked.

Kale frowned, majorly put out. "Carbonate."

"The stuff barnacles make their shells out of?" I asked.

Eel nodded. "Makes the skin over your knuckles pop out and delivers a punch that feels like you got black-jacked with a sack of ball bearings."

"Well, that's not fair," Gemma said angrily. "Where's Mayor Fife? We have to tell him."

"Anything goes," I reminded her.

"Whatever draws the tourists and their money," Pretty quoted with disgust.

Just then Gabion's fist connected with Shade's face, slicing open his cheek like ribbon. Eel hissed in air while Gemma jerked back and clamped her hand over her mouth.

Shouts of "first blood" whipped through the decks above, and money changed hands. I saw Tupper fork over a wad of cash to Fife. My heart sank as I realized there was a very real chance that Shade wouldn't win this match. Which meant that Levee wouldn't tell me what he knew about Drift and I'd be as stymied as ever on how to track down my parents.

"Why is he doing this?" Gemma demanded. "For the prize money?"

"Why else?" Eel asked.

"There are better ways to make money," she replied. "Safer ways."

"Not when there's a bounty out on you," Hatchet said.

"And bounty hunters who only back off if they get paid off," Kale added evenly.

"Told him not to turn twenty-one," Eel said, returning to the railing.

"You don't have to watch," I whispered to Gemma, who was looking like she might pass out. She shook her head and kept her eyes pinned on Shade as if she could protect him through sheer force of will.

The fighters regained their balance and straightened. There was no fancy footwork in this match. No dancing around. One wrong step could send either one tumbling into the water. Shade's skin darkened as if he were being charred over coals, until he was pitch-black and difficult to see.

When Gabion's fist shot out again, Shade sidestepped it and landed a punch to Gabion's kidney. Gabion let out a bark of pain, and I caught a glimpse of his tongue. Not only was it blanched whiter than white, it appeared swollen to three times its natural size. No wonder he couldn't talk.

Shade jackhammered both fists into Gabion's gut and then tried heaving him into the water, but Gabion grabbed him around the legs and brought them both down in the center of the raft.

Suddenly boots pounded through the crowd, accompanied by shouts of "Move!"

On the raft, Shade and Gabion continued to grapple though neither could get a firm grip on the other because of the oil slicking their skin.

"Freeze!" a voice rang out. Across the pool, Captain Revas put a foot on the railing. "This match is over."

As soon as Shade spotted her, his skin paled. Redoubling his efforts, he pried himself out of Gabion's grip and got to his feet. Revas snatched a crossbow from one of her troopers. As Shade dove for the pool, she took aim and fired. The thin spear sliced through Shade's right thigh, its point splitting into a double barb.

Jamming back a lever, Revas switched on the crossbow's automated spool. With a hiss, the line pulled taut while its barbed tip kept the spear embedded in the outlaw's leg. Revas gripped the crossbow tight as the line retracted, dragging Shade across the water in a geyser of spray as if he were a thrashing swordfish.

Fife watched with stunned fury as two troopers climbed to the other side of the railing and hung off, hands outstretched, waiting for their catch to arrive.

"You did this, didn't you?" Pretty hissed. "Called the Seaguard."

I realized his ice blue eyes were on me and my pulse quickened. "Why would I?"

The crowd roared its indignation as Shade was hauled onto the deck. He collapsed, holding his thigh, grimacing in pain. Food and cups rained down on the pool, flung by angry spectators.

Pretty angled closer, his hand resting on the hilt of his knife. "To collect the bounty."

I refused to back up. "Money is about the last thing on my mind right now."

Gemma stepped between us. "Ty would never do that."

"Ease up," Eel said, beckoning Pretty back. "Those flyers went out all over. Anyone could have recognized him."

Hand still on his blade, Pretty eyed me as if unconvinced.

Suddenly I remembered telling Levee and Krait about Shade before the match, and guilt stabbed through me. I'd told them that he was the leader of the Seablite Gang. What if they had called it in to collect the bounty?

On the other side of the drill well a trooper tended to the spear in Shade's leg. After slicing open the outlaw's pant leg, he snapped the hinged barb back into the spearhead and yanked the shaft from Shade's thigh. Blood welled from the wound until the trooper sprayed it with artificial skin—a temporary fix, which would do nothing for the pain.

Jaw clenched, Shade heaved himself to his knees and then stood, leaning against the railing. The crowd shouted its approval, but he didn't respond. As the troopers handcuffed him, Shade's eyes scanned the crowd, his expression furious. Clearly he, too, thought someone had turned him in.

Suddenly Fife sparked to life, shouting, "There is no ordinance against bare-knuckle fights on the ocean." He stormed toward the troopers. "Rip Tide might be stationary, but it is off coast. As in surrounded by water. Officially."

Captain Revas met him halfway. "Federal law applies everywhere, Mayor. This isn't about an ordinance. It's about harboring a fugitive. Now I suppose you're going to tell me that you didn't know there's a bounty out on him."

In a blink, Fife turned conciliatory. "Shocked to hear it." He slipped his hand inside his cassock. "But I ask you, Captain, what's the difference between arresting him now versus after the match?"

I was standing close enough to see Fife offer her a thick stack of bills.

With a flick of her fingers, Revas called two troopers forward. "Arrest him" — she turned her gesture to Fife — "for the attempted bribery of a Seaguard officer."

"What . . . this?" Fife waved the money at himself. "Just using it to cool myself down. But I'll put it away since it's obviously given you the wrong impression, Captain."

Revas said nothing until Fife tucked the money back into his cassock. Then she spoke. "Rip Tide has a jail cell." It was a statement, not a question.

"Bottom deck. But why not just take him with you now?"

"Because we're here for the night." She held Fife in a steady gaze, daring him to argue.

"Glad to have you. Though you should know we only rent out rooms on deck four, and they're all taken."

"I'm not here to sleep."

With a shrug, Fife drew a key ring from his pocket. "You're not planning to put the kibosh on all of our fun, are you, Captain?" Freeing a key, he tossed it to Revas.

"Confine yourself to legal activities, and you don't have to ask."

As soon as she headed back to the troopers holding Shade, Fife's pleasant expression hardened. "And I thought *I* put on a good show."

Pushing Shade in front of her, Captain Revas disappeared down the last stairwell.

"Except for the uniform," Eel said, watching them go, "she's adorable."

"Tell me you're kidding," Kale snapped. "She just arrested Shade!"

Eel shrugged. "Didn't say she was perfect."

"All that lost revenue," Fife murmured while gazing at the decks above.

A voice cut through the silence. "The rules say a second can fight in his stead."

I looked over to see that Representative Tupper had offered up that little fact. Now he ducked his slathered white head as if wishing he hadn't called attention to himself.

Clapping with gusto, Fife said, "Now, that's some polished thinking." He stepped onto the announcer's platform and picked up the microphone. "This match isn't over," he told the crowd. "Shade's second will replace him as the challenger." Joining the Seablite Gang on the deck, he asked, "Okay, who's going in for Shade?"

I held my breath. One of them had to volunteer to be the challenger. Even more important, whoever it was had to win. The only way Levee would tell me what he knew about Drift was if he collected on his bet.

"Come on, boys," Fife prompted. "I know Shade needs the money."

"He only needed it to keep the law off his back." Eel lounged defiantly. "Not much point in earning it now, is there?"

I looked from outlaw to outlaw, took in their truculent expressions, and my hope faded.

Fife was slower to catch on. "Hatchet, I've seen you in plenty of brawls."

"That's for fun," he scoffed. "Not pay." As if that was something to be proud of.

"Pretty, what about it?" Fife asked. One glance at Pretty's very unpretty expression had him turning back to the rest of the gang. "Guys, help a fellow out."

What had Levee said? That only surfs were desperate enough to end up in that ring. But he was wrong.

"Come on," Fife cajoled. "Who's it going to be?"

I stepped forward, before the insanity of it could sink in. "Me."

FOURTEEN

"The people want to see boxing, not murder," Fife said, looking me over. "Well, not in the first minute anyway. I need someone who can land a punch or two before going into the drink."

"I'm not going to end up in the drink," I said firmly. "I'm going to win." Or die trying. I needed a lead if I was going to find Ma and Pa.

Fife faced the Seablite Gang again, but no one stepped forward. "Okay," he said crisply. "You're in."

I nodded, though the truth was that I was close to puking from fear. Without another word, Fife headed for the announcer's platform that jutted a few feet over the drill well.

"No!" Gemma cried.

As if he hadn't heard her, Fife picked up the microphone and told the crowd that as Shade's second, I was now the official challenger and all wagers would be honored as such.

"Ty, what are you doing?" Gemma pointed at Gabion,

who lounged on the raft, eating a mango that someone had tossed him. "He will pulverize you."

"Thanks for the vote of confidence."

"She's right," Kale said. "Gabion's reach is twice as long as yours. You'll never get in a punch."

Eel stopped cleaning his teeth with a crab claw and grinned. "And even if you do, Gabion is used to worse than anything a sea squirt like you can muster."

He had nerve calling me a squirt; he wasn't that much bigger than me—and Gabion dwarfed us both. "I don't have to get in a punch. I just have to stay on the raft while spilling him off."

"How?" Gemma demanded, hysteria tingeing her words. "He's got a hundred pounds on you. Maybe more. All muscle."

"That's to my advantage." At least I hoped so. "He's heavier, so his side will drop closer to the water."

"Not if he stands in the middle and throws you in headfirst," Trilo pointed out.

Hatchet laughed. "And when the lampreys get done sucking on you, you'll weigh nothing at all."

As he stepped off the platform, Fife gestured to me. "You've got five minutes to wash off that zinc and get greased."

Moving fast to keep myself from thinking, I scrubbed off the blue zinc-paste with handfuls of wet sea salt. Now the surfs would know I was a pioneer. But if they made money off their bets, maybe they wouldn't care. Maybe I could still get the answers I needed from them. All I had to do was win. No small order, that. I tried to come up with a strategy, but all my brain could conjure was Gabion's fist colliding with my face.

As I drizzled fish oil down my arms and across my chest, a stark white head glided through the crowd toward me. Representative Tupper in all his zinced-out glory. "I had a thought," he said while beckoning Fife over. "You grew up subsea."

"So?" I said defensively.

"So . . ." Tupper paused until Fife had joined us. "You have some secret ability, yes? Like the outlaw. What you settlers call a Dark Gift."

Fife's eyes widened with delight. "Now we're talking."

"I'm not asking so that you can turn the boy into a sideshow," Tupper snapped. "I'm trying to help him."

He swung his attention back to me. But when I kept my mouth shut, he *tsk*ed with impatience. "Now is not the time to be coy, Ty. If you can do anything that could give you an advantage in that ring, tell us and let's think of how you can use it."

I didn't hide my Dark Gift anymore. Or deny it. But I wasn't keen on showing it to the world, either.

I glanced at my opponent and that decided me. "Biosonar."

"Which means what?"

"I can see using echolocation."

His brows rose in surprise. "All right, then," he mused. "That would give you an advantage in the dark. . . ."

"Yeah." But with spotlights trained on the raft, I didn't see what difference it made.

Fife shot Tupper a reproachful look. "I know where you're going with this, but these people paid good money to *see* a fight."

"They won't see anything if it's over in two seconds," Tupper retorted.

"Point taken." Fife sighed heavily. "I'll tell them to dial down the lights."

I watched him hurry off, knowing that dimming the lights wouldn't make much difference. The drill well was too loud to hear my own clicks or echoes and the fight would probably move too fast for my sonar to be of any use. Still, I didn't want to rule it out.

I realized that Tupper was studying me and stiffened. *Here it comes*, I thought. Some slam against my parents for raising me subsea.

His eyes flicked over the people around us. "Can you use it as a weapon?" he asked in a hushed voice.

"What?"

"Your sonar. Ever tried directing it at a person and, you know, amping it up a bit?"

Amping it up? "What would that do?"

"I'm thinking of those crowd-control guns that the

Seaguard uses. They shoot sound waves or some such thing. Send people running." He shook his head as if dismissing the thought. "Never mind. I don't know what I'm talking about. Good luck out there," he said, giving my shoulder a squeeze.

He headed back to his seat while I let his question sink in. Use my Dark Gift as a weapon? I'd never tried, though I'd seen dolphins and whales stun fish with bursts of sonar plenty of times. But those noises were rapid low-frequency bangs, not the clicks used in echolocation.

Could I make such an intense burst of sound? "Amp it up" enough to disorient a fish? I'd give it a try the next time I was in the ocean, I promised myself. But not now. No matter how scary Gabion was, I wouldn't try it on a human.

Suddenly, lights cut out all over Rip Tide and the applause started up. I could even hear cheering coming from the distant shore.

"Everyone, back to your seats," Fife said into the microphone. "Let's get this show on the raft." He waved to the guy in the rowboat.

Gemma looked a hundred times more worried now than she had while watching Shade's match, which I both liked and found a little insulting.

"Don't die," she instructed, giving me a quick hug.

With a nod, I climbed over the railing and dropped into the waiting rowboat. When I tossed my towel up to Eel, his eyes widened.

"Oh, chum," he said. "Not your best move."

"What?" I asked, but the boatman began to row me toward the raft. As I settled onto the bench, I saw what had startled him.

My shine.

I liked to think I didn't glow. Or kid myself that it was just a faint shimmer. But in some instances, it was impossible to deny. In the dark, I glowed. As bright as the full moon on a summer night. As if to prove it beyond a doubt, when I leapt from the boat to the raft, a gasp went up in the crowd, which then turned to one long collective, "Ohhh."

"Why did we dim the lights?" I heard Fife ask. "How does that help him?"

It didn't.

As the evil grin on Gabion's face could attest. Seeing that he had my attention, he opened his mouth wide. I stumbled back in horror. Instead of a tongue, a swollen white parasite lived inside of his mouth. I'd seen it in fish . . . but how had a human not noticed that a parasite had taken up residence in his mouth, feasting on his tongue as it grew, finally attaching itself to the bloody stump?

Before I could stop myself, I heaved the contents of my stomach onto the raft. The conch fritters that Eel had pushed on me tasted even worse the second time around. Gabion roared with laughter as I wiped my mouth on my arm. Hate surged through me. Hate for the lowlifes on

Drift who'd taken Ma and Pa and for surfs in general, including the ugly one in front of me.

"Ty," Fife shouted from the announcer's platform, "do you need some time?"

"No," I said hoarsely, and then raised my voice. "I'm fine."

Before I had a chance to talk myself into that lie, the gong reverberated across the water and Gabion's fist shot forward. I ducked, moving faster than I have ever moved in my life, and felt a whoosh of air ruffle my hair. As I scrambled back, he opened his mouth wide and waggled the parasite at me as if it were his tongue. I dodged around him as much to avoid looking into his mouth as to avoid his punch.

Twilight turned the spectators into a haze of color. Which is why the sleek blue jumpsuit caught my eye as it cut through the delicate clouds of clothing. Nudging the tourists aside, Revas stepped up to the railing. Upon spotting me, she froze.

When a slash of movement blocked my view, I dropped into a crouch. Gabion's fist sailed over my head, his height working against him. If I kept low, made him lean down to get me, he'd have a harder time staying balanced. I shot another look at the railing but Revas was gone.

When I spotted her again, she had a handful of the front of Fife's cassock and a finger jabbing in my direction.

Even though I couldn't hear her words, her meaning was clear — *"Stop the fight!"*

Gabion roared with frustration when I rolled under another jab. On the deck, Revas rounded on her troopers and sent them running for the crank that pulled in the raft.

Knowing I had just seconds to bring in a win before the match was closed down, I stayed crouched and let Gabion close in. Clearly, he was done throwing punches. Knuckles bulging, he reached for me, intending to hurl me into the pool. I hunkered even lower, forcing him to bend. Then I shot upward, cracked my skull into his chin, and sent him staggering backward.

Like a flying fish, I leapt into the air and landed hard on his side of the raft, crouching fast to grab on to the edge. Our combined weight sent his side plummeting into the water. The raft went vertical. I held on, while Gabion crashed into the pool. As the raft flipped over completely, I never lost my grip. Making sure that my fingers showed every inch of the way, I dragged myself hand over hand along the side. The splashdown had cleared away the eels momentarily. But they were back just as I reached the center of the raft. I felt them winnowing between my legs, trying to find flesh. Hoisting myself out of the water, I sprawled alongside the barrels that ran down the middle of the raft.

I spit salt water, shook an eel out of my pant leg, and got to my feet. A spotlight lit up with a pop, blinding me.

Then noise filled the drill well. Hollering and cheering loud enough to wake the comatose.

With a jerk, the raft was cranked in. A hand reached from the shadows—Fife's—as he offered to help me onto the deck. He kept my arm aloft as waves of cheers engulfed us and hats flew into the air. I blinked against the lights, wishing I could shoot sonar at Levee up on the sundeck—see if he seemed satisfied. But I'd never hear the echo from my clicks in this mayhem.

Guiding me onto the announcer's platform, Fife gestured to Ratter to hand him the microphone. Below us, men clambered onto the upside-down raft and hauled Gabion out of the pool. The water sluiced from his body but the slick gray eels remained, a dozen at least, wriggling wherever they'd latched.

Ratter offered Fife the microphone, but Captain Revas snagged it. Expression steely, she said, "Well done, Ty. Too bad you can't collect the prize."

Panic gripped me. She couldn't be serious. I lowered my arm, pulling Fife's down, too.

"What are you talking about?" he demanded, pushing past me to step off the announcer's platform. "The boy won. Fair and square."

"The *boy* shouldn't have been in the ring," Revas snapped. "Tell me you don't know about the law against using minors in commercial sports."

"Nobody planned this, you hauling off Shade. This

was a onetime circumstance. So have a heart. Let me declare Ty the winner. He earned it."

"He's underage. You're going to declare this match invalid." She thrust the microphone into Fife's hands. "Now."

"No!" I stepped off the platform. But when I saw her expression harden, I amended my tone. "Don't give me the prize money. That's fine. But at least let Fife declare me the winner so the surfs can collect on their bets."

"Sorry, kid. The law doesn't make exceptions." She lifted her gaze to Fife. "For anyone."

Fife opened his mouth to reply, but Revas cut him off. "Another word out of you, Mayor Fife, and I'll charge you with child exploitation." She pointed at the announcer's platform. "Now tell the crowd there's no winner and return their bets and entry fees." She stood back, fully expecting to be obeyed.

Seething, Fife stepped onto the platform and instantly the crowd quieted. He motioned to someone above and lights all over Rip Tide came on, signaling that the event was over. All eyes were on him. "Unfortunately, due to a technicality, I have to disqualify the challenger and declare this match invalid."

Groans, complaints, and boos echoed through the drill well.

"The bookies will return your bets. And you'll get your entry fee back as you depart Rip Tide." Fife turned to Ratter. "Finish pulling eels off him"—he pointed at Gabion—"then get the strongbox and return their money."

"That's the government for ya," Ratter said bitterly. "Always meddling in people's business."

"Just take care of it." Fife glared at Captain Revas's retreating back. "And I don't want to hear about how much we lost." Wincing at the thought, he sat down hard on the edge of the platform.

"I know, boss. No details," Ratter assured him, and bent over Gabion to pry off another eel.

Leaning over the railing, I scanned the sundeck. I hoped Levee would talk to me anyway. With the town lights blazing, I quickly spotted the surf I'd made the deal with. The one who knew something about Drift. Who had information that might help me find my mother and father. Or give me a clue as to how to save them.

Levee stared down at me impassively, tore up his betting stub, and tossed the pieces over the railing. His message was clear; he'd tell me nothing now.

As I watched the bits of paper float down to the pool, my hope sank with them.

FIFTEEN

I knew who I had to thank for snatching away my one chance at getting information. All because of my age. And while Captain Revas was so busy sticking to the letter of the law, who was tracking down my parents?

Gabion grunted as Ratter yanked another lamprey from his blood-slicked body and tossed it aside. Despite his obvious pain, Gemma closed in on the slumped boxer. "You could have really hurt him out there," she said, pointing at me. "He's only fifteen, you know."

Yelling at the guy who'd lost didn't strike me as very sportsmanlike, but Gabion was going to have to defend himself against her scolding.

"I'm almost sixteen," I told her as I passed to catch up with Captain Revas.

"Okay, he's almost sixteen," she amended, "but he's still half your size."

I smothered the urge to turn and correct that overstatement as well, and instead focused on my anger at the captain. I blocked her path. "I was close to getting information about Drift."

"You're out of line. Step off," she said, without a trace of anger.

"Why are you even here? I thought you were out trying to save thousands of surfs. Isn't that why you couldn't spare more than three skimmers today?"

Though her dark eyes flashed, her tone remained cool. "Kid, I told you to go home. Last thing I need is a settler making some stupid comment that riles up the surfs."

"I know better." Even though I'd thought plenty of offensive things about surfs since the morning—with good reason.

"The way you knew how they felt about the ordinance?" she asked pointedly, and then stepped around me.

Okay, maybe I didn't know what got surfs riled, but I'd mingled with them today and managed not to incite an uprising. I matched her pace. "There's a surf on the sundeck who knows something about Drift."

"A lot of them do. And so do I."

"What?" I demanded. "What do you know?"

She didn't answer.

"At least tell me why you think the Drift surfs did it—if they're not asking for ransom."

Stopping short, she faced me. "I tried putting it nicely, kid. But now I am officially ordering you off Rip Tide. Is that clear?"

A movement nearby caught my attention. Gabion had

hoisted himself into a sitting position on the deck. With his beady eyes pinned on me, he was obviously listening with interest.

"Is that clear?" Revas repeated in a military snarl.

"As dewdrops on a summer day." Fife pushed himself up from his seat on the platform. "Ty needs to hurry back to the territory. He gets it." He joined us. "Go do your Seaguard thing, Captain Revas, and I'll make sure the boy gets off safely."

Revas gave me a look like she wanted to crack open my head and see what I was planning, but all she said was, "I'll contact you when I have news." She stalked away then, barking orders at her troopers.

"Never cross the young ones, Ty," Fife advised. "They're always out to prove themselves, and it's never pretty."

"Depends how you define 'pretty,'" Eel said, his eyes following Captain Revas.

"I can have Ratter take you two back to your Trade Station in my airship," Fife offered.

"We have a sub." All the energy leaked out of me. I just wanted answers—or at least assurance that my parents were going to be okay. And she expected me to go home with nothing.

"Don't know how you folks do it. You can't get me to travel a mile underwater. And living down there . . ." Fife shivered. "If the only wilderness I see is steamed and served on a plate, I'm a happy man. Anyway," he went on, "the line for the cable car will be a mile long. Go get some dinner at the café, champ. The girl, too. On me. You can take off when the crowd clears out."

"Mayor Fife, can I go down to the jail and see Shade?" Gemma asked.

"Ask Captain Revas," he said, strolling away. "While she's on Rip Tide, I'm a guest in my own town."

When Gemma took off to ask the captain, I slumped to the deck, feeling shipwrecked—smashed and run aground. An eel writhed, inches from my hand. With a swat, I sent it skidding back into the water and then noticed that Gabion was gone. I'd won the match fairly and yet had nothing to show for it. Not a single lead to pursue. How was I going to find Ma and Pa?

Bodies closed in on me, forming a circle of boots. Looking up, I found the Seablite Gang—minus Eel and Shade—glaring down at me. Now they looked as dangerous as I remembered.

"Seems you did bring the Seaguard here after all," Pretty said. His tone was smooth, which was far more ominous than if he'd yelled.

"Making Shade's arrest your fault," Hatchet snarled, putting his sharpened teeth on full display.

"My fault?" I said, incredulous. I spotted Eel against the railing. He shrugged as if there was nothing he could do.

"Either you spring Shade tonight," Kale warned, "or we will hunt you until you're dead."

"What did he say?" I asked Gemma when she returned from stopping by Representative Tupper's table in the open café. We settled into a dark corner of the sundeck as far from the musicians as we could get. I'd retrieved my shirt and bandana from the slather shop but was too worried about my parents to eat. And too angry to follow Revas's order to go home. So for now, I was staying out of sight.

The moon was bright and the party was in full swing. Not a single surf remained on Rip Tide. They'd been ushered off in droves the moment the boxing match was over. Only Topsiders were invited to this shindig, to laugh and dance on the sundeck under swaying ropes of tiny lights. Their zinc paint long since smeared. Their silky clothing stained. I wondered if the permanent residents of Rip Tide were lying in their beds now, cursing the racket that had to be echoing through all seven levels of the town.

"That only the president of the Assembly can issue a pardon for an outlaw," Gemma said glumly. "And that she'd need a really good reason to do it."

"Did you remind Tupper that the 'wealth locked the Seablite Gang in an underwater reform home and let a doctor experiment on them? The president should issue Shade a pardon for that alone, and let him start fresh."

"I said all that and more." Gemma sounded broken-hearted. "But Tupper says President Warison isn't going to stick her neck out for some fugitive, because she's already under constant attack."

"Attack from who?"

"I didn't bother to ask. I'm sure Tupper meant the scientists who are demanding that the 'wealth repeal Emergency Law because the Rising is over."

"They'll never do it," I scoffed. "If we're not living under Emergency Law, the states could hold elections again and all those Assembly representatives would get ousted. Including President Warison."

Gemma shrugged, not caring one way or the other.

"Captain Revas should have let you see Shade." As soon as the words were out, I felt bad for reminding her of her dwindling options. With Shade in prison, she couldn't exactly live on the *Specter*.

"She said no even after I told her that I was his sister."

"No surprise. She's heartless."

"I just wanted to talk to him. We didn't get much of a chance before the match."

And in the little time they'd had together, Gemma had told him about my crisis, even though hers—finding a place to live—had to be weighing on her.

"I guess you were right," she said. "The 'wealth doesn't care about families."

I winced inwardly because I knew that fact better than most. The 'wealth had tried to rip my family apart when it came out that I had a Dark Gift. Topside doctors took my parents to court in an effort to get them declared unfit, all because they'd raised me subsea. Ever since hearing Shade's story, I'd often thought that if I had been made a ward of the 'wealth, I probably would have ended up in Seablite as well.

I looked out at the ocean as panic rose in my chest. If I didn't find my parents, Zoe and I could still end up as wards of the 'wealth. I shook off the thought. There was no way that I would let that happen. Especially not to Zoe. With her Dark Gift, someone in the government would take an interest in her and nothing good could come of that.

A gunshot rang out close by, making us both jump. We whirled to see a couple of Topsiders shooting skeet a little ways down the wall. With a *ker-chunk*, another glow-in-the-dark pigeon sailed into the night sky, followed by another shot. A hit this time, and the clay pigeon exploded over the ocean.

As the glowing dust drifted downward, an enormous fin broke the waves. The skeet shooters shouted, freaking over the size of the shark. Gemma and I exchanged a glance, knowing it was the Seablite Gang's sub, the *Specter*, circling Rip Tide, waiting for me to deliver Shade. I should probably have taken their threat seriously, but right then I didn't care about my own well-being.

At least that's what I thought until a hand grabbed me from behind and dragged me into the shadows of the stairwell. Gemma's horrified expression gave me some prep for what I'd see when I turned. Still, my heart flipped over when I found Gabion scowling down at me.

And worse, he spoke.

A guttural, unintelligible string of words flew out of him and sent me stumbling back to avoid his spittle. But his grip on me tightened, keeping me close. When he opened his mouth again, my gaze locked on the white parasite within, which looked like an oversized sand flea. The creature waggled and flapped, almost as if dancing to his grunts.

Gemma stepped up beside me. "Try again," she said matter-of-factly. "The first word is 'go,' right?"

When Gabion nodded, I nearly fell over from shock.

He let go of my arm and spoke again. Still unintelligible but, I now realized, not angry. He wasn't looking to clout me for taking his title. With his black eyes boring into mine, he was desperately trying to tell me something. But for the life of me, I couldn't guess what.

"I-I'm sorry," I stammered. "I don't understand."

He looked to Gemma, but when she shook her head as well, he growled in frustration.

"Can you write it down?" she asked.

He winced, and I guessed that was a sore subject. I'd heard that a lot of surfs were illiterate. I wondered if asking him to act it out would be too insulting. But then another thought hit me. "Can you sign?"

His face lit up, and he pointed at me hopefully.

"Yeah, I can." And in sign language I told him, *All the settlers can sign.*

He looked astonished at that, and I realized there was a lot that surfs and settlers didn't know about each other.

Raising his hands with their bulging knuckles, Gabion signed, *Most surfs can't.*

A tick of pain tightened my throat. How awful to have no one understand you. How lonely. *What did you want to tell me?* I asked before realizing that *I* didn't need to sign. Gabion wasn't deaf.

Footsteps clanged on the metal stairs below us. At least two people were coming up to the sundeck. Gabion shot a worried glance behind him as he quickly signed, *Go to the black market.*

"Is that where Drift is?" I asked.

He shook his head. Then he seemed to reconsider and lifted his hands, palms up to show he didn't know.

Gemma nudged me. "What did he say?"

"Why should I go?" I asked him. "What's at the black market?"

Voices drifted up the stairwell as the footsteps climbed higher. Gabion jerked as if he'd been poked with a shock-prod. He spun to look down the stairs.

"Because he's your prisoner until dawn," the woman on the stairs snapped. "So station someone outside his cell." I recognized Captain Revas's voice.

Clearly Gabion did, too, because he motioned that he had to go.

I wondered why Revas had him running scared. "Wait," I whispered, even though the footsteps were nearing the top of the stairs.

"Why can't one of your troopers guard him?" asked a second voice, sounding very put out. Not surprisingly, it was Mayor Fife.

Backing into the shadows, Gabion signed, *Hardluck Ruins tomorrow night*, and vanished just as Captain Revas appeared.

I glanced at Gemma, who was frowning at the spot where Gabion had been. Brows pinched, she seemed suspicious of something. I beckoned her into the darkness of the covered walkway. The last thing I needed was another confrontation with Captain Revas.

SIXTEEN

Gemma and I watched from the shadows as Captain Revas paused at the top of the stairs and took a key from her pocket. "We're leaving, and our sub can't accommodate a prisoner. If Shade escapes before I return," she said as Fife joined her on the deck, "I will hold you responsible." She thrust the key into the mayor's hand.

"Whatever you say, Captain." Fife's smile barely concealed his irritation. "How's the hunt going for the other two townships?"

I saw Revas's expression tighten, and then without a word, she left him. As soon as she strode past, I slipped out of the shadows.

"I still don't see how this is my job," Fife groused, pocketing the key. "I didn't arrest Shade," he called to Revas's retreating back. "I didn't even want him arrested!" When that got no reaction, Fife gave me a what-are-you-going-to-do shrug.

Joining us, Gemma frowned at him. "The captain didn't appreciate your township comment."

"Just amusing myself at her expense."

"It's not funny, though."

Fife looked at Gemma with surprise. "You think I don't care about those surfs? I'm the only one who noticed that they were missing. I'm the one who—Ratter, no!" he shouted, waving frantically past us.

We turned just as Ratter tipped a man over the side of the wall and sent him screaming into the ocean. There was a distant splash, but no one else on the sundeck seemed to hear it above the music.

In answer to Fife's astounded glare, Ratter shrugged. "You told me to take care of the troublemakers." Snatching a life preserver off the wall, he flung it into the waves without looking. "He'll make it, boss. He wasn't that drunk."

As Ratter shoved off, Gemma and I hurried over to the wall and saw the man below, gripping the life preserver, kicking his way to shore. Instead of taking a look for himself, Fife watched us slump with relief and relaxed. "Sit," he said, waving us toward the café tables. "And I'll tell you about the missing townships if you're interested."

The fact that he didn't fire Ratter or even yell at him irked me. But I did want to know about the townships, so I followed Fife through the crowd. Matching my stride, Gemma seemed to have let curiosity muffle her annoyance, too.

As we settled at a table, I noticed that the people around us all had glowing blue lips and teeth. *Another weird Topside fashion?* I wondered. Then I spotted the center table piled high with clams—piddocks, to be exact. The kind that squirted phosphorescent slime. At the surrounding tables, people were happily cracking open the piddocks, slurping them down, and roaring with laughter as luminous goo dripped from their chins.

Oblivious to the partygoers' antics, Fife launched into his explanation. "Rain or shine, on the first of the month, the townships show up at Rip Tide to collect their rations. When Fiddleback didn't show up one month, I told the Seaguard that something tragic must have happened. These townships need the supplies too much to skip a month. But the Seaguard did nothing. Six months later, Surge stopped coming. Called that in—nothing. Finally, this month when Nomad didn't show, the Seaguard sent young Captain Revas to investigate. Can't say I'm too impressed. Heard you two found Nomad." Fife hailed a waiter. "Bring me a glass of sugar kelp wine. And for you," he said looking at us, "carrageen milk shakes?"

"No, thanks," I said, knowing Gemma hated the mossy red seaweed, especially when served as a spicy, gelatinous drink.

"Why would someone do it?" Gemma asked him. "Kill all those people?"

"I think I'll keep my mouth shut on that subject or *I* might end up anchored to the seafloor."

"We won't repeat it," she assured.

With a sigh, Fife leaned across the table. "It's a guess, that's all, but I think certain government officials might be tired of fulfilling a treaty that was made eighty years ago."

Gemma shot me a told-you-so look.

"The past few years, the 'wealth has been sending fewer rations. The surfs are barely scraping by. When I asked about it, I was told that the order to cut back came from on high. Wouldn't surprise me if other orders got passed down as well."

"To anchor a township?" I asked, disbelieving. "No one would obey an order like that."

"History says otherwise," Fife countered. "Look at it this way: Who stands to benefit if the surfeit population goes down? Only the government." Suddenly a hearty smile spread over his face. "Well, hello, Rep. Care to join us?"

I turned to see Representative Tupper coming up behind me. Fife sent us a conspiratorial look — as if we needed to be told not to criticize the 'wealth around Tupper.

"No, I'm heading back to the mainland now," Tupper said. His streaky zinc slather gave him an unsettling look — like his face was melting. "But when I saw you with the Townson boy," he went on, "I had to come over. You're telling him all that he wants to know, right?"

Fife met eyes with me. "I think I've told Ty more than he wanted to know."

Tupper thumped me on the back. "Good. Because I've been giving your parents' situation some thought, young man. If the surfs are brazen enough to abduct two of the territory's founders, how does that look to the public? Why, it could slow down the seaward expansion. And I can assure you, no one wants that."

I felt my resentment rise. In Tupper's view, my parents' kidnapping was a public relations problem.

"Which is why I've instructed Captain Revas to keep me apprised," he went on. "If she isn't able to recover your parents in the next twenty-four hours, I will bring up the incident on the floor of the Assembly. I'll call it an act of terrorism," he finished grandly.

"What good will that do?" Gemma asked.

"My dear, a terrorist incident cannot be ignored. Not by the state representatives or the public. The surfs will have to choose: return your parents or become an official enemy of the Commonwealth."

"Why wait twenty-four hours?" I twisted in my seat to face him. "Why not put the pressure on now?"

"What a rustic life you lead on the great plains of the ocean floor," he said with amusement. "I can't throw around a word like 'terrorist' without getting the Assembly's approval first. Off the record, of course. Wouldn't want to spoil the 'shock effect' of my speech. Well, good night, all."

The party on the sundeck was growing louder. The music, laughter, even cheers.

Fife regarded me with undisguised interest. "I didn't know that your parents were such important people."

"They're not," I said. "They're just subsea farmers. But they're important to me."

"And me," Gemma said.

Fife got to his feet. "Well, I have to go find someone to guard our fugitive." He shot me a sympathetic look. "Shade is a friend of yours, I know. Mine, too. But my hands are tied. You understand that?"

I nodded while Gemma focused on rewrapping her sari.

"Can I ask you something quick?" I asked.

"Of course," he said, beckoning us to walk with him.

"I need to go to Hardluck Ruins." Ignoring Fife's raised brows, I asked, "You know where that is, right?"

"I do. . . ." His surprise turned into suspicion. "What exactly are you looking to buy?"

"Nothing. I just think I might find answers there. About Drift."

Fife stopped short. "Who put that idea into your head?"

"Good question," Gemma said, pointedly tossing the loose end of her sari over her shoulder.

"Who cares? What matters is finding my parents."

"There's no information booth in Hardluck Ruins," Fife said. "It's a place where 'dangerous' and 'unsavory' describe a good day."

"I'm old enough to decide what I can handle."

"There's a term for that, son: famous last words."

When I didn't crack a smile, he studied me.

"All right. Tell Revas to send a few troopers to check it out. That *is* their job."

"I'm done asking Captain Revas for help. She's got other priorities."

"Won't argue with you there," Fife said. "But I'm not going to help you set off on a goose chase that could get you killed. Especially when you won't tell me who pointed you in that direction. Makes me think you're being set up." With a tip of his hat, he started toward a table of raucous men, which included Ratter.

"Gabion," Gemma said.

Fife turned. "Excuse me?"

"What?" she said, catching my look. "He didn't say anything about not telling."

Because Gabion hadn't had time to say much at all, but it had been obvious that he didn't want to be caught talking to us.

"What makes you think Gabion knows anything about anything?" Fife asked me.

"It's the only lead I've got."

"Which is no lead if it's a trap," Gemma said. "He tried to knock you senseless out on that raft. Didn't pull a single punch. And now he wants to help you?"

"Smart girl," Fife said. "And I'll tell you why she's right to be suspicious. You just bumped him off the best-paying gig he'll ever have. The man can't talk. Can't read or write. The surf boxing circuit was his only shot at earning real money and you, a boy—a *settler*—humiliated him. I'm sure he's looking for payback."

"He didn't seem vindictive," I said.

"Because he's trying to lure you someplace dangerous so he can punch you to a bloody pulp," Gemma said as if it was obvious.

"Or worse," Fife added pleasantly.

A chill passed over my heart. Laid out like that, their suspicions made far more sense than Gabion taking a friendly interest in my problems.

"Sorry, son. But you're not going to get the coordinates to Hardluck Ruins from me. I don't dabble in assisted suicide."

My hopes collapsed as he strolled off. Who else would know where to find the surfs' black market? No settler, that was for sure. And if Captain Revas knew, she was even less likely to tell me than Fife was.

Gemma met my eyes, but I couldn't read her expression. "What?"

In answer, she opened her hand to reveal a key.

I inhaled sharply. "You picked Mayor Fife's pocket." Really, I shouldn't have been surprised. I'd seen her perform that trick before.

"If we don't help Shade escape, the Seablite Gang will come after you."

I suspected that wasn't the real reason she wanted her brother free, but didn't say so.

"And besides," she went on, "he might be able to tell us where Hardluck Ruins is."

After her dramatic warning about Gabion, I couldn't believe she wanted to find the place.

Seeing my skepticism, she sighed. "It's the only lead we have."

"Why would Shade know anything about Hardluck Ruins? He's not a surf."

"When his gang was robbing supply ships, they had to sell the goods somewhere. Like maybe a black market . . ."

I nodded. That made sense.

"But we can't just ask him for directions," she said firmly. "He has to promise to come along as your bodyguard."

I had to admit, Shade's protection would be no small thing. I could have kissed her for being so smart.

Well, and for other reasons. But I forced myself to focus on the problem ahead of us—breaking Shade out of jail.

"Okay, I'm in."

As I hurried down the stairs, I scanned each deck, wondering how we should get off Rip Tide. The cable car was out—at least for Shade. By freeing him, I knew I was officially throwing my lot in with outlaws. But he was the only person who might be able to help me get to Hardluck Ruins. And even that wasn't guaranteed.

As I stepped onto deck three, I heard, "Hey, kid!" and turned to see Captain Revas striding toward me. "What are you still doing here?"

Before I could stammer through some lame excuse, a trooper called to her.

"Captain, we're all boarded." He stood by a grappling hook that hung over the wall.

"Go," Revas told him. "I'm right behind you."

I was surprised to see the trooper drop over the side of the wall and disappear. I crossed and peered over in time to see him shinny down a rope and into the hatch of a massive Seaguard sub.

"Where are you going?" I faced Revas.

"Following a lead."

I couldn't help but wonder if Gabion had told her to head to Hardluck Ruins as well. But considering Gabion's obvious avoidance of the captain earlier, I decided it was unlikely.

"About my parents?"

Her look was as clear as if she'd said, *"You know better than to ask"* aloud.

"There's a lot I can't tell you, Ty, but I do want to make sure you understand why I couldn't let Fife name you the winner today."

I shrugged like it didn't matter, though truth was, I was still simmering over it. I had won, fair and square. Something as trifling as my age shouldn't factor in.

"I couldn't let it slide, exploiting a kid. Not even once," she said. "Because then a scumbag like Fife will think he can get away with it." She paused, then added, "And maybe the next boy wouldn't be so lucky out on that raft."

I clenched my jaw to keep from pointing out that the next boy was nothing more than a theory, while the danger my parents faced was real. Not that she cared.

"But if the law cracks down every time," she went on, "then the scumbags know that it's not worth it to even try."

"Sure. I understand," I replied stiffly.

"Go home," she said again, though with less vehemence than before. "You have my word that I'm doing all I can for your parents." Then she swung her legs over the wall and shinnied down the rope to the sub waiting below.

I unclenched my hands, surprised at just how clammy they were.

Without a second to spare, I crept down the last two stairwells and into cold water that came up to my chest. How I wished I had on my diveskin. But at least I'd talked Gemma into letting me come down to the jail. She thought Shade would be more likely to say yes to her, while I'd argued that I could navigate in the dark and she would be better at stalling a guard on his way down. Now that I knew the light down here wasn't just dim, it was nonexistent, I was glad she'd given in. Besides, if Shade wanted out of his cell, he'd strike a deal with any stiff who held the key.

The farther in I went, the creepier it got. Without my Dark Gift, I would have been lost, to say nothing of jumpy, between the maze of pipe-lined passages and all the hissing, rumbling, and clanking. Clearly this was the mechanicals level.

Navigating the darkness with sonar, I picked the narrow corridor that headed toward the exterior wall for no good reason other than that it led away from the deafening bangs. I considered swimming rather than walking, but the water was slick with oil and scum. Nothing I wanted to put my face in.

When I turned a corner, steam blasted out of a pipe and sent me slamming into a wall, which hurt more than it should have. Stepping away, I ran my hand over the corrugated metal and discovered that it was crusted with barnacles—as sharp as barracuda teeth. If Rip Tide's prison housed any permanent residents, I pitied them. No one—no matter what he'd done—deserved to be stuck in this wet, dark, deafening nightmare of a jail.

I paused at a cross section of passages, wondering which way to turn and whether shouting for Shade was a stupid thing to do during a prison break. Probably. But I didn't know how long Gemma would be able to keep a guard from coming down—especially if Fife discovered the key was missing. And throwing sonar clicks down the passageways revealed nothing except sloshing water and hard walls.

Then I became aware of another noise under the mechanical din. A thumping sound. Irregular. Punctuated with a metallic rattle. Like someone shaking a sheet of aluminum siding . . . or a cage.

Following the banging, I slogged through the flooded halls until I reached the exterior wall. Visibility was better in this section thanks to the moon, which gleamed off the metal stalls that lined the corridor. The jail looked hastily constructed. Especially the grating that covered the gap between the deck's exterior half wall and the ceiling. Not that an inmate could punch through the metal grille, but given unlimited time and the will to escape, eventually the bolts that held it in place could be worked out of the steel girders.

Now that I was in the correct area, the irregular thuds were louder and the rattling more alarming. I sloshed through the shadows, past empty stalls, toward the noise, which had become so ferocious, so crazed, my nerves were up and stretching. Who or what could be making such a racket?

A minute later, I spotted the answer: A huge bull shark was battering the grille above the half wall. With its broad head just under the water and both large and small dorsal fins exposed, the beast pounded and ripped at the metal grate. All while Shade lounged on his bunk with seawater lapping at his chest and his skin glowing so brightly he lit up the room.

SEVENTEEN

I gaped at the scene inside the jail cell. The thin metal grille buckled under the bull shark's ramming. But Shade didn't look like he cared one whit that the crazed beast was moments away from breaking through.

"Knew you'd be the one to fetch me." He grinned. "Bet the boys weren't too happy with you."

I couldn't take my eyes off the shark, which had torn up its own snout as much as the grate. Though only about ten feet long, the animal was heavily built and aggressive as all get out.

"He got a whiff of my bloody leg and came knocking," Shade said.

I looked back at the outlaw who was sitting in the flooded cell, relaxed and luminous. No shine could give him skin that radiant. But his Dark Gift could. "I want to make a deal," I told him.

"I'm listening."

But with one loud metallic crack, the thrashing shark had my attention again.

"I'm letting him do all the work," Shade explained. "Cutting me a way out."

"And what happens when it breaks through?"

"Things will get interesting." Lifting his fist above the water, he uncurled his fingers to show me a piece of sharpened metal. Probably taken from the bed frame. "Unless you got a better offer."

I held up the key, and his smile widened.

"Like I said, I'm listening."

Another crash from the shark changed my plan. I felt for the keyhole under the water and then jammed the key into the lock, turning it as fast as possible. Just as I yanked open the door, the shark bashed its snout through the grille and worked its snapping jaws into the stall.

Shade rose. "Thought you wanted to make a deal?"

"Just get out of there!"

"If you insist." He waded past the frenzied shark, with its head wedged through the hole, and out of the stall like he hadn't a care in the world.

I slammed the door shut and relocked it.

"You're not real good at negotiation, are you? 'Cause I don't see what you're getting out of this deal. Unless you wanted to turn outlaw."

"We're still in negotiation. Otherwise, I'll head upstairs and tell Mayor Fife that you're free. Maybe you'll get away in the *Specter* in time, maybe not."

"Can't tell anyone anything if I kill you." He crossed his arms and leaned against a wall. His expression was dead serious.

I wished I could call his bluff, remind him about giving Gemma a home. But a small part of me wasn't convinced that he was bluffing. Or that his sense of gratitude would win over his desire for freedom. Just then the shark burst through the grille, leaving a gaping hole, and plowed into the flimsy stall.

"I need a ride to Hardluck Ruins," I said quickly, not sure which alarmed me more—the bull shark or the outlaw. All I wanted was to get out of there.

"Could have just asked," Shade said in a lighter tone.

"I need to go to the Ruins tomorrow and I want you to come in case Gabion is planning to kill me."

"Heard you won today."

I noted that Gabion wanting to murder me didn't surprise him. In fact, he took it a little too much in stride. As if fearing for my life was the natural consequence of winning a boxing match. "Does that mean you'll do it?"

"I'll let you know when I feel inconvenienced."

Taking that for a yes, I sloshed back down the passageway, ready to put some distance between me and the bull shark that was now ramming the cell door.

At the top of the stairwell, Shade paused and his skin turned pitch-black. His eyes, too, which was more than a little unsettling when he turned them on me and asked, "The *Specter* still circling?"

"I think so."

"Get Gemma. Take the cable car back to the docks. We'll pick you up from there."

I said nothing, suddenly wondering if I could trust him to show. Once he was aboard the *Specter*, he might decide to head for the open ocean.

Footsteps clanged above us. Descending. Then Gemma's voice rang out, "Come on, Ratter, let me sneak one peek at the outlaw. I didn't get a good look at him in the ring."

"Can't do it, little girl," Ratter replied. "Fife said not to let anyone down."

"I'll have you know that Mayor Fife is a friend of mine," she announced.

"Fife don't have friends," Ratter said with an ugly laugh. "You either work for him or you're nothing to him. That's about it."

In a crouch-run, Shade and I crossed the deck and slipped behind an empty deep-fried shrimp stall.

Shade had limped on his wounded leg as he'd run, and now he grimaced in pain. "Change of plan."

As Gemma and Ratter appeared at the foot of the stairs, I saw her glance around and knew she was looking for us.

Shade nudged me. "No reason for you to hide."

I rose from behind the shrimp stall and gave her a wave as Ratter disappeared down the stairs.

"Get her," Shade ordered. "We're going to dive for it."

"Off Rip Tide? She's not going to want to do that." That was the understatement of the century. Still, I waved her over.

"Fine, we leave her." He stood. "Safer here anyway. But if you want a ride, you dive. That guard will sound the alarm as soon as he spots my empty cell."

We intercepted Gemma by the drill well, and Shade quickly relayed his plan.

"I'm coming," she said firmly.

"I don't have time to wait for you to take the cable car and climb down a cliff," Shade said roughly.

"I'll dive."

I shot her a look, remembering what had happened the last time she was in the ocean.

"Ty taught me how to swim," she added, as if that was the issue.

Shade tipped his head as if to say *whatever* and took off toward the far side of town.

"It's closer this way," I hissed, pointing at the half wall just past the stairwell.

He paused. "There, we'd hit the water near the jail. After we left, that shark probably headed back into the ocean."

"Shark?" Gemma asked.

"Shark!" a voice screamed. A second later Ratter barreled out of the stairwell.

"Or maybe not," Shade conceded.

At that moment, Ratter spotted us and gawked. "You!" he shouted.

Shade hooked Gemma by the elbow and took off.

"Stop there!" Ratter whipped his speargun off his back and aimed it at Shade, even though Gemma was running alongside him. "Stop or I'll pin you to the deck!"

I dove for Ratter, tackling him to keep him from pulling the trigger. A good sight heavier than me, he tried to shove me off, but I grabbed ahold of his speargun. As I tried to yank it from his hand, he rolled, using his weight to loosen my grip.

Now he had me pinned, crushing me. But when he attempted to push himself up with one hand while holding on to his weapon with the other, he floundered. He had to release all the pressure on me to get himself to his knees. I shimmied out from under him and grabbed the butt of the gun. In trying to pull it out of his hand, I unintentionally helped him up. Then a tug of war began, each of us gripping the speargun.

But he had the wrong end.

I could easily pull the trigger and send a shaft into Ratter's gut—but I wouldn't. Not that he knew that about me. Most people would have let go the second they saw that they were gripping the barrel end of a gun. Not Ratter, though, who was clearly too stupid to understand the danger he was in.

Suddenly, he tried to swing me off, using his bulk to his advantage. I went with it, letting him heave me around in a circle, figuring that he'd get dizzy first or exhaust himself well before I was spent. I wasn't *that* lightweight. It wasn't like he could get me up in the air. He had to throw his whole body into each heave, while lurching haphazardly.

On his second tipsy rotation, I realized he'd circled us to the edge of the drill well—right where there was no railing. In that split second, I knew I had a choice: let go of the gun or get thrown into the eel pool. But one glance at Ratter's dogged expression and I knew there was a third option. I went with the next lurch, tightening my grip on the speargun as I sailed off the edge of the deck. And sure enough, Ratter stubbornly refused to let go of his end of the gun, only to realize too late that by holding on, he'd be pulled into the pool with me. And so he was—splashing down one second after me.

As I sank, I released the speargun and felt it drop away. Ratter must have finally let go. All at once, a wriggling mass of eels enveloped me. Covering my face with my arms, I tried to kick away but there was nowhere to go. The lampreys were everywhere, winnowing through my clothes, seeking out bare flesh. *Use it as a weapon*, a voice in my head shouted.

I clicked rapidly but the eels only increased their writhing.

Amp it up.

This time I blasted out the lowest-pitched sound I could muster and instantly all movement around me ceased. I knocked aside the limp coils in front of my face and kicked for the surface. *It worked!* I'd stunned the eels like a dolphin stunned prey. Why hadn't I tried it before?

I surfaced just long enough to fill my lungs with air. A few yards away, Ratter thrashed toward the pool's edge. Without attracting his attention, I dove again and swam below the drifting eels.

Sending out clicks, I sensed where the net wrapped around the town's legs. Not far at all. Above me, Ratter splashed and kicked as he attempted to heave himself out of the pool.

I drew out my dive knife and tore into the net. The blade strained for only a second before cutting into the woven metal. Luckily, not titanium. The cold gnawed at my skin as I slashed a hole big enough to wriggle through. Too bad I wasn't wearing a diveskin.

I'd just made it past the net when the lampreys poured through the hole and swarmed around me. Alert once more and on the attack. Pain broke out along my neck and below my ear as eels bored into my skin. I tried blasting them with sonar again, but those that had already dug in didn't loosen their bite. By now my lungs felt scorched from needing air. But I was trapped under Rip Tide.

I swam toward the edge of the town, head dizzy, extremities cramping with cold. Had Shade and Gemma made it to the sub?

I had to get clear of the town. Had to surface *now*. I pushed my speed. Didn't even break my stroke to pull off the lampreys, though their bite burned and their heavy, soft bodies thumped against my chest.

My eardrums throbbed as I swam against the tide, yet I couldn't make any headway. A powerful undercurrent was keeping me pinned beneath the town. I dove deeper to escape its drag, only to find that the undertow was even stronger closer to the seafloor. So strong I was nearly swimming in place, unable to reclimb the water column, and I was growing weaker by the second. Close to blacking out. Only terror kept me conscious.

Lampreys ripped from my skin and vanished in the current. Which was wrong, I realized with a start.

The undertow should be moving out to sea, not toward the coast. I turned to shoot sonar over my shoulder and lost ten feet as I was whipped backward. And that's when I saw it in my mind's eye—a hulking underwater turbine, which sucked in the tide to power the town. Its housing would keep me from getting mangled, but without air, I wouldn't have the strength to pull myself away from its grille. Frenzied, I tried to swim faster, harder, anything.

Water pressed down on me as something large descended. The bull shark! I gasped, sucking in seawater. Even while choking, I threw up my hands to defend myself . . . and cracked my knuckles against metal, not the flesh of a sea creature. For a second my brain couldn't categorize the gray mass above me, then understanding hit. That was the *Specter* hovering over me.

Gagging, I began to scrabble along the underside, seeking entry, while fighting back the darkness that threatened to eclipse my thoughts. Registering that the hatch was still closed, I realized that had been Shade's plan all along—to let me drown. A burst of light appeared and something brushed the back of my neck. Another lamprey, here for the feast. I tried to knock the eel away, but it tightened its bite and jerked me upward. *Big lamprey* was my last thought before I blacked out.

The impact of hitting a floor jarred me back into consciousness, and I rolled to my side to cough up half the ocean. When my eyes could finally focus, I looked up to see that once again the Seablite Gang had me surrounded.

Shade's smile was wry. "Welcome aboard the *Specter.*"

EIGHTEEN

Most of the outlaws disappeared through the hatchway as Pretty set to work yanking the two remaining eels off my neck. The pain was sharp and intense. But I gritted my teeth to hold in my shout. Pinning me down with a boot on my shoulder, he opened a bottle of alcohol and doused me with it, and I bit down harder. He may as well have set fire to my open wounds. Seeing Eel smirking at my efforts only increased the sting.

I looked around me at the chaos that was the *Specter*'s gear room. Equipment swung precariously from hooks overhead; weapons had been piled haphazardly on the rack, while a jumble of diveskins, helmets, and boots covered the bench and floor. Even worse than the mess, the air stank of old socks and sweat.

The *Specter* picked up speed, but hearing no hum of propellers, I guessed that she was a stealth sub, powered by artificial muscles embedded between the inner and outer hulls, which let her glide through the ocean, silent as a shark.

"Where's Gemma?" I asked. Eel's smirk vanished, and he nodded at the hatchway that led into the next room.

I pushed myself up, and my body winced. "Is she okay?"

"Getting there," Eel replied. "Moved from scared stiff into shaky."

"She's fine," Pretty said as if he were the resident medical expert.

Eel shoved open the hatch and I followed him into the sub's common room, which had the feel and smell of a whale-hands' bunkhouse. Weapons and taxidermied sea creatures adorned the walls, while a punching bag swung in one corner. The lights were embedded in the ceiling like vertebrae and set on dim so that no glowing viewports gave away the sub's presence. As my eyes adjusted, I saw Gemma tucked into the corner of a padded bench.

Shade, still in his damp clothes, tossed me a towel. "Got your breath?"

I nodded, noting that the towel wasn't exactly clean—but at least it was dry.

Now I could see the blur of ocean through the dark viewport opposite the table. Whatever our destination, we were heading there fast. Hardluck Ruins, I hoped.

"Okay," Shade said as if getting down to business.

I looked over, but he was facing Gemma. "He's here." Shade hooked a thumb at me. "He's alive. Now talk."

Despite being wrapped in a blanket, she shivered. Her eyes met mine, and I read in them a silent plea for assistance.

"She gets nervous in the ocean," I told Shade, heading for her. When I was close enough, I whispered, "It happened again?"

She nodded, looking miserable.

"Nervous?" Shade scoffed. "She stopped moving. Curled up in a ball and let herself sink."

"Passive panic," I told him. "That's what it's called. Happens to new divers all the time."

"I've heard of that," Eel put in from his perch on the wall ladder.

"Can I just lie down for a while?" Gemma asked. "Then I'll be fine."

"Not till you explain," Shade said, crossing his arms over his chest.

"She doesn't want to talk about it," I snapped.

He was unfazed. "I don't care."

"You want to know what's wrong with me?" Gemma burst out. "I'm not tough, that's what. Not in the ocean. Everything about it scares me, and everything in it."

"See," Shade said calmly, "all I wanted to know." He looked over at Pretty, who, with a shoulder propped against a wall, radiated boredom. "You can take care of that?"

Pretty nodded.

"Take care of it how?" I asked.

"Pretty can hypnotize people," Eel answered. "And not just with his dazzling personality."

Kale and Hatchet spilled in from the far corridor where they'd clearly been lurking while Trilo dropped out of a hatch in the ceiling, bypassing the wall ladder that Eel had claimed for a seat.

"Pretty can make you forget your own mother," Trilo told me, and then shot a wary look at Gemma.

"Really?" She twisted on the bench to look at Pretty.

He remained impassive. "Fear is easy to take away."

"Can you make a person not see something?" she asked.

"Like what?"

Exactly my question.

She cleared her throat. "Things that might not be there . . ."

"You're seeing things?" Shade demanded.

"I see ghosts," she admitted softly. "In the ocean."

The room fell utterly silent until Shade repeated, "Ghosts?" in a tone that echoed the same disbelief I was feeling.

I wondered if she was making it up to get him off her back about being scared to swim.

"Yes." Lifting her chin, Gemma met his look. "The ocean is filled with ghosts."

Shoot. She wasn't making it up. In fact, she believed

it with the conviction of a New Puritan. "Is that what freaked you out this morning?"

She nodded.

"Why didn't you tell me?"

"I didn't want you to think I'm crazy. I know you don't believe in ghosts."

"What do they look like?" Eel threw himself onto the table to get near her. Clearly, he believed.

"They're just movement. Shapes just at the edge of my vision."

As she started to say more, Hatchet plowed forward, pushing me aside to listen.

Other than Shade, only Pretty hung back, his expression skeptical, which bugged me. Not because his skepticism wasn't warranted. I just hated knowing that he and I felt the same way about something.

"They disappear when I try to look at them directly," Gemma went on. "But it's more than that. I feel them, too."

"You mean, inside you?" Trilo's acid green eyes were aglow. "Like you're possessed?"

She shook her head. "At first I'm just aware of something around me. All around me. My skin prickles before I realize what's happening. And then that feeling turns awful."

"It hurts?" Kale asked.

"No. It's not pain. It's just . . . my whole body feels bad. Worse than bad. And that's when I see them, moving, blurry shapes, hovering next to me. But when I turn to get a better look, they vanish."

Shade turned to Pretty. "Well?"

"Maybe" was all he would commit to.

Gemma threw off the blanket, revealing her wet, ruined sari. "You can hypnotize me into not seeing them?"

"Maybe," he repeated. "I can definitely take away your fear."

"Make her not see them," Shade said firmly.

"Do both," Gemma said. "How do we start?"

"Hold up," I demanded, facing Pretty. "You're going to mess around with her mind?"

"She can undo it," Pretty said as if it were no big deal. "If she concentrates really hard on feeling and seeing what she did before."

"But if I don't do that," Gemma pressed, "I'll stay hypnotized, right? Never see them again or feel them or be afraid to swim in the ocean?"

"Can't say." Pretty pushed off from the wall and strolled closer. "I've never tried to stop someone from seeing ghosts before." Irony soaked his words.

"Can I talk to you?" Nudging aside the outlaws, I offered Gemma a hand up. "Alone."

Her gaze shifted to Shade, who swept his arm toward the gear room. "Go ahead. Let him tell you all the reasons why it's a bad idea."

"It's only a bad idea if Pretty is mad at you," Eel said,

punching Hatchet in the arm, "and you don't want to spend the day thinking you're a pig."

As the other outlaws broke into oinks and jeers at Hatchet's expense, Gemma and I retreated to the gear room.

The moment I closed the hatch, I asked, "Since when do you ask anyone for permission for anything?" At her look of confusion, I added, "Shade. You checked with him before you'd agree to come with me." And it burned me up.

She waved my point aside. "It *is* his sub."

Knowing that she wanted to live with him, it shouldn't surprise me that she'd act like his gang and treat him with deference. I had to get to what was really important. "Listen, you can't let Pretty hypnotize you."

"Why not?"

"Because there's something wrong with him."

She had that look she got whenever she didn't want to be talked out of something. "He was locked up in a reformatory when he was young. We can't all be lucky enough to have a family like yours."

"That's not the point. You read people faster than I can read a depth gauge. You know that Pretty has as much human feeling as an icefish. Probably has see-through blood and a bleached heart like one, too. And that's who you're going to let mess with your head?" When she didn't reply, I said, "We'll find another way to get you help."

"What way?" she scoffed. "A doctor will say I'm brain-baked. And maybe I am, who knows?" Shivering, she sank onto the bench. "I don't want to wait for some cure that might never come. Not when there's a chance that Pretty can fix it now."

"Because that's what Shade wants?"

"What? No," she sputtered. "I have my own reasons. Ghosts!"

"But you're doing it his way because you want his approval, want to live on the *Specter*. It's okay, I get it. He's the only family you have left."

She went very still. "I thought I was part of your family now. That's what your parents said. What you said. No matter where I bunk."

"You are." I couldn't get the words out fast enough. "But wasn't that your plan — to ask Shade if you could live with him?"

"I don't have a plan. I told you I didn't want to deal with my problem until we find your parents. Because I don't care where I end up so long as your family is back together — the way a family should be, together — even if I'm not part of it anymore."

"You *are* part of it," I told her, ignoring the throb of pressure behind my eyes and tightening throat. "I didn't realize. . . ." I paused and took a breath. "You know I want you to live with us."

She gave me a faint smile. "Because Zoe gets bored exploring shipwrecks with you. And I don't."

"And a million other reasons."

"Which is why I'm going to let Pretty hypnotize me—so I can live subsea again. And because no matter where I go, I never want to see another ghost."

What could I say? It was her decision, even if I didn't trust Pretty to do right by a goldfish.

"Would you stay in the room while he does it?" she asked.

"You couldn't keep me out."

Her smile was sad. "Make sure he doesn't put any extra crazy in my head, okay?"

"We'll hit Hardluck Ruins at daybreak," Shade said to the cluster of outlaws as we reentered the common room. "But we're not going in till sunset."

"Can Pretty hypnotize me now?" Gemma asked.

"Dry off first," Shade told her, then looked over at Trilo. "Find her something of yours to wear."

Frowning, Trilo fingered the charms around his neck.

"Don't say it again," Shade warned him.

I shot a questioning look at Eel, who now lounged on the bench, his feet propped on the table.

"He thinks having a girl on board is bad luck," Eel explained with amusement.

Trilo's frown deepened until Kale clamped a hand on the back of his neck and said pleasantly, "Or we can give her the clothes you've got on."

Trilo thrashed out of Kale's hold and glared. Though by the time he met Shade's gaze, he'd dialed down his attitude by several clicks. "Okay, I will," he said, without moving.

"And you give her your bunk," Shade told Pretty.

If Pretty had had a tail, it would have swished. "Why mine?"

"You're the cleanest. And while she's on board, you're going to look out for her. Anything happens to her, it's your hide."

"I can take care of myself," Gemma said with annoyance.

Shade smiled. "You're welcome to try."

"She can have my bunk," Eel offered.

"The one that stinks so bad even you won't sleep in it?" Kale asked with disgust.

"If I get rid of the dirty clothes and sea urchin shells, it'll freshen right up."

"Let him look out for her," Pretty said without so much as a glance in my direction, just a jerk of his head.

"If these chum-suckers get outta line, you think they're going to listen to him when he says 'stow it'?"

"Pretty doesn't say 'stow it,'" Trilo complained. "He just throws a knife at your head and calls it a warning."

"That way I don't have to ask twice," Pretty said coldly.

Once Gemma had returned to the common room after changing into Trilo's shirt and pants, Shade kicked everyone else out except me, Pretty, and Eel. Gemma sat in a chair with her eyes closed, and Pretty stood a few feet behind her. Eel handed me two wax earplugs.

I shook my head. "I want to hear what he says."

He started to protest, but Pretty cut him off. "It won't work on him if he's aware and resists it."

"Did the guards in Seablite try to resist it?" I asked. At Pretty's raised brows, I said, "That was how you escaped, right? You hypnotized them into falling asleep for twenty minutes."

"It was a part of how we escaped," he admitted.

"Can we get on with it?" Gemma asked. Suddenly she clamped her hands to her ears. "What was that?"

I hadn't heard anything.

Pretty seemed taken off guard. "You can hear it?"

"That trembly sound? Yeah, you can't?"

Eel pulled out his wax earplugs. "What are you guys talking about?"

Gemma clapped her hands over her ears again and twisted to look at Pretty. "Are you doing that?"

Again I'd heard nothing, but this time I was attuned enough to feel the vibration. So much harder to pick up in air than water but definitely there. Like the low notes of whale song. Too low for the human ear to register, but still, you can feel the sound roll over you if you're paying attention. "Are you making some kind of low frequency sound?"

He nodded. "It's what puts people in a trance. But no one I've tried it on has ever heard the sound. Even I can't."

Gemma shrugged. "I've got good hearing."

"Better than good," I said, remembering how she'd heard Zoe approaching in the Slicky even though we'd been above the water. "What if you go lower?" I asked Pretty.

"I can't. And even if I could, frequencies that low mess with your guts, eardrums, eyeballs . . . then you puke."

"Let's not go that low," Gemma said.

"You know, it shouldn't matter that you can hear the noise," Pretty said. "Like drumming or chanting. You hear them, but those sounds can still put you into a trance state."

"Why?" I asked.

"Sounds can change your brain waves," Eel said as if it were no big deal. "That's what Doc said. Pretty *induces theta brain waves in the listener*. The kind you have right before you fall asleep."

Pretty shot him an evil look at the mention of Doc. And I couldn't blame him. If a doctor had cut into my brain trying to figure how my Dark Gift worked, I'd be bitter, too.

"Is that why people feel calmer after they swim with dolphins or listen to whale song?" I asked, knowing that I sure did. "Because of the low frequency sounds they make?"

Pretty considered it, actually looking interested in something for a change. "That makes sense."

"So hypnotize me already," Gemma said.

This time when Eel offered the wax earplugs, I took them. Though the second it looked like Gemma was in a trance state, I pulled them out. "You're done making the sound?" I asked Pretty.

He nodded and started talking to Gemma in a totally normal voice. He told her that she wouldn't see the ghosts anymore. Wouldn't even know they were there. Wouldn't feel them or sense them in any way. He went on like that for about ten minutes and made her repeat it back to him. Then he brought her out of the trance.

Of course she wanted to test the results immediately and rushed into the bridge to ask Shade to stop the *Specter*. He refused, wanting to put serious distance between us and any Seaguard skimmers that might be searching for him.

"You can swim in the morning," he said. "Show her your bunk," he told Pretty. "And keep the others away from her."

"The diving will be better on the shelf anyway," I told her as we left the bridge. "There's nothing much to see in the open ocean."

With a nod she headed off with Pretty.

"I never get the fun jobs." Eel sighed. "Hey, if it came down to me or Pretty, who do you think she'd choose?"

Exactly the kind of conversation I did not want to have. Ever. "He's human freezer burn, and you're a slob."

He grinned. "Giving me the edge, don't you think?"

"I'm going to look around, unless that's a problem."

"She's a beauty," he said, sounding completely smitten.

"Gemma?"

"The *Specter*."

I made a quick tour of the sub but didn't climb the ladder to the second deck. Eel had told me the sleeping berths were up there but that I would be bunking on the padded bench in the common room. He'd also told me to take my pick of the diveskins in the gear room, so I set aside two that looked like the best fit for Gemma and me and were also the cleanest. When I finally settled onto the bench, I couldn't sleep. Worry about my parents ate at me.

Now that I had nothing to occupy my mind, it really hit me that there was a chance that I would never find them. That they would never come back because the worst had occurred. I gave up trying to sleep and headed into the small galley. Dwelling on those possibilities would only cripple me with grief.

I'd just opened an apple barrel when a dot-dash pattern flashed in my peripheral view. I straightened to face a large viewport, which was entirely taken up by a dark gray background marked with pale yellow spots and vertical stripes: it had to be the flank of a passing whale shark. I moved in for a better look at the largest fish in the ocean, only to walk smack into an invisible wall. No, not a wall. *Shade.* I stumbled back. The outlaw had claimed a place by the viewport and was nearly impossible to spot because his skin so perfectly matched the rippling pattern outside.

"Sorry," I muttered, but he didn't seem to care.

Shirtless, he watched the whale shark plow past and I wondered if he knew that his skin was mirroring the passing fish or if it was unconscious.

Without turning he asked, "What do you think she's really seeing?"

"No idea." I moved to his right and watched the whale shark disappear from view.

"Could be a Dark Gift." He faced me as the spots and stripes on his skin faded.

"Maybe," I agreed. "But she only lived with us three months."

"Where's she been living since?" he demanded. No surprise that his swirling tattoos reappeared with his temper.

"The Trade Station. But the Seaguard took it over, so she can't bunk there anymore."

Shade looked out the viewport again and his skin settled into the brown shade he seemed to favor, even though he was really as pale and freckled as Gemma. After a moment he said, "Kale was in Seablite only three months before we broke out. He got a Gift."

I decided to take advantage of his relaxed mood to ask a question that I'd wondered about. "Do you know who's behind the missing townships?"

"Didn't even know they'd gone missing till today."

I figured that meant no.

"You want something to chew over?" he asked. "Try this: Word got out beforehand about your deal with Drift. Got all the way to people who make their living selling to the surfs on the black market."

"Who?"

"Same people who buy from us. Our main source of income. Means I can't afford to throw names around." His voice turned bitter. "You saw firsthand just how many options we have for making money."

"If you're not going to give me names, then why bother telling me anything?"

"The boys and I were asked to bust up the deal with Drift. Steal the crop. We said no, it being settlers and all."

He sent me a sidelong look, and I remembered that after I'd saved his life from the lynch mob, I'd asked him to promise not to steal from any more settlers. Guess he was keeping that promise.

"You might think about whether the surfs on Drift could," he added.

"Could what?"

"Say no."

I looked at him blankly, not understanding.

"People, situations," he added, "aren't always what they seem."

Got it. Shade was implying that someone might have forced the Drift surfs to do it. Someone who went so far as to outfit them with a sophisticated sub. "This is just a theory, right? You don't know anything for sure."

"If I knew who took your parents"—his tone had turned icy—"I would've mentioned it on Rip Tide."

I'd offended him. Great. When a laugh floated down from the upper deck—Gemma's—followed by a guy's, I was relieved that Shade had somewhere else to take his irritation. He swung onto a ladder and climbed the rungs two at a time. I followed at a slower pace, knowing that Gemma had the right to laugh with anyone she chose—even if hearing it squeezed the air out of my lungs.

The ladder ended beside a railing that looked out over the bridge. I spotted the empty pilot seat and hoped that the *Specter*'s computer was a reliable autopilot.

To my left, double-decker berths lined both sides of a passageway. Each compartment had its own privacy curtain, though now most were drawn back. Halfway down, Shade stopped short at Trilo, who was sprawled on the passageway floor, while other outlaws leaned out of their berths, all silent and listening. Golden light spilled from one of the top compartments, along with Gemma's voice. I couldn't make out her words but recognized Hatchet's guffaw.

"Need a hand down?" Shade growled at whomever was in the berth.

Sure enough, Hatchet tumbled out, landing on top of Trilo. Both scrambled to their feet.

"If I see you," Shade warned all of them, "it means you're awake and looking for something to do. . . ."

En masse the outlaws retreated into their berths.

"It was my turn next," Eel complained as he flopped into the compartment next to me.

"Turn for what?" I asked.

"Gemma was telling our fortunes with cards. She said Kale is going to be president of the Assembly one day."

Now that the passage was clear, Shade paused in front of Gemma's compartment long enough to say, "Simplify my life; shut the curtain."

Then he spotted Pretty digging into a locker. "You call that keeping them away?"

Pretty shrugged. "Didn't have my knife."

Once Shade disappeared down the passageway, I paused by Gemma's berth, figuring his edict didn't apply to me. She was on her knees yet had plenty of headroom as she slid the curtain closed. Spotting me, she beckoned me up—but I knew better than to push my luck with Shade, so I shook my head.

"Isn't it perfect?" she whispered, leaning toward me with her hair spilling around her face.

I couldn't help but smile. While roomy for a berth, it was half the size of the Surface Deck storage closet. Maybe the built-in drawers and cubbies appealed to her, who knew? At least Shade had been right about Pretty. His compartment was spotless.

"Perfect," I agreed, and backed away from her. "Good night."

She waved good-bye and slid the curtain shut.

As I headed down the passage, I saw that Pretty had been watching us, which turned up the voltage on my shine. Especially since he was looking at me with a slightly puzzled expression.

"What?" I demanded.

"Nothing." He slammed his locker shut. "I just can't tell if you're indifferent or stupid."

He headed off, leaving me to light up the passageway with my overheated face.

The subsea valley spread out below us, shimmering like a mirage where an icy current joined the warmer water. Surrounded by ocean, I felt like myself once more. Could move the way I liked—in all six directions, fluidly, easily. I glanced at Gemma. I didn't want to seem like I was hovering, but I had to know if the sweeping view had sent her into panic.

When she smiled at me, my whole body relaxed. She wasn't afraid. She could dive again. Swim in the open ocean with me like she used to.

We had hours to kill before nightfall, but I didn't want to test the limits of Pretty's hypnosis. I gestured that we should head back to the *Specter*, but she shook her head and strung Hatchet's borrowed crossbow with a barbed arrow of brass wire, ready to try hunting again like I'd taught her months ago.

I grinned and slipped Eel's spear from a loop on my borrowed diveskin. With a twist, I extended the shaft until a five-foot spear gleamed in my hands. Lightweight, sturdy, with a razor-sharp triangular tip—a good spear. I couldn't wait to give it a try. Unlike using a speargun, spearfishing required stealth and a deft hand, which was a far more exciting way to bag lunch. Plus, it gave the fish a sporting chance.

The valley lay hidden among a series of seamounts. I doubted anyone else even knew of its existence, which meant the resident fish would be numerous and bold. Determined to erase the memory of Gemma's last dip into the water, I'd been proceeding cautiously, so she took me by surprise when she launched herself over the edge of the cliff and floated into the valley below.

Following in her wake, I drifted down the cliff wall, where masses of colorful sea anemones crowded the overhangs while neon blue crabs scuttled underneath. Just beyond my reach a shoal of golden snapper darted in perfect sync.

When I touched down, Gemma had a fat dorado already in her sights. Over six feet long. Keeping her bow arm rigid, she took aim, only to have a school of silvery palometa engulf her before she could release her arrow. Round and flat, the fish reflected the sunlight like a thousand mirrors as she shooed them away. By the time they'd scattered, the dorado was gone. I laughed at her look of frustration and pointed to a mushroom-shaped guyot some distance away where the dorado had headed.

Together we swam the length of the valley. Protected by the channel's high walls, soft coral flourished, as did sponges and sea plumes. As we neared the rock formation, I dropped to the seafloor. Most likely the dorado would hide along the bottom, so when Gemma touched down beside me, I pushed aside the waist-high seaweed. Spotting the metallic green fish under an outcropping with its forked tail poking out, I beckoned Gemma closer.

Just as she lifted the crossbow and took aim, a voice blared into our helmets simultaneously.

"We're coming," Trilo shouted through the receiver. "Be ready to jump in."

Though I wanted to type on my wrist screen that we weren't ready to come back, something about his agitation worried me.

Upon seeing the sleek outline of the *Specter* above us, we kicked our way up to the bottom hatch and hoisted ourselves in. The moment Trilo slid the cover back in place, he shouted into an intercom. "They're in. Go!"

TWENTY

"What's going on?" I asked as soon as I'd cleared my lungs of Liquigen.

"Nothing you need to know about," Trilo said, heading for the hatchway.

I blocked his path. "We'll find out soon enough, so tell us now."

He considered it and then shrugged. "While you two were out playing, we spotted a mark."

"A what?" Gemma asked.

"A fishing trawler. So a couple of the boys went to check it out. Now we're swinging back to get them."

I didn't step aside. "Check it out? What does that mean?" Though I could guess the answer.

Gemma inhaled sharply. "Are they robbing some ship?"

"We gotta bring something when we go to the Ruins." He shoved past me but then paused at the hatch. "Showing up empty-handed would be . . ." He searched for the right word. "Rude." With that, he banged out of the gear room.

"Guess that's a yes for robbery," I said.

As I pulled off my dive boots, I thought hard about how I was the one who had let Shade out of his jail cell. Had I kidded myself for even a second that he was going to give up being an outlaw? No. Truth was, my only concern had been getting Shade to agree to take me to Hardluck Ruins. Looking at the consequences down the line—the way Captain Revas had done with the hypothetical boy on the boxing raft—hadn't factored into my thinking at all. And now some fishing trawler was suffering the consequences.

When I looked up, I was surprised to see Gemma smiling. "You're not upset that your brother is off robbing a ship?"

She shrugged. "He's not going to change. But I did," she said, beaming. "I didn't see or feel a single ghost."

I wondered once again what she had really seen. Could I be so certain there were no ghosts in the ocean? Certainly enough people had died in it.

"And you can come live with us again," I finished with a smile.

She nodded as she tugged off her boot. "Now that I can do what you like doing again."

Something about her phrasing brought me up short. "That's not why you stopped living with us before, is it?"

"Not the only reason."

"That shouldn't have been a reason at all," I said, feeling put out. "Yeah, I like spending time in the ocean, but I don't care if you go in or not."

She hesitated. "I think you do, even if you don't realize it."

"You're wrong," I said firmly. "I don't write people off based on what they can or can't do. Only a complete jerk would. Think about it. You like to talk. If some parasite eats my tongue, are you going to cut me off cold?"

A smile pulled at her lips. "Could we pick a different example?"

I remained serious. "Why did you think it mattered to me? Did I say something?"

Her cheeks turned so pink, so fast, I was stunned. I'd struck a nerve.

"No," she said, backing off. "I was just being dumb."

"About what?"

"Nothing." Stepping over piled boots, she headed for the hatch. "It's stupid." When I got there first, she stopped short and sighed. "Okay," she relented. "I noticed that after my first freak-out, you didn't like me as much."

"You're right," I said, and she stiffened. "That *is* stupid."

"Well, that's how it seemed," she said defensively.

"Why?" And then it dawned on me. "Oh. Because I didn't kiss you again." Her flush deepened and I knew I'd hit the mark. "I thought maybe I'd caused your freak-out."

"I told you it was the ocean."

"You could have been just saying that. I figured if you wanted me to try again, you'd give me a sign."

"A sign?" Her tone was incredulous.

Now *I* felt stupid, though also relieved, knowing for sure that I hadn't set off her panic attacks. "I was trying to be considerate."

"Okay, there's considerate. And then there's dense beyond belief."

"Hey—"

"Exactly what kind of sign were you looking for?" she asked. "Ten feet tall with blinking lights?"

I leaned in and kissed her, partly to stop her teasing but mostly because after squashing the impulse for so long, I'd finally gotten a go-ahead—even if it was roundabout. Her response, however, wasn't roundabout at all. As soon as my lips touched hers, she slipped her hands around me and kissed back. A soft kiss. Lingering . . . until something heavy slammed into my leg.

We broke apart in time to see a helmet surface in the hatch, while a bulging sack lay at our feet, having just been thrown there.

"What a haul!" Eel hoisted himself into the gear room and gestured at the sack. "Wait till you see the size of those oysters."

As we followed Eel into the bridge, I asked, "Big fishing boat?" I couldn't help wondering if the outlaws had targeted some poor floater who depended day to day on his catch.

"About as big as they come," Eel said, motioning to Kale to take the *Specter* topside. "Just look at that monster. She's strip-mining the sea. Ain't right," he said with a shake of his dark head.

Gemma and I moved into the bridge's rounded viewing dome as the *Specter* broke through the waves off the starboard side of a massive ship. One glance at the giant chute mounted on the ship's stern told me Eel was right. I knew how these trawlers operated. They came equipped with enormous nets that scraped along the ocean floor, scooping up everything from clams to fish to dolphins—whatever happened to be in that stretch of ocean. Then a winch would haul up the net and empty it into the chute so that its contents spilled straight onto the deck for sorting. Nothing got tossed back.

A trawler like that could easily haul in two hundred tons of fish an hour. If the captain kept off the Seaguard's radar, his ship could scoop up far more marine life than the official limit. And almost all of them did. Too bad there weren't enough skimmers on the ocean to enforce the regulations.

Suddenly the irony of that hit me, and I grimaced. I'd just wished for more Seaguard. *To bring justice to the ocean frontier,* like the trooper had said.

When the *Specter* closed in on Hardluck Ruins, Gemma and I returned to the bridge as the sub surfaced again. Stacked rubble formed a wall, topped with a fence of barbed wire, surrounding what had once been a city. Now the buildings stood semisubmerged in the clear water of a lagoon.

"No way to get past the wall in a ship," Shade said. "We moor on this side."

"What about those?" I asked, pointing at an open patch of water on the other side of the barbed wire where a flotilla of small boats bobbed. Instead of true sails, long swags of colorful sheer material hung from their masts.

"The surfs keep those to use in the lagoon," Pretty said with a nod at the odd sailboats and their ineffective sails. "Those are their market stalls."

"That's the black market?" I asked. "A bunch of boats?"

"That's where the surfs sell things. What they've caught or made."

From the pilot seat, Kale pointed out the remains of a large building some distance away, once mostly glass— now mostly scaffolding. "That's the main market."

"What's the difference?" Gemma asked.

"That's where they buy."

"You have to pay to set up a counter in there," Pretty explained.

"So how do we get in?" I asked him.

"There's a break in the fence up ahead. We'll drop anchor as close to it as we can."

"Shade," Kale called, sounding alarmed. When Shade came forward, Kale pointed in the distance where several vehicles zipped across the waves, heading for the ruins. "Those are moving an awful lot like Seaguard skimmers."

Though they were barely more than dots on the horizon, I saw what he meant. The back halves swung out as if separate but tethered to the front. And then one popped up on a wave. Definitely wasp-waisted skimmers.

"Take her down," Shade ordered.

Kale jammed the throttle forward, tilting the *Specter* into a near-vertical dive.

"What are they doing here?" Pretty wondered. "They can't cross into the Ruins without a warrant. This city was deeded to the surfs. Same as their garden."

"Drop her in there." Shade pointed at a mass of plankton.

Kale buried the *Specter* within the thick green cloud. Not only was the sub well out of view, but the plankton was so dense, it would show up as solid on a sonar screen, without revealing what was hidden within.

"Give the skimmers time to circle to the other side, then take off," Shade told Kale.

"Take off for how long?" I asked.

"Not coming back tonight," he said firmly. "We'll try tomorrow."

"Gabion told me to come tonight," I protested. "I'll go alone."

"Don't want to do that."

"I'm not scared of Gabion."

"He's not the only thing that can kill you in the Ruins," Shade said.

"I'll take my chances."

I turned to head for the gear room, only to see Pretty blocking my way with his knife drawn. "Those skimmers are here because of *you*. Shade escapes. You're nowhere to be found, but your sub is still bobbing by the cliff. . . ."

"So the Seaguard guessed that I came *here*?" I scoffed.

"Not guessed. You told someone back on Rip Tide that you were itching to get to Hardluck Ruins. Maybe asked for a ride. No way the *Specter* was your first choice."

I stiffened, remembering how I'd begged Mayor Fife for the coordinates. Would he have passed that information on to Captain Revas? Maybe. If she'd blamed him for Shade's escape and he needed to save his own hide.

"We'll wait until tomorrow," Gemma said, pushing aside Pretty's knife. "I don't want to go in there without you guys. And neither does Ty, even if he's not thinking straight right now."

Pretty looked like he wasn't buying what she was selling.

She turned to Shade. "Will you at least take us to the surf's community garden tonight? So we can maybe find out what it is that they know about Drift that Captain Revas wouldn't tell Ty."

I wasn't going to settle for that even if she was. I saw Shade's gaze flick to Pretty.

"The garden is between here and the coast," Pretty told him. "Due west."

Shade nodded in answer to Gemma's question. "So long as no skimmers show up."

"Okay," she said. "We have a plan. Okay, Ty?"

Pushing past them, I left the bridge. I heard Gemma quietly say, "Give me a minute to talk to him."

I paused in the galley, listening to them.

"You shout if he tries to dive," Shade ordered.

"He won't," I heard her say. "He'll listen to me."

Anger shoved my feet forward. I *was* going to dive. Just let her try to talk me out of it. The only question standing was whether she would yell for Shade.

When she came up behind me, I didn't acknowledge her. She slipped a hand under my arm that I was about to shake off when, instead of trying to pull me back, she pressed me forward.

"Hurry," she hissed in my ear. "Pretty will check on us before a minute is up. Hey," she called to Eel as we crossed through the common room where he and Hatchet were throwing daggers at a dartboard.

When he glanced over, she smiled. "Be right back," she told them, while nudging me toward the gear room with a hand on my back. "We're just going to talk privately for a minute."

It wasn't until she closed the gear room hatch and jammed a fishing spear through the wheel that all doubt about her washed from my mind. I didn't even know how to begin an apology of the magnitude I wanted to make.

"Don't just stand there," she ordered. "Get your helmet on. Let's go."

"Shade is going to be really mad at you," I warned.

"He better get over it. We broke him out of jail." She sealed her helmet with a snap and shimmied through the hatch in the floor.

TWENTY-ONE

Following Gemma, I dropped soundlessly out of the *Specter*. As she disappeared into the viscous darkness, a column of green light appeared in her wake. Then I noticed the bright tracer lines all around me made by fish darting past. *Shoot*. Disturbing the plankton turned it bioluminescent. I swam after Gemma, sending plumes of translucent green swirling into the darkness with every kick and stroke. Beautiful, yes — but also a neon sign advertising our departure. After a moment, I checked over my shoulder. As far as I could tell, no outlaws were coming after us.

We surfaced and swam along the piled rubble that formed the wall until we spotted the break in the fence that Pretty had mentioned. The rubble was slicked with rock snot and silt, which made climbing it difficult, but we finally clawed our way to the top of the wall and slipped through the gap in the barbed wire.

On the other side of the fence, a rope net hung over the water, leading from the rubble wall to the shell of what had once been a three-story building; now two levels were submerged. We scrambled across the net and into the abandoned building.

There was no glass in the windows and no interior walls. Probably torn down long ago to salvage the wood struts. As we splashed through puddles toward the other side of the building, I wondered what it had been before the Rising. Maybe a bank or city hall. Something important, judging from the inlaid marble floor. Now tall weeds sprouted in the cracks, making it hard to spot rats until we were nearly on top of them.

"Wait," I said, slowing my pace. "I need to apologize. I thought . . . I didn't realize you were lying to them back there. On the *Specter*."

She raised a brow. "You just forgot that I love your parents and want to find them?"

"I . . ." I wanted to promise never to doubt her again. But after my about-face, I wouldn't blame her if she scoffed. "I'm sorry."

"Forget it," she said, seeming unoffended. "I'm a great scammer; you fell for it. So did my brother, who's good at reading people."

"And I'm dense beyond belief," I conceded.

"Only sometimes." She smiled. "Come on. By now they'll have figured out that we're not on board."

She took off through the open building and I followed, still feeling guilty about my lack of faith in her. Ahead of us, a section of the wall had been knocked out. A ladder dangled in the opening. We'd have to climb to the roof to get onto the hanging bridge, which crossed the lagoon.

"Does this setup look safe to you?" She gave the ladder a shake and frowned. "This is definitely not safe."

I followed the jerry-rigged bridge with my eyes to where it ended at a platform by the moored boats. "Not safe at all," I agreed. The water, on the other hand, looked inviting—crystal clear and not more than twenty feet deep. Leaning over the edge of the building, I could make out an ancient street under the water, with rusting cars covered in seaweed. "It'd be quicker to swim."

I turned to Gemma, but she was studying the path of knotted rope nets that were strung up through what was left of the city. "They all lead to the market," she concluded.

"Let's try to get there before sunset." Which wasn't long off. Winding through the half-submerged ruins at night would be like navigating a maze, even with my Dark Gift.

"Okay"—she reached back to flip up her helmet— "swimming it is."

"You don't want to do that," a voice warned from behind us. "You're inside the wall now."

I turned to see a rough-looking man, clearly a surf, sloshing through the puddles, hefting a sack. His expression turned to one of surprise upon getting a look at my shine, followed by a scowl.

"Why?" I asked, despite his obvious hostility. "What's in the water?"

"Things that bite," he snarled, and swung himself onto the ladder.

Every inch of the ocean contained things that bite. Why this lagoon should be so much more dangerous, I couldn't guess. But remembering all the surfs with scars, I decided to take the man's advice. Gemma eyed the water warily as she followed me up the ladder.

From the rooftop, the hanging bridge looked even less safe. Pieces of railing had been wired together and dipped at odd angles. Planks cut from old doors had been laid over the rungs haphazardly. In the gaps — nothing but bars. The surf seemed to cross it easily enough, so we ventured on, gripping the cable that hung along one side.

Halfway to the boats, I looked down and spotted the remnants of a playground under the water. Something round and rusted spun in a circle. Swings drifted upward, caught in a light current. And then a shadow glided past the far end of the clearing. I didn't get a look at what cast the shadow, but a chill crept over my skin. Whatever it was, it had been big, at least fifteen feet long. Plenty of fish came that size. But something about the way the shadow moved told me it was no fish.

"What do you see?" Gemma paused, holding on to the cable with two hands.

The ancient wood by her foot caught my eye. The plank was shorter than the rest and its ragged edge was lighter in color, meaning that part of the board hadn't been exposed to the elements as long. When I knelt and nudged her foot aside, we inhaled in unison. A tooth was sticking out of the wood. I wiggled it free and held up a daggerlike fang.

"Is that from a shark?" Gemma asked with alarm.

"The biggest shark tooth I've ever seen was three inches long. This is at least five. And look at the shape. I don't know what it's from." I peered down at the water and felt my nerves grow taut. "Something down there can launch itself at least twelve feet into the air," I said, judging by the height of the bridge.

"Let's get to the boats now."

She got no argument from me. We hurried to the platform on the far side of the lagoon and climbed down another rope ladder. At the bottom floated a walkway made of tethered barrels that ran between the boats, which looked even less safe than the hanging walkway. At least the boats were moored bow to stern, forming something of a barrier on either side. Some were little more than rafts, while others resembled pontoons and catamarans, yet all the hulls were crafted from salvaged ship and sub parts—from many time periods—all soldered together. Brightly colored mosquito netting hung from the masts, draped to provide shade. I always preferred nature to any kind of man-made beauty, but I had to admit there was something appealing about the hodgepodge crafts.

"So where do we start looking?" Gemma asked.

"Here." I nodded at the boats.

"Okay, you go in one and I'll go in another. But you keep your eyes peeled for Gabion in case this was all a setup."

He was the least of my worries. Boarding the closest boat, I ducked past the mosquito netting and saw three women inside the makeshift tent, sitting behind piles of clothes made from feathered bird pelts. The moment they saw me their eyes narrowed. Probably because of my shine. "Hi," I said, trying for a polite smile.

Their reply, resounding silence. I plowed on. "I'm trying to track down a township. Drift. Have you seen—"

"We don't do business with you people!" shouted the oldest woman, though I was within feet of her. Either she was hard of hearing and hadn't understood me . . . or she really hated pioneers.

"I'm not here to do business." I raised my voice, hoping it was a hearing issue. "I'm trying to find—"

"Get out!" she shrieked. "We don't buy from pioneers. Never will!"

"Okay, got it," I said, backing out fast.

Gemma jumped onto the barrel walkway an instant after me. "Any luck?" I asked.

"That was weird," she said, looking disturbed.

"And you don't even have a shine."

"The guy was normal—well, for a surf—until I asked if he'd seen Drift. Then he told me to get off his boat or he'd throw me into the lagoon."

"Yeah," I agreed. "Weird."

"No. The weird part was that he was terrified."

"You wouldn't think that was strange if you got a look at the surfs from Drift."

"Ty, he was scared of *me*. Like I was going to hurt him."

"What? No. It's just 'cause you mentioned Drift."

She shrugged, having no explanation, but wasn't buying mine.

Thinking about it, I wondered if the old surf woman could have been shouting at me out of fear, not anger. She'd known that I was a pioneer. Could the surfs be afraid of us? Then I glanced at Gemma with her bounty of freckles, ponytail, and borrowed diveskin that was so oversized, she looked like a kid playing dress-up. I'd seen scarier seagull chicks.

Not ready to give up, Gemma and I boarded a dozen other boats where surfs from different townships sold a wide variety of goods. Carved beads of shell, clay, and halibut vertebrae; clothes handmade from cured fish skins; awls and needles of bone; walrus stomach gear bags and bladder water pouches; and whale sinew, split and combed into fine thread. As different as their crafts were, the surfs' reactions were nearly identical upon seeing my shine or hearing any mention of Drift — fear flashed across their faces and we were told to disembark pronto.

"Okay," I said finally, though there was nothing okay about any of it. "Whatever Gabion wanted me to see, I don't think it's here. Let's move on to the main building."

The sun had just slipped past the horizon when we entered the market building by way of another cable bridge. Tarps were strung up between the exposed girders, sectioning off the stalls. They reminded me of the fish vendor tents that circled the Trade Station's promenade, except that those were colorful and inviting, while these tattered sailcloths and fishing nets were just sad.

After walking through one level of the open building, my fear of running into Gabion had dried up completely. There were plenty of people in the market. And not just surfs. The booths were operated by fishing companies, dry goods vendors, and other businesses. What astounded me most were the prices.

"They're charging triple for sea lettuce here what we negotiated with Drift's sachem," I said, stopping by a girder to look at the darkening sky. "And about ten times more than what the 'wealth says it's worth."

Gemma stayed farther back from the edge. "That makes no sense. Why would a market with the poorest customers have the most expensive goods?"

"Because the surfs have nowhere else to buy things," I guessed. "They either pay these prices or they go without."

"Why can't they go to the coast to buy things like the settlers?"

I figured out that one easily. "Because the townships aren't allowed to get close to the coast except near Rip Tide." I looked around at the windblown stalls. "This really is the only place they can shop."

Gemma inched a little closer to the girder to look out over the lagoon. "Those don't belong to surfs." She pointed at a marina's worth of boats in the distance, moored outside of the rubble wall where it was interrupted by a stadium. All small yachts and sailboats.

"Probably came from the coast," I agreed. A glow emanated from the open-topped stadium. "Something's going on there."

"And they're going to it." She pointed down at the flotilla of scrap boats. Now loaded with surfs, the boats cut silently toward the stadium. "Could be another boxing match."

A click went off in my brain. "Gabion didn't just say go to Hardluck Ruins. He said go *tonight*. Whatever it is that he wants me to see—it's in the stadium."

Only one hanging walkway headed that way, and its entrance was one floor down. I took Gemma's hand. "Let's see what's going on in there."

We climbed down another rope ladder and started

toward the hanging bridge. But as we passed a stall that took up nearly half of the floor, I paused. Not only was it ten times bigger and fancier than any other stall we'd seen, it was bursting with customers.

I slipped in by the fluttering tarp and saw baskets and buckets of seafood but also tables heaped with other goods—bolts of fabric, tools, even engine parts. In the back, a thickset man in an apron threw a skipjack onto the chopping block, and using a fillet knife, he separated the fish's flesh from its bones with one slice.

"What are you looking at?" Gemma asked from behind me.

"Nothing." Curiosity satisfied, I turned to go and noticed the trough by my knees. The seaweed piled into it was freshly harvested. The filmy fronds ran from brownish green to purple-black. As the son of subsea farmers, I knew seaweed. This was laver. Good boiled or pickled in vinegar. Good baked into bread. More important, it didn't grow naturally on this side of the Atlantic. A lot of settlers had fields of laver on their homesteads, but none had planted as many acres as my family. Now, looking at the three long, overflowing troughs of it, I knew beyond any doubt this was the seaweed that Pa and I had harvested two days ago.

"Who runs this stall?" I demanded.

Setting aside his knife, the sweaty man stepped from

behind the chopping block. Too well fed to be a surf. "What do you want?"

"Where did you get this seaweed?"

"What's it to you?"

"It's fresh. Meaning it didn't grow on the other side of the Atlantic. So where's it from?"

"Come here and I'll tell you." He snatched up his knife and started for me.

"Run!" Gemma cried, taking off for the hanging bridge with me on her heels.

"Heading for a dead end, boy," the man yelled. "Only way back is the bridge, and I'll be waiting right here to give you that answer."

TWENTY-TWO

We clattered along the hanging bridge toward the pair of lampposts at the other end. Satisfied that we weren't being pursued, we paused to watch the surfs tether their boats under the bridge and climb a dangling ladder to a ledge that ran under what were once upper-story windows in the stadium.

When the surfs scrambled through a large window without glass, Gemma and I hurried across the bridge to catch up. But before we'd reached the end, a man's voice brought us up short. "Well, look who it is." A husky figure moved out of the shadows on the ledge into the glow of the lamps. Lockbox in hand, Ratter radiated delight. You'd think he'd just won a lifetime supply of chewing-weed.

I paused before reaching him to consider who was more dangerous: Ratter or the seaweed thief with a fillet knife? *A toss-up*, I thought.

"Here for the show?" Ratter asked.

Last night, I'd broken an outlaw out of jail and helped Ratter into an eel pool. Yet now he grinned like we were old friends. Not suspicious at all . . . provided I was brain-dead.

"What kind of show?" Gemma slipped in front of me as if she could hide me from Ratter's view.

"You want to know," he taunted, "gotta pay to get in."

"Those surfs didn't pay," she pointed out.

"Because they're not here to watch. They're the main attraction."

I knew then that this had to be where the surfs got their scars. Easing past Gemma, I strode to the end of the bridge. "At least tell us what kind of animal it is," I said, trying to seem nonchalant. "It's not a shark, but it's big. Must have a three-foot jaw at least. And a bite like I've never seen."

"Been paying attention, have you, pioneer?" he mocked.

"Yeah, we noticed the surfs with missing limbs. So, impress us. What is it?"

Ratter's beady eyes glittered in the torchlight. "You know, let's call this your lucky night. No charge. You can go see 'em for yourself." He hefted the lockbox into his arms, climbed through the window, and hopped down with a clatter. When he straightened, he stood level with our waists now that he was inside the stadium. "What are you waiting for? Show's about to start."

Curiosity drew me forward, but Gemma caught up and slipped her hand into mine. "You know this is a bad idea, right?"

"Stay out here," I whispered. "I just want to see what's happening in there and then I'll come right back."

"Nice try." She turned to Ratter, who was peering up at us. "Is this one of Mayor Fife's events?"

"His favorite," Ratter said as if divulging a secret. "But he don't want people knowing it's his operation, so he don't come around much. Leaves it to me to run, though I ain't no big show-off like him."

So when I'd asked Fife for the coordinates to Hardluck Ruins, I'd unknowingly gone to the right person . . . or possibly the worst person, depending on what we found in the stadium. Gemma and I exchanged a look that confirmed our determination to press forward despite the risk. We climbed through the window and dropped into a dark corridor.

"As I heard it," Ratter said from beside us, "Mayor Fife warned you to keep away." I spun to see him snatch a harpoon gun from the rubble-strewn floor. "You should have listened to the man," Ratter said, and aimed the gun at me.

After taking our dive belts and patting us down, Ratter forced us through an archway and into the night air, which buzzed with the noise of a thousand spectators. The stadium was flooded but more intact than any other building in Hardluck Ruins. Only the upper part of one section had collapsed. A razor-wire fence stretched across the rubble, spanning the breach. Beyond the gap lay the ocean. Too bad we didn't have a boat.

Until Gemma and I came up with a plan, we had no choice but to let Ratter march us down the steep stairs toward what had once been the playing field, which was now under water, along with over half of the stands. In the dim stadium lights, it looked as if Topsiders filled the rows above the waterline, except for the section Ratter had herded us into. The rows around us were packed with surfs, who seemed startled and suspicious at our presence — as if Gemma and I were going to add a new, unpleasant complication to the event. From what I could tell, the surfs sat in clusters based on their townships, like cheering sections, though I had an uneasy feeling that there wouldn't be any reason to cheer at this event.

When we'd almost reached the razor wire that encircled the flooded playing field, Ratter pushed Gemma into a seat at the end of the row. I moved to take the one beside her, but he stopped me. "Not you," he said with gleeful malice. "You're on the other side with the rest of the heroes."

"Other side?"

That's when I looked past the razor wire and saw the men and women — at least thirty of them and all surfs — standing on the seats of the last row above the water. Judging by their clothes, no two were from the same township. Some were grizzled and battle scarred, others young and fierce. All carried knives and had tridents or harpoons lashed to their backs.

Gemma scrambled to her feet. "Ty's not going out there."

"Don't worry about him." Ratter shoved me toward a platform that straddled the fence. "He beat Gabion in the ring. What can a saltie do to him?"

"A what?" I asked.

He jabbed the harpoon's tip into my ribs. "Get climbing."

I couldn't exactly outrun a fired harpoon, so making a break for it was out. I glanced at the surfs studiously ignoring us. No doubt they'd had other dealings with Ratter and knew better than to interfere.

"Finished thinking it over?" Ratter asked. "Figured out that the only place you're going is over that fence?"

"At least tell me what I have to do," I insisted as he pushed me along the bottom aisle toward the slanting ladder that led up to the platform. If I got him talking, maybe I'd buy time to figure out how to get away.

"Not much. Just bag yourself a saltie. Be the savior of your township."

"I don't have a township," I said, refusing to put a foot on the ladder.

"You got Nomad," he snapped.

"Is that why you're doing this?" I demanded. "Because Nomad was my salvage?"

His grin returned. "That, and I don't like Dark Life."

I saw Gemma edging past the seated surfs one row up to keep pace with us.

"But being as I'm the generous type, I'm giving you a chance that any surf would jump at," he went on. "Only if you kill the saltie, you don't have to share that sweet white meat with the stinking surfs back on your township. It's all yours. Over a ton." His laugh was ugly. "Bet you never tasted croc. That's some good eating. 'Specially the tail."

"'Croc' as in crocodile?" Gemma gasped from where she stood.

"Saltwater crocodiles," he confirmed. "Big as a shark and just as hungry. Main difference, you're no safer out of the water."

I frowned. "There are no saltwater crocodiles in the Atlantic."

"Maybe they swam here from down under." His smirk widened into a sickening green smile. "Or maybe someone imported them."

Why would anyone do something so stupid? The odds of keeping the creatures confined in this lagoon forever were worse than bad.

"Get up there," he ordered.

"At least give me a weapon."

Instead he aimed his harpoon gun at my chest. Seeing no other option, I climbed the ladder to the square platform above the razor wire. From that perch, I surveyed the flooded stadium. Boulders and rubble had been piled high to create mini-islands here and there.

"Keep going!" Ratter shouted. "I got a show to start."

I stayed put, lying low on the platform. He'd have to climb the ladder to get an angle on me, and I planned to have a hold on his gun before he could pull the trigger.

Below me, Ratter snorted with laughter. "Think I'm coming up there? Look around you, stupid."

Lifting my head the barest fraction, I saw only the rows of disinterested surfs.

"Look higher," Ratter shouted.

I lifted my gaze to the shadowy archways above the stands and then saw the ancient box seats at the top of the stadium. A whole line of them, glass long gone. In every third one stood a dark figure hefting a harpoon launcher twice the size of Ratter's—now all directed at me.

Reluctantly, I climbed down the ladder on the other side. Each surf moved over a chair to accommodate me.

"Even think about climbing back," Ratter yelled to me, "and one of the croc handlers will spear you through the gut." With that he hustled up the aisle to a booth near the top. Suddenly, the lights brightened all over the stadium, hushing the spectators. I squinted, trying to get my eyes to adjust to the light, when I heard the distinct whiz of metal on a zip line. Glancing back at Ratter's booth, I saw a hook baited with a decapitated tuna flying along a cable that stretched across the stadium. When the hook reached the center, a rubber ring stopped it in place. The headless tuna twisted in the breeze, dripping blood into the water below—clearly calling forth the "salties."

All around the stadium the spectators remained silent. Waiting.

I seriously considered climbing back over the razor wire, figuring the "croc handlers" would be focused on the water. But a glance at Ratter's booth nixed that idea. His beady eyes were locked on me and he had a clear shot at the platform. I didn't know how good his aim was, but I decided not to chance it just yet.

Someone on the far side gave a yell, and the Topsiders leaned forward in their seats to look down into the water. I was too far away to see what they were pointing at and gasping over. Probably dark shadows, like the one I'd seen in the lagoon earlier, streaking into the flooded area through underwater passageways. I shivered and wondered how Ratter could have forced so many surfs onto this side of the wire.

A man on my right, shirtless and sunburnt, placed a knife crossways between his teeth and bit down. An inflated seal bladder dangled from the handle, though I couldn't guess why. Then I noticed all the surfs' weapons were adorned with the sheer brown balloons. Two more surfs chomped down on their blades, freeing up their hands, which sure wouldn't have been my choice if Ratter had let me keep my knife.

On my left was a woman who kept her hair back with yellow mud, which had been smeared along her hairline. When she untied her trident, I caught sight of her necklace—a strip of leather studded with five-inch teeth like the one I'd pried out of the plank.

"Stay out of the water," she told me, with her trident now in hand.

"I plan on it."

"If one is coming for you, climb the razor wire."

So, getting shredded by razor wire was preferable to facing down a saltie? Good to know.

Suddenly, a mud-colored creature rocketed out of the water, teeth glistening in its open mouth. The sound of the crocodile's jaws closing on the tuna reverberated through the stadium like the slamming of a vault door. I nearly swallowed a tonsil. No shark could shut its mouth with such explosive force.

The crocodile ripped the tuna from the hook and crashed back into the brackish water, sinking under the surface with its prize. Adrenaline blasted through my body, leaving me shaky. When Ratter had said that a saltwater crocodile came as big as a shark, I'd pictured a tiger shark. But the beast I'd just glimpsed had to have been twenty feet long and weigh well over a ton. As in, the size of a great white . . . but with legs. I twisted on the seat, searching for another way over the razor wire. No way was I going toe-to-toe with a predator that massive.

A gong rang out, and splashes erupted along the edge of the flooded area as the three surfs who'd been holding their knives between their teeth dove into the water. I froze, unable to comprehend what I was seeing. The other surfs dashed along the row of submerged seats, tridents raised, scanning the water. Ratter must have pulled these lunatics out of mental institutions. They were suicidal—every last one of them.

Across the stadium, spectators lurched to their feet, hollering encouragement. Seeing the Topsiders screaming for blood didn't surprise me. But then I noticed that the surfs on my side of the stadium had risen as well and were also cheering.

That's when I understood.

These people hadn't been forced to cross the razor wire. They *wanted* to be on this side. One crocodile provided over a ton of white meat, according to Ratter. Enough to feed a whole township. No wonder the surfs displayed their scars with pride. They'd risked life and limb to feed their townships and survived. Which made me wonder how many people hadn't.

A pair of knobby eyes broke the water's surface and I saw that the crocodile had catlike pupils—a fact that kick-started my heart. Not only was the beast close, but vertical pupils meant it had excellent night vision. As if a two-thousand-pound reptile needed another advantage.

TWENTY-THREE

"On the other side of the settler, Plover," a voice behind me called to the woman.

She nodded in response. "Coming through," she said to me.

I leaned back against the razor wire and felt it slash my diveskin. It was the only way to give her enough room to pass safely, which she did in a blink. But as soon as she raised her trident, the creature submerged.

"Thank you," said the voice behind me. I glanced back to see a girl not much older than Zoe, with yellow mud plastered along her hairline like the woman. "Most hunters won't let another go by," she explained. "Or sometimes they pretend that they will and then push the other person in."

"Ty isn't a hunter," Gemma said, stepping over the last row to join the girl by the razor wire. "He was forced to climb in there."

"We saw. But no surf is going to cross one of Mayor Fife's goons." The girl stopped talking to watch as Plover scanned the water with her trident held high, but the croc showed no sign of resurfacing. The girl exhaled with relief and said, "I'm Eider. And that's my sister, Plover. We're from Shearwater."

Pressed as close to the razor wire as I dared get, I waited for Gemma to ask her about Drift. I would've, but figured shouting it over my shoulder wasn't going to get results. And I wasn't about to take my eyes off the water.

"Does this go on every night?" Gemma asked Eider.

Another worthwhile question.

"Oh, no," Eider replied. "Only at sundown on the fifteenth. When our rations are gone and the next delivery isn't for another two weeks."

Gemma gasped. "No one forced them in there?"

"Course not," Eider said, surprised. "The meat tides us over and the leather is worth a lot. But we can only hunt them inside the stadium once a month, one hunter per township. As soon as one croc is killed, the match is over."

"That's crazy," I heard Gemma sputter.

In the center of the stadium, the water thrashed and churned. A moment later a woman scrambled onto an island of rocks. A crocodile dashed after her as she climbed to the top. Luckily it stopped about halfway up. When the woman lifted her trident, I saw that her arm had been badly mauled. The second she hurled her weapon, the crocodile whipped around and crashed back into the water. The trident grazed the submerging crocodile's back but must not have pierced its skin because the animal swam off. I felt a stab of pity for the woman who'd now lost her trident on the bottom of the stadium. But then an inflated seal bladder popped up. When she easily fished out her floating trident, I understood why the surfs attached the bladders to all of their weapons. They couldn't afford to lose them.

A new bout of thrashing erupted on the other side of the stadium. A man whirled out of the water, knife raised, only to crash under again as the enormous crocodile he was wrestling rolled over. The churning water took on a red tinge—blood. But whether it was the man's or the crocodile's I couldn't tell. The spectators jumped to their feet, shouting and cheering. I felt sick watching it. Knowing that it was just as likely to be the man who floated to the surface, lifeless.

The surfs who'd been standing along the perimeter now dove into the water as if fearing the opportunity to kill a crocodile was about to end. The woman, who I'd thought was trapped on top of the rock pile, caught hold of a grip bar sent to her via the zip line. Grasping it, she kicked off from the rocks. With her arm so bloody and sliced up, I was sure she'd lose her hold, but she drew up her knees and held on, flying over the crocodile pool. She could have easily sailed past the razor wire and into the stands, but she wiggled the grip bar to make it slow.

When she was over the row of seats inside the fence, she let go and resumed hunting.

On the other side of the stadium the thrashing and rolling continued. With each passing moment, I thought it was less likely to be the surf who emerged the winner. But I was wrong. The man surfaced with a whoop, holding his knife in the air. Beside him the crocodile floated upside down, revealing the long gash down its pale underside.

When the gong sounded again, the surfs scrambled out of the water. Many were cut and bleeding. Grip bars whizzed along parallel zip lines. Each ran directly over several boulder piles. The surfs who were trapped on top of the mini-islands seized the grip bars and flew to safety while crocodiles circled below.

Something bright splashed into the stadium near me. I jerked, thinking a crocodile had swum close. Then more glowing objects streaked down from the stands. Like falling stars, they hit the water and sank.

"What are they throwing?" Gemma asked Eider.

She scowled. "Money. The tourists put it in glow-in-the-dark pouches to make it easier to find underwater. Supposedly it's a consolation prize. But really they just want to see more—no, Plover, don't!"

I turned to see Plover dive into the water.

"No!" Eider clutched the razor wire, cutting her hands. "It's not worth it!" she cried.

That's when I saw a line of rippling water heading that way. A crocodile had seen Plover go under, and now it was homing in on her like a shark following a chum trail.

Without another thought, I hit the lagoon's surface in a long dive. Once under the water, I released the fins in the tips of my boots and power stroked toward Plover. Using sonar, I sensed her scooping up the pouch. What she didn't see in the brackish water—couldn't see—was the enormous crocodile swimming right for her.

I didn't know which sense was a crocodile's sharpest. Sight, hearing, smell? So I thrashed like a wounded animal and once again mimicked a dolphin's distress cry. And it worked. The crocodile angled away from Plover and headed for me. I saw its long, pointed snout perfectly in my mind's eye. And its powerful body cutting through the water, propelled by a whipping tail as long and wide as me.

Did I dare try using a sonar blast to stun the beast? I seriously doubted that it would work. Not the way it had on the eels. As massive as the croc was, it would probably do no more than blink.

I swam as fast as I could toward the edge of the arena. But when I sent clicks over my shoulder, I saw that the crocodile was gaining on me. I'd never make it out of the water in time—not that being on land would help much. Sucking Liquigen from the tube in my neck ring, I filled my lungs as I dropped. Now I didn't have to worry about breathing, but as I touched down between two rows of seats, I realized I'd crossed into the flooded stands. It would be harder to maneuver here.

Just as I sent out more clicks to see how close the crocodile was, I saw a pouch hit the water. The croc snapped it up like a fish taking a hook. The moment was over before I'd had a chance to use the distraction. And the croc was back on track, plowing toward me. But now I had an idea.

I unhooked my helmet from the back of my neck ring and found the manual switch for the crown lights. Holding the helmet in front of me with shaking hands, I waited for the croc to close in. As an apex predator, it would fear nothing. But any creature with a nervous system could be startled.

When the croc burst forward, jaws wide, I switched on the helmet lights—cranked to blinding—while blasting out sonar, amped way past "up."

And it worked!

Hit with the explosion of light and sound, the crocodile froze. Tail midwhip, jaws agape. I'd probably bought myself two seconds at most. Enough to jam my fist inside my helmet and thrust it into the beast's open mouth. I was counting on the flexiglass to protect my arm from those five-inch teeth, and it did. I drove the helmet as far down the croc's throat as I dared and snatched back my hand, leaving the flexiglass orb behind. I kicked away just as the beast thrashed back to life. Hoping the flexiglass could withstand the pressure exerted by those jaws for more than a millisecond, I stroked for the surface.

Gemma's scream rang in my ears the moment I emerged. I swam for the edge and felt many hands haul me out of the water.

"You're insane, you know that?" a woman's voice scolded.

Surprisingly, not Gemma's.

I looked up to see Plover. "But thank you," she finished.

The other surfs, who'd helped pull me out, now retreated down the row of seats, clearing a path to the ladder for me. The stadium lights had grown dim again as the stands on the opposite side began to empty. I picked my way across the row of wet seats toward the platform, only to jerk to a halt when the pool erupted to my left.

The crocodile burst out of the water and belly flopped with a smack so loud it echoed through the stadium. And then the beast threw itself against the water again. Flinging itself back and forth, the croc pounded the pool's surface with growing violence — in the throes of death or attempting to dislodge the helmet? I didn't know. But it was agonizing to watch. I'd shoved the helmet down the croc's throat out of self-preservation, yet seeing the animal's torment sickened me to the core.

Coming up beside me, Plover said, "Go," while putting a hand on my back, urging me forward.

"Lend me your knife," I said, turning to her. At least I could end the creature's suffering.

"You can't!" Her tone held a vehemence that startled me. "The match is over. Kill it now and you'll be arrested for theft."

I jerked my hand toward the pool. "It's suffocating because of what *I* did. I have to—"

My words were cut off by screams from every direction. And I saw why. The crocodile had stopped flailing and was now cutting through the water toward us—jaws shut—clearly having spit out my helmet or swallowed it. Crazy as it seemed, I could swear the croc was coming solely for me, bent on revenge.

I wasted no time in scrambling for the ladder, leaving room for Plover to climb alongside me. Just as we heaved onto the platform and rolled away from the edge, the crocodile ripped into the ladder from below.

With the sound of crunching aluminum in my ears, I dropped to the other side of the razor wire, where Gemma was waiting. Throwing her arms around me, she squeezed so tight, I couldn't breathe—not that I was complaining— and then she shoved me. "Must you always swim with monsters?"

The stadium seemed to have grown darker still as Eider stepped forward and offered me the glowing money pouch. "You earned it," she said solemnly. Plover and the other surfs from Shearwater joined her, radiating their approval.

"Thanks, but I'd feel better if you kept it."

When Eider continued to hold out the pouch, I added, "I didn't know how bad the surfs have it. None of the settlers know." I wished I could promise to do away with the ordinance that prevented them from fishing in Benthic Territory, but that was nothing I had a say in.

"Ain't you noble?" mocked a voice from one row up. It was Ratter, of course, with his harpoon gun aimed at my head once again.

"He didn't break the rules," Plover snapped.

"Stay out of it," Ratter warned her. "'Less you want another cut in Shearwater's rations." He waved me toward the stairs. When I didn't budge, he flipped off the harpoon's safety clasp.

Plover whipped out her knife. "We're not going to let you kill him."

By the time she'd finished the sentence, the other Shearwater surfs had taken out their weapons — rough-hewn blades and tridents — to face off with Ratter. The surfs were to my right and Ratter on my left. Gemma rounded it out by slipping behind me. With one tug of my diveskin, she persuaded me to retreat.

Before we'd shuffled back more than a few yards, Ratter shouted, "Where do you think you're—" His words cut off sharply as something over my head caught his attention.

In unison, the surfs lowered their weapons—even Plover—as they too stared at the stars with alarm.

Before I could turn to look up, a voice boomed from the heavens: "What the heck is going on down there?"

TWENTY-FOUR

Gemma and I whirled to scan the night sky, though I already knew who we'd see, having recognized the voice that had boomed down at us. And there he was—Mayor Gideon Fife—leaning out a window of his striped airship, a megaphone to his mouth.

"Ty, Gemma, stay right there," he ordered, voice blaring. "I'm coming down."

As soon as the airship swung toward the top of the stadium, Plover and the other surfs scattered. I figured they had the right idea. Noting that Ratter was headed back to the booth as if he had work to attend to, I met eyes with Gemma. "Let's get out of here."

"What, you don't trust Fife's intentions?"

Her question was rhetorical, yet I asked, "Do you want to stick around to find out if they're good?"

"Not for a second."

With that, we sprinted up the steep aisle between the rows, heading for the corridor that would take us back to the hanging bridge. But before we could make it to the top, a dark figure appeared in the archway. When I stopped short, Gemma bumped into me from behind.

"Why—" Without finishing the question, she followed my gaze and saw the large man descending toward us. His face was still too dark to make out, but with each step down he favored one leg—Shade.

He paused on the stairs above us. "See you two are still alive." He didn't sound angry, but he wasn't smiling, either. He looked off to the left. "Been keeping an eye on them?"

I turned to see Fife strolling between the seats one row up. "Just arrived myself," he told Shade. "You must admit, when I say I'll take care of you, I always do."

"Was just at your stall, dropping off my thank-you," Shade replied as they clasped hands. "Fresh oysters."

Fife grinned. "Now that's my kind of thank-you."

"You have a stall in the black market?" I asked Fife. That seemed wrong somehow, since he was the 'wealth's surf agent.

"Of course," he said. "Who knows better than me what the surfs need? Shade and I have been working together for years. He and the boys provide the supplies, I sell them, and the surfs buy them. Everyone wins."

"*You're* the one who asked Shade to bust up our deal with Drift and steal our crop."

Fife's brows rose in surprise. "That's a strong accusation."

I noticed that he didn't deny it. "That was your stall selling the laver, wasn't it? But Shade didn't steal it for you. So what, when he refused, you forced the Drift surfs to do it?" My anger mounted as I began to see how all the elements fit together. "You've known where my parents were all along because you forced Hadal to kidnap them."

"Whoa, whoa," Fife exclaimed, holding up his hands. "You're going to have me assassinating President Warison next. Look, I admit that when I buy goods to sell in Hardluck Ruins, I don't ask how they were obtained." He and Shade exchanged a look of amusement. "So as far as I know, it's all legit. Now kidnapping, well, that doesn't even have the patina of legal. Wouldn't do it. Wouldn't ask someone else to."

"You got us to break him out of jail." Gemma pointed at Shade.

"I didn't ask you to," Fife replied smoothly.

I knew my shine must be glowing over how stupid we'd been. How easily they'd used us. Forcing myself to stay calm, I asked Shade, "How did you know that we'd free you?"

"Didn't think you'd let me sit and rot." His gaze settled on Gemma. "Not when someone is so good at picking pockets."

Fife grinned. "I never even felt you lift it."

She flushed with anger. "Why couldn't you just let him out yourself?"

"A mayor set loose a fugitive?" Fife said with mock horror. "Besides, this way a hundred mainlanders can swear that during the time of the breakout, I never left the sundeck. I didn't even tell Ratter the plan. He's a great thug, but a terrible actor." He looked at me. "Sorry about the dunk in the eel pool."

"The eel pool?" I scoffed. "What about the crocodile pool? Are you going to apologize to *those* people?"

"For what? I'm providing them with an opportunity. Don't recall you having a problem with the boxing match."

"People don't die in a boxing ring."

"On the surf circuit they do. All the time. But it's the surf's choice to step into the ring. Same with the stadium. No one forces them into that water."

"Their circumstances force them," I said coldly.

"And what caused their circumstances?" Fife asked pointedly. "Maybe an ordinance that keeps them from fishing on the continental shelf?"

Shame tore through me. I had no answer for that.

"There's our ride," Shade said, pointing toward the part of the stadium that had collapsed into a wall of rubble. Now the purpose of the razor wire strung across the breach was obvious — to keep the crocodiles from escaping into the ocean. Beyond the fence, an enormous fin cut through the waves. The *Specter*.

Fife sighed and cast a look at Shade. "Breaks my heart to think you won't enter the ring again anytime soon."

"Anytime ever."

"You would have drawn them in by the hordes. Oh, well. So, we're back to our usual arrangement?"

"Should have something for you within the week," Shade confirmed.

Just listening to them made me want to dive in the ocean to scrub off.

With a wave of his hat, Fife signaled his airship, which was holding its position over the stadium. At the same time, Shade took off in the opposite direction, heading for the breach.

"I'm thinking about ocean rodeo next," said Fife, looking at me. "Dolphin roping, bucking orcas," he went on as a ladder unfurled next to him, dropped from the hovering airship. "What a show it could be. Shame you're not eighteen." With a tip of his hat, Fife mounted the ladder and climbed toward an open hatch in the floor of the airship's compartment.

Spinning on her heel, Gemma hurried to catch up with Shade, who stood at the edge of the breach. He jumped before she reached him. Racing over, I saw that the edge was not a sheer drop-off but a steep incline of cement and debris. Below, Shade leapt from chunk to chunk until he'd reached the top of the razor wire, where he dropped to the rubble wall on the ocean side. Moving at a more careful pace, Gemma and I followed.

The *Specter* had circled back and now Pretty stood on the pectoral fin, swinging a grappling hook at the end of a rope. When the sub reached the gap, he let the hook fly. With a thud, it landed in front of the fence and scraped along until it caught in the wall.

"How can you do business with a man who runs an event like that?" Gemma asked Shade the moment she'd alighted onto the rubble.

"Ease her in closer," Shade shouted down, then he turned to her. "Fife pays the most for our goods."

"What kind of excuse is that? This is happening right in front of you" — she jabbed a finger toward the flooded stadium — "and you're doing nothing about it."

"Never threw a coin," Shade replied, unfazed. "Never will."

Below us, Pretty used the dangling line to climb up, hand over hand. At the top, he hauled himself onto the wall and stood, with his long hair glowing like silver in the moonlight. "We need to make wake," he told Shade, and handed him the line. "Those skimmers are still circling."

"I'm not going with you," I told them.

"You going to fly out of here?" Shade sounded amused.

"I'll borrow one of the surfs' scrap boats and row out."

"Suit yourself." He held out the line to Gemma. When she didn't take it, he frowned. "I'll drop you where you want."

"I'm staying with Ty."

"Think I'm going to let you paddle out of here on a heap of trash? Think again."

Several members of the Seablite Gang stood on the *Specter*'s fin watching as Gemma backed away from him.

"You got five seconds to get aboard the easy way," he warned her, "or we do it the hard way."

"Dark Life," Pretty said abruptly. "Know how to sail?"

"What?"

"Boat. On top of the water. Sail," he spelled out in a dry tone.

"Yeah, I can sail." I'd learned on the *Seacoach* when I was young, practicing on supply runs to the coast.

"The surfs keep sails and rigging in the back of the first building south," he told me. "Just follow the wall and you'll find it."

"Thanks," I said, while wondering if his information was on the level. The last time Pretty and I talked, he'd threatened me with a knife.

Turning to Shade, he said softly, "Hauling her aboard kicking and screaming . . . You really want to set that example?" He tilted his head fractionally toward the watching outlaws.

"Didn't know I needed a conscience." Shade's tone had a dangerous edge.

Pretty eased back. "You don't pay me enough for a job that hard. Do what you want."

Shade leveled his gaze at Gemma. "Buck me on this and you don't get another chance. You understand?"

She nodded.

"So, are you coming?"

"No," she said firmly.

He tipped his head as if saying *"so be it"* and turned to rappel down the dangling line onto the *Specter*'s fin.

"That's chum," Pretty scoffed, facing me. "If anything happens to her, he'll kill us both."

"I won't let anything happen to her."

"Then take off now before Fife decides you've seen too much. He didn't hire Ratter for his math skills."

"Pretty!" Eel shouted. He stood on the fin alone, holding open the hatch. "You better jump or he's going to leave you swimming with the crocs."

Cursing, Pretty took a flying leap onto the fin. The hatch barely closed behind them before the sub sank under the water.

"I was wrong about him," I said, watching the *Specter*'s dorsal fin disappear.

"Do you mean you underestimated Pretty or overestimated my brother?" Gemma asked sadly.

"Come on." I took her cold hand in mine. "Let's get out of here."

No guard watched over the boats tethered together by the rubble wall. Resolving to return it at my earliest opportunity, I chose the sturdiest among them, and Gemma and I climbed in. Paddling away from the light of the stadium into the sweltering darkness, we headed south.

"I don't understand," Gemma said from the front of the boat. "Why did Gabion send us here?"

"He heard me ask Captain Revas why Drift would have done it. I think he was showing me why."

"No one knows how bad the surfs have it."

"Because little things added up—settlers passing the ordinance, states not letting townships near the coast, and the federal government cutting their rations. No one saw the total effect."

"Or cared to," she added.

We came to the first building south of the stadium. It was perched on higher ground, yet only one story was visible above the water. Circling, we spotted a wide entryway in the back that led into a cavernous room, probably a warehouse at one time. Flashlights dangled from cords tied to the support beams above and created eerie pools of light on the water.

Though we'd stopped paddling, our boat glided forward in the still water. Docks floated at the back and along the sides of the enormous space. All three were crammed with equipment—masts and sails, stacked fish traps, paddles and crates. We tethered our boat to the dock in the back and climbed out.

"I'll bet they moor all of the boats in here at the end of the night," I said, noting the line of cleats that edged each of the docks. "Which means we better hurry. I don't want to be here when the surfs come back."

Gemma untied one of the flashlights and held it while I dragged a rolled-up sail off a pile by the wall.

When I heard her gasp, I looked up to find her staring at me with horror. "What?" I glanced around but saw only piles of rigging.

"On the wall," she said in a choked voice. With her flashlight directed over my shoulder, she spotlighted a word painted across the cracked cement in large, scrawling letters—SURGE.

Before I could make sense of it, Gemma tracked the flashlight's beam over the wall until she discovered another: FIDDLEBACK.

Finding no more on that wall, she directed the light to the other side of the loading bay. She said the next township name aloud even before she found it: "Nomad."

And there it was, in scrawled letters just above the floating dock.

The heat inside the warehouse grew oppressive. "Maybe the surfs painted the names of the missing townships as a way to commemorate them," I suggested.

"Does that writing look respectful to you? Or does it look like it's intended to scare people?"

"Scare or warn," I agreed. "Let's get out of here."

After one last look around the dark, dripping space, I pulled the mosquito netting from the boat's mast and rigged the sail in its place. Gemma continued to shine her flashlight across the mountains of stuff, until something caught her eye behind a curtain of fishing nets that had been hung up to dry. When she ventured toward that corner, I called, "Gemma," in a hoarse whisper. "Come back." I didn't need the light, but she felt too far away for my peace of mind.

"I think I see more writing," she said.

"Come back," I insisted. "I'm finished. Let's get out of here." I glanced at the entryway, half expecting to see the flotilla of surf boats arriving. They weren't. But what I did see there stopped my heart.

"Ty, look." Gemma had pulled the fishnets aside. "'Drift' is painted here."

"Chum," I muttered, whirling around to look for a weapon.

"What?" she asked.

I pointed at the water where a wake streamed into the docking area as if made by an invisible boat. "Crocodile." Only its nostrils poked above the water. But judging by the size of its ripple and the width of its snout, the croc had to be nearly twenty feet long.

Gemma let the fishing nets fall back into place. "Oh, crap."

The creature made a wide circle and headed back toward the entrance.

"It's okay," she whispered as much for herself as for me. "It's leaving."

But no, the crocodile didn't leave. It took up a spot in the center of the entryway and floated, daring us to come near.

"Even if we're in the boat, it can get us, right?" she asked, although it was clear she already knew the answer.

"I wouldn't try cutting past that beast in a speedboat, forget trying to sail by when there's no wind in here."

"It can climb up here anytime it wants, can't it?" She surveyed the floating dock. "Don't answer that."

"Look for a harpoon or a speargun," I said, backing toward the far corner.

When I turned, my legs were knocked out from under me. My head cracked onto the dock as I sprawled. Thinking the crocodile had somehow flown across the distance, I pushed up with a choked yell, only to see a man standing over me, his rusty trident at my throat. Hadal, who looked more monster than human with his scabbed, hairless skin and horns.

"I have no choice," he ground out as he lifted his arm to impale me.

"It's anchored, isn't it?" I sputtered, putting the pieces together in a flash. "That's why 'Drift' is painted on the wall."

He froze, weapon still raised but not smashing into my chest.

"Someone chained the hatches, disabled the engines, and sank her deep." I was guessing, but it felt right. "And you don't know where."

"Yes," he said, so softly it might have been a released breath. "With all of them trapped inside," he added, running a hand over his scaly head as if to erase a thought, "Even my daughter."

"Who?" I asked, without trying to get away. "Who is scuttling townships?"

Hadal lowered his trident. "Fife."

No big surprise there. My dip in the crocodile pool had altered my vision. Now I saw Fife's good-natured act for what it was—an act. "He ordered you to kill me?"

With a nod, Hadal stepped back, allowing me to rise. "At Rip Tide. But I came here instead, thinking that maybe the Seaguard could find Drift in time. . . ." His words rolled off as he regarded the crocodile floating in the entryway, its eyes and snout visible.

Quietly, Gemma joined us.

"Where are my parents?" I asked.

Turning from me, Hadal moved to the dock's edge. "Fife planned to leave them at the surfs' garden tonight. That way, we'd be blamed."

His words sliced me open. "They're dead?"

Still and silent, Hadal watched the crocodile slip under the water without a trace. "I don't know," he said finally.

I forced myself not to react—no panic, no grief, nothing—to think above my mind's noise. I had to get to the surfs' garden fast—how? Call back the *Specter*?

Hadal faced us, looking so haunted, my thoughts stuttered into silence. "Killing you won't save Drift." His voice sounded raw, as if he were in a stranglehold. "Fife will never free Drift. They're a warning to the rest—while I'm the living reminder."

When he lifted his trident again, I pulled Gemma behind me, cursing myself for dropping my guard.

He rolled the weapon in his hands. "It's Fife I should kill. . . ." He spat, tightening his grip on the shaft. Then his eyes found me. "But maybe it's not too late for you. Maybe you can still save your family, but only if you sail now." He flipped the trident tines down. "Get there before high tide."

At that moment, the crocodile exploded out of the water.

Spinning, Hadal slammed the trident down on the creature's skull, but the razor-sharp prongs bounced off as if they'd hit rock. In a flash of movement, the crocodile closed its jaws on Hadal's leg and yanked him off the dock. All that remained a heartbeat later was a swirl of blood in the churning water.

I staggered back and heard Gemma's choked cry, felt her arms circle me. I turned to cling to her.

TWENTY-FIVE

"The boat's light enough to lift over the wall," I said as we sailed toward the break in the barbed wire. Hadal's words urged me on — *Get there before high tide.* Which meant within the half hour. Maybe less. My nerves were taut as a winch line and yet, for the first time in two days, I had real hope.

Gemma had not taken her eyes off the dark water around us since we'd sailed out of the docking area. She swept the flashlight beam across the lagoon in a repeating arc. I understood completely. The thought of encountering another crocodile was unbearable. Luckily, by the time we reached the break in the fence, we hadn't seen so much as a ripple.

She scrambled onto the rubble, taking the paddles while I rolled up the sail.

"Ty," she said, pointing into the darkness. "Something is cruising over the waves out there. A boat?"

It was too far away for me to see with sonar. But something Kale had said on the *Specter* came to mind. "It's moving like a skimmer. Can I have the flashlight?"

I knew the beam wouldn't help us see that far out on the ocean, but with luck it would *be* seen. I flicked the light on and off—three short, three long, three short. SOS in Morse code.

Within minutes, the skimmer pulled up alongside the rubble wall. Both front and back pods had tinted viewports, making it impossible to see who was inside. Then the viewport on the first pod slid back to reveal a trooper, staring at us with disbelief.

"We need to get to the surfs' community garden as fast as possible." I dropped the rolled sail, ready to abandon the surfs' boat.

"You're glowing," the trooper said.

"Yeah, I know." His comment didn't prick me at all. In fact, I couldn't imagine ever caring about such a minor thing again. "My parents might be hurt. Please give us a ride."

"Hop in." He waved us into the front pod with him, even though it was designed to hold two people, while the back pod had seats for three. "You're the Townson kid?"

"Yes," I said, squeezing in next to Gemma.

He punched a button on the control panel and the viewport slid closed. As the skimmer took off at top speed, hopping the waves, he said, "Captain Revas will be glad to hear we found you."

"Found us?" Gemma asked.

"We're here on her orders."

At Gemma's confused look, he explained, "There are two more skimmers on the other side. We can't cross into the Ruins without a warrant. But Captain Revas told us to circle the area all night in case you showed up."

"How did she know we'd be here?" I knew now that Fife wouldn't have told her.

"Some boxer got hold of her. Said he told you about the Ruins, but then he started worrying about your safety."

"Gabion," Gemma said.

I realized it wasn't Captain Revas that Gabion had been afraid of the previous night, but Fife. "The captain understood him?"

"We all know sign language." The trooper sounded offended. "It's part of our training."

As he radioed the captain and told her where we were headed, Gemma and I stayed pressed together. Not talking.

I didn't have words for what we'd seen that night. Or a reaction, it seemed. I froze up every time Hadal came to mind, which was just as well. I needed to stay calm at least until I knew that my parents were okay. Then I could think about him. And Drift . . . Suddenly the memory of Nomad's chained hatches swept through my mind on an icy current.

No. I couldn't think about what the people on Drift

were going through, either. Not now. Not if I wanted to be able to function.

Two skimmers arrived at the surfs' garden from the south, just as we reached the entrance. One pulled up alongside us, and the front viewport slid open to reveal Captain Revas.

When the trooper retracted our viewport, she beckoned to me. "Jump in," she said, though it didn't sound like an order. Gemma must have decided not to squeeze Captain Revas because she opted to stay with the trooper.

Once we were inside the garden, Revas told the troopers in the other skimmers to split off to either side, while we headed down the narrow center canal with our viewport open.

Like Hardluck Ruins, the surfs' garden was a flooded city, though much smaller. And unlike the skeletal wreckage of the black market, these ancient buildings had purpose. In the bright moonlight, I could make out vegetable-bearing vines winding up the exposed girders and hydroponically grown fruit dangling from balconies. Even though I was impressed by the surfs' inventiveness, I paid no more attention to the flora around us. All my focus went into finding Ma and Pa.

"Hadal told you that Fife's men left your parents here?" Revas asked.

I nodded, knowing that the trooper had given her the report over the transmitter on our way here. I guess she was checking to see if I'd left something out . . . which I had.

"Hadal is dead," I told her. "One of Fife's crocs got him."

Revas stiffened but didn't reply.

"He contacted you right after the kidnapping, didn't he?" I asked as I continued to search the surroundings for some sign of my parents. "Told you how he'd been forced to do it."

After a moment's consideration, Revas nodded. "I went to Rip Tide to meet him face-to-face. It was the only way he would talk."

"That's why you told me to go home yesterday," I guessed. "Because Hadal was there."

"Yes, and by the time you finally left Rip Tide, *hours later*," she said pointedly, "he'd already gone into hiding at the Ruins. Then Gabion tells me that's where you've headed." Her expression turned grim. "I was afraid that Hadal might decide that killing you was his last shot at getting Fife to release Drift."

Hadal had thought that and almost acted on it. He'd also considered taking vengeance on Fife. But in the end, he'd done something very different. He'd chosen to help me — a settler. "He made sure that I could get here in time to save my parents — before high tide."

She glanced at me. "High tide was over an hour ago."

"It might not have reached its peak," I said, while refusing to look too closely at the crumbling concrete and exposed girders as we glided past them. No barnacles or limpets clung to the wreckage above the waterline. If I saw sea life growing just under the waves, then I'd have to face the truth—that the tide had risen to its highest point.

We continued in silence for a while. As much as I wanted to block out everything but the search, my conscience kept poking me.

"There's something I need to tell you," I said finally, and turned on the seat to face her. "I let Shade out of jail so he could take me to Hardluck Ruins." I'd been so desperate to save my parents, I'd willingly broken the law. But now I wondered if I could have accomplished the same thing without Shade's help. I sure didn't try very hard to find another way.

Captain Revas studied me. After a moment she asked, "Did you see the shark?"

"What? Yeah. A bull shark. It ate right through the grille."

"Is that why you unlocked the cell door?"

"I would have unlocked it anyway," I admitted. "But yeah, the shark was ten seconds from breaking through."

"Then you did the right thing," she said. "No one deserves to be eaten alive by a shark. Not even an outlaw.

I shouldn't have left a prisoner in that poor excuse for a jail. As I see it, your actions were due to exigent circumstances." She gave me a stern look. "But it can never happen again."

"It won't," I assured her.

Suddenly an eerie tinkling noise filled the night. I glanced up to see hundreds of old glass bottles swinging overhead. Green vines sprouted from the bottles and wound over crisscrossing cables. As the wind picked up, they tinged like wind chimes, which may have sounded pretty to some, but seemed ominous to me.

"Ahead," Revas said sharply.

I followed her gaze to where two ropes were tied side by side on a horizontal girder. The ends disappeared beneath the water's surface.

Revas maneuvered the skimmer closer, clearly intending to pull up alongside the dangling ropes, but I didn't wait. I dove off the seat, shooting sonar the moment I hit the water. What came back to me shouldn't have made my stomach curl up inside of me. I wasn't seeing my worst fear—my parents' bodies hanging from those ropes. Nothing dangled before me other than the ropes themselves. But it was the ends that freaked me out. They were frayed as if cut with a serrated knife. Or serrated teeth.

That meant nothing, I told myself. Someone had tied a pair of fish traps here and simply cut them loose once the traps were full.

I couldn't hold my breath much longer, yet still I swam closer to the ropes. Catching the ends in my hand, I kicked for the surface.

The skimmer bobbed nearby. "What did you find?" Revas called from where she stood in the pod.

When I held up the ropes' frayed ends, she seemed to breathe a sigh of relief. However, my heart beat faster than ever now that I knew the ropes were made of braided whale tendon. A surf had crafted these, putting in time and skill. Too valuable to leave behind after fishing. If I'd learned anything in the past two days, it was that surfs were the least wasteful people on earth, whether it meant eating every part of a seal or finding new uses for the ancient bottles that littered the ocean floor. Someone else had left these ropes here.

What had Hadal said? That Fife planned to leave my parents at the garden, so that the blame would fall on the surfs. These ropes had been part of that frame-up, I was certain of it. But if Ma and Pa had been tied here — where were they now?

Dropping the ropes, I inhaled Liquigen and dove. I kicked my way down to the submerged cityscape that someone had tried to turn into a kelp field. The water wasn't cold or deep enough for kelp, so what should have been lush thirty-foot stalks were barely ten feet and had a mangy look. With my sonar all I saw were fish, darting under the drifting fronds.

I sank until I could see the kelp's holdfasts clinging to the rocks and in the sand. I sent out a series of clicks, not knowing what I was looking for until I saw it: A dive belt lay among the sea stars and anemones that covered the ground. I snatched it up, pushed off from the seafloor, and kicked my way to the surface.

"Ty, stop doing that!" Revas shouted the moment I broke the waves. "Get back in the skimmer now."

I treaded water and lifted the dive belt to see it with my eyes in the moonlight.

"What's that?" Captain Revas demanded.

My mother's dive belt, that's what. Unmistakably hers. My throat closed off as I studied the loops and holsters, which weren't crammed with weapons like other settlers' belts. Hers were filled with aquaculture tools, including a special clipper designed for her by my father. The front buckle was still fastened. The belt had been sliced open on the side—again by something with a serrated edge.

TWENTY-SIX

I rode back to the Trade Station alone in the back pod of Captain Revas's skimmer. She hadn't questioned my choice, just let me know that she would inform the troopers, Gemma, and my neighbors of what we'd found. I was glad she'd volunteered to pass on the news. I couldn't even begin to put it into words.

I sat alone in the pod, staring out at the moon-streaked waves, and felt . . . nothing. It was as if my body didn't believe the obvious conclusion.

Ma and Pa were gone.

I tried considering the situation from every angle. Maybe Fife's men had tied my parents to that girder only to change the plan and cut them free. Not likely. No doubt what happened to Ma and Pa was exactly what Fife had intended. They'd been tied up and dropped into water up to their necks, and when the tide came in, they'd either drowned . . . or were devoured by sharks.

The air inside the back pod thinned, and without warning the pressure plummeted as if a storm were brewing.

But I could see outside the pod. Could have counted the stars if I wanted; the night was that clear. So why was it so hard to breath?

They're gone.

I tried to shake off the thought, only to send a prickling numb feeling down my arms and into my fingers. Nothing was definite. I hadn't found their bodies. Leaning back, I closed my eyes.

They're gone!

With every nautical mile, the air pressure seemed to increase until I felt close to shattering, all while my brain fizzled and popped with that phrase. But no matter how insistent the words, how irrefutable the logic, I couldn't quite believe it. Not all of me anyway.

When Captain Revas's skimmer surfaced in the moon pool on the Access Deck, I took a moment to collect myself before sliding back the viewport of my pod. Gemma's skimmer had arrived first, and she was waiting for me as I climbed the ladder to the wet room floor.

I braced myself, thinking that she'd throw her arms around me or cry. Instead, she offered me her hand, which I took with a rush of gratitude. Had she done more, my composure might have cracked and I didn't want that to happen here, even though at nearly midnight, there were only a handful people in the vehicle bay.

As Captain Revas stepped off the rim of the moon pool, a trooper rushed to attend her. Ignoring him, she paused by me. "Ty, so much of this situation has been a setup—the kidnapping, framing Hadal as the villain—I'm not about to jump to conclusions because of a convenient piece of evidence. You shouldn't, either."

I nodded. But really, if someone wanted to plant evidence, would he drop it on the seafloor where it could be swept away by the outgoing tide?

Lars was waiting on the Access Deck as well. He'd probably come as soon as he'd gotten Captain Revas's call. He joined us, looking solemn.

"Does Zoe know?" I asked him.

"No. I thought you ought to be the one to tell her."

He may as well have been asking me to impale her with a harpoon. How could I possibly inflict that kind of pain on my little sister? Pain she'd never get over.

"You two always have a home with us," Lars went on. "You know that."

"Thank you." I sounded like a bad actor in a traveling stage show—but none of it felt real.

"We'll join our farms so the 'wealth don't try to claim your land because you're underage," Lars went on. "Not after all the work your folks put into cultivating it."

I looked away, retreating from his words.

A trooper jogged across the access bay to Captain Revas. They moved off to talk.

"Have you found Drift?" I asked, following them, because I had to know. But also because I refused to talk logically about what to do with Ma and Pa gone.

The trooper seemed appalled by my interruption, but Captain Revas said, "Not yet. We've set up a grid across the trash gyre, near where you found Nomad. Starting on the north side, we're searching mile by mile, heading south."

"We won't even cover a tenth of the gyre by daybreak," the trooper told her. "That's how long we figure they have until the cold kills them — daybreak. Provided they have air. If they couldn't get their backup generator running, they're already dead."

I shivered. Daybreak didn't seem so far off.

"Leave it," Revas ordered the trooper who'd maneuvered a clamp on to her skimmer and was about to haul it out of the moon pool. "I'm going out again. And you're coming with me," she told the man before her.

"We're joining the search?" he asked.

"No, we're going to arrest Mayor Fife. I can't pin the missing townships on him. Not yet. But I can arrest him for keeping animals that led to Hadal's death, and anything else I can think of between here and Rip Tide."

"Is Fife stealing part of the surfs' rations?" Gemma asked.

Revas shook her head. "I suspected that, too. But no, he hasn't taken a thing. The 'wealth really did cut the surfs' rations by half several years ago."

"I want to help search," I said.

All of them looked at me—Captain Revas, Gemma, Lars, even the trooper.

"Son, you should take it easy, after the shock you've had." Lars put a hand on my shoulder. "Come home with me and rest up. Be there when Zoe wakes."

"Hadal gave his life so that I could try to save my family. The least I can do is try to save his."

"That's the Seaguard's job," Revas corrected, though not unkindly. "Take care of yourself and your sister, Ty. No one expects any more than that."

She was giving me a pass—without judgment—but I didn't want it. "I know the trash gyre better than anyone. If Drift only has till daybreak, you need my help."

"Our help," Gemma put in.

"You're sure you're up for it?" Lars asked me.

"My parents would want me to," I said. "I want to."

"You're right about your parents," he said with a sigh. "They'd want all the settlers to join the search."

"Well?" I turned to Captain Revas and was surprised to see a trace of a smile on her lips.

"Think you can you drive a skimmer?" she asked.

As a trooper readied a vehicle for us, I assured Lars that I would get over to his homestead first thing in the morning to be there when Zoe woke.

Lars climbed into his sub. "Anchored, huh?" he said as if unable to believe it. "I'll make some calls. See if I can rouse a few people from their beds to pitch in."

"That would be great."

"It's the middle of the night," he warned. "I may not get any takers."

"I know. But if anyone does want to help, tell them we'll be on the south end."

"You do know that gyre is the size of a state, right?"

I nodded.

"Good luck. You're going to need it."

After getting a quick lesson about skimmers from a trooper named Escabedo, we headed for the moon pool that took up more than half the access bay. Gemma stood on the submerged ledge by the skimmer, which had been dropped into the water by a mechanical clamp.

"Do you understand what we're supposed to be watching the screen for?" she asked as she climbed into the front pod.

"A low frequency noise. We won't hear it, but the reading will be repetitive. Nothing like whale song."

As I started to climb in after her, I heard someone call my name. Turning, I saw Escabedo coming back our way.

"I almost forgot," the trooper said. "Captain Revas said to give you this." He handed me a small metal square. "It's the title card for Nomad. It's all yours now. We even fixed the engines."

"The Seaguard is done with it?"

"We learned what we needed. Drift has the same backup generator as Nomad. It's ancient, but if they got it to work, they have oxygen. Just no heat."

"Like on Nomad," I said, remembering all the bodies curled on the floor, wrapped in blankets.

He nodded. "That's how we figured out how we might locate Drift. When we got Nomad running, we noticed its backup generator had a low frequency hum. Too low to hear, but the equipment picked it up."

"And that's the noise that we're supposed to watch for on the screen," I guessed.

"Yep." He backed away from the moon pool. "The irony—here, we're hoping that the surfs on Drift got their generator to work. But if they did, that hum is so low, it's making them sick." With a wave, he headed toward the elevator.

"Okay," Gemma said. "Let's go."

I nodded, though my thoughts were suddenly racing along a different track. "Be right back."

I leapt onto the moon pool's rim. "Sick how?" I called after Escabedo.

He turned, though the elevator doors had opened.

"How does the hum make people sick?" I asked.

"It shakes up their insides without them knowing it," he said, now impatient.

"Including their eyes?"

"I don't know, kid. I've got to go." He stepped into the elevator.

When I turned to scramble down again, I found Gemma standing knee-deep in water on the submerged ledge.

"I know what you're thinking," she said. "That I feel sick in the ocean because I've been hearing noise from those generators."

"Sound travels farther and faster in water than it does in air," I said, wading over to her. "If you can hear things other people can't on the Topside, imagine what you're picking up subsea."

"What about the ghosts?" she asked. "How do you explain those?"

"If your eyeballs are resonating in their sockets, you'd see all sorts of things. Blurry things."

"So you want me to undo the hypnosis? Make myself see them again?" Her voice rose sharply. "What if you're wrong?"

I was asking a lot of her; I knew that.

"And even if you're right," she went on, "knowing that I'm sick from a sound won't make that feeling go away."

"If we find Drift in time and shut off the old generator, the feeling will go away."

She was close to tears. "And if that's not the cause? I'll undo it and never be able to go in the water again. I won't be able to live with your family. . . ." She paused and then shook her head as if she'd realized something obvious. "Of course I'll do it."

"You're sure?"

"I won't be able to live with *myself* if I don't try."

TWENTY-SEVEN

"Why do you think Fife is doing it?" Gemma asked as we sped through the ocean in a skimmer, heading for the south end of the trash gyre. "Anchoring townships?"

"Greed," I said. "He can't keep selling goods to the surfs at triple cost if they start buying from us."

"So he terrifies the surfs by making examples of the townships that go against him," she finished. "Nice."

And making examples of my parents to prevent future sales. I shook the thought away. I'd decide tomorrow whether to have hope or grieve. For now, finding Drift would be all I would concentrate on. I owed Hadal that much.

Outside the viewport, the blades of an old wind turbine slowly cartwheeled past. I figured I'd have to be more careful about plowing through trash in a skimmer. Fortunately, the head beams were powerful and the viewport automatically tinted for ultraviolet viewing, so I could see the debris in time to avoid it.

I studied the control panel. "Escabedo said our

monitor should pick up the signal from at least three miles away. But maybe you can sense it from even farther."

"Farther than sonar equipment?"

"Whales can hear low frequency sounds from one hundred miles away. *Feel* the sounds, really. Sonar equipment doesn't register feelings. But if you're really sensitive to infrasound, maybe you'll feel queasy even outside the signal range."

"Queasy. I should be so lucky." She smiled, though I could see that she was pale and shaky.

"I'll turn on the skimmer's autopilot so it holds its position. That way I can dive with you."

With a nod, she reached behind the bench for her helmet.

"Ready?" I asked.

She sealed her helmet, clearly set on toughing it out. "Ready."

I dropped out of the hatch first and treaded water until she emerged. She wore the expression of someone listening intently. I couldn't hear anything except the usual creaks of the derelicts piled up on the seafloor and the distant grunting of a male toadfish. Watching her, I began to feel queasy myself. Not from any vibrations, but remembering how bad it had been for her last time. And what if I was wrong? What if her terror didn't come from some old generator? She'd never dip a toe in the ocean again, and I'd only have myself to blame for asking her to undo the hypnosis.

She closed her eyes and treaded water for ten long minutes. When she opened her eyes again, she shook her head and pointed to the skimmer.

We pushed through the port in back and climbed over the bench. After she caught her breath she said, "I feel slightly sick but it could be just nerves."

"Let's go in farther. Closer to the gyre's center," I suggested.

We stopped again and pushed through the port. Again she floated with her eyes closed. This time she made a sour face. But back in the skimmer she said, "I don't think it's working."

"You didn't look happy out there."

"I'm not. And I do feel worse. But I don't think it's because of some vibration."

We continued to head toward the middle of the gyre. Next time we stopped, she popped out first. Just as I emerged from the skimmer, she waved me back in. "What?" I asked as soon as I cleared the Liquigen from my lungs.

"I don't feel as bad here. Let's go back to where we were."

"You could just be getting used to being in the water."

"Maybe," she acknowledged.

But when we were farther south again, she told me to stay inside the pod. "I'll hold on by the viewport."

Almost instantly, she gripped a handhold by the viewport and waved me east. Driving very slowly with her hanging on to the skimmer, I could judge from her expression that she was starting to feel bad. She motioned for me to stop and climbed back in.

"Let's go a couple miles east. Then I'll go out again."

The next time she popped out, she climbed back in less than a minute later. Pale and shaky, she nodded and waved me to keep heading east without even bothering to clear the Liquigen from her lungs. We kept at it mile by mile, and then she began directing me north—into the wide eye of the vortex.

"Stop here and I'll try again," she said. She pushed through the hatch. When she didn't appear beside the viewport, I assumed she would crawl back inside. But long seconds passed, and I panicked. I couldn't see her, and I had no idea whether she could hear me through her helmet's receiver. I fumbled to put the skimmer into autopilot, then sealed my borrowed helmet and sucked in Liquigen simultaneously.

I shoved through the back port and didn't see her anywhere near the skimmer. Sonar clicks weren't much help. There was so much debris around me, twirling slowly in place—I couldn't see past it. Frantic, I swam among the junk, looking for her. Hating myself for having sent her out here. And still I couldn't find her. Much of the wreckage had nooks and cavities, where dangerous sea creatures could lurk. Anything might have snatched her up.

I fought the crosscurrents to swim farther from the skimmer, leaving it behind in the darkness, wishing I could yell for her. Then something large and gray darted past, just on the edge of my vision. By the time I turned and sent clicks in that direction, there was nothing—it must have slipped past a piece of debris. My anger at myself and my terror for her were messing up my thinking. I couldn't stay oriented, wasn't sure which direction the surface lay. And with junk and pieces of vessels creaking around me, it was impossible to tell.

I focused on the swirling water currents, feeling for the powerful upwelling that kept all the wreckage afloat. It was easy enough to single out. Swimming against it was hard, yet I kicked deeper as I searched for Gemma among the debris.

But there was no sign of her. Not even when I sent my sonar as far and wide as possible. Had she curled into a ball again? At least with the upwelling, she wouldn't sink. But even so, there was a good chance that I'd never find her in this whirlpool of refuse. The thought made me feel so sick, *I* wanted to curl up and sink.

Another gray shape swam past on my left. I spun, but again, it was gone before I could tell what it was.

I shot a series of clicks into the darkness, but suddenly I knew — even before the echo bounced back — that there would be nothing there. And there wasn't. Because I was seeing Gemma's ghosts firsthand. Exactly as she had described them.

Knowing that I was experiencing a physical reaction to infrasound didn't make the overwhelming feeling of despair go away, though. Or ease my worries. If we were so close to Drift that *I* could pick up on the vibrations, how much worse must it be for Gemma?

Knowing her determination, I reasoned that she would have headed toward the source, not away. So I tried to still my racing thoughts and concentrate on my body. I moved to my left and felt no change. But when I pushed against the current to swim deeper, my skin prickled as if a thousand ghosts were whispering in my ears. I could almost hear their voices. Almost. I shook away that horrifying thought and clicked in every direction, focusing on the pictures in my mind.

And there she was.

Far below me, Gemma lay still on top of something massive. I flipped over and stroked downward as hard and fast as I could. Now I could see her with my eyes as my helmet lights penetrated the dark. Her body lay limp and oddly strewn across a mountain ridge of blue flexiglass.

She'd found Drift.

Concentrated beams of light blinked on and off inside the dome. Flashlights, I realized. The people inside had seen Gemma's helmet lights and were trying to signal back. But Gemma was incapable of responding. I touched down next to her and was alarmed to see that she'd vomited inside her helmet. All I could see behind the flexiglass were her eyes resonating under the lids—which meant she was alive.

Pressing her wrist screen, I turned off her crown lights so that only mine were visible through the dome. Then I began flicking my helmet lights on and off. I hoped the people inside knew Morse code. Twice I spelled out: *Will come back. Turn off generator.*

Then I swept Gemma up in my arms and kicked off. Swimming while holding her wasn't hard with the powerful current pushing us upward. At one point she rolled in my arms and then thrashed as if waking from a bad dream. I held on tighter, wishing more than ever I could talk with Liquigen in my lungs. But she blinked and focused on me and that was as good as words. She wrapped her arms around my waist and kicked with her fins. Together we made it back to the skimmer.

As soon as we were inside the pod, I zoomed for the surface. We broke through the waves, and I was momentarily surprised to see that it was still nighttime. It felt as if hours had passed.

Gemma slid back the viewport and jumped into the ocean to rinse out her hair while I got out the red and white signal buoy.

After flipping on its radio beacon, I dropped the buoy's long weighted chain into the water. "There's no wind tonight, so it should hold its position."

"I think they turned off the generator," Gemma said as she bobbed on the moonlit waves. "I don't feel anything."

"That's good. But I'm not getting any response from the Seaguard. They're too far away."

"Do you hear that?"

I smiled. "All I can hear are the waves. What are you hearing?"

She ducked under the water. When she popped up, she scrambled onto the bumper of the front pod and pointed past me. "A sub, coming toward us fast."

The words were just out of her mouth when I saw the speeding wake with no boat—meaning a sub was traveling just under the surface. And Gemma was right: It was headed directly at us.

"Dive!" I hollered.

We both hit the water swimming just as a sub broke the surface and rammed into the skimmer at full force, flipping it over with the front pod open.

TWENTY-EIGHT

As I paused to look back at the upside-down skimmer, Gemma surfaced next to me. A cloud covered the moon, making us nearly invisible as we treaded water on the dark ocean.

"There." I pointed at the sub that was now circling back. I'd only seen it once before, but would never forget it—the sickly green narwhal. "It's Fife's sub."

"He didn't come all this way for us," Gemma said.

I watched the sub circle the capsized skimmer. Probably looking for the driver. "He's here to sink Drift," I guessed.

"Why? They're close to death now."

"He must have heard that the Seaguard is searching the gyre."

The top hatch flipped open with a bang and a dark figure clambered onto the small circular deck amidships.

"Hide in the pod," I whispered to Gemma, and then added, "I'll be right behind you." Though first I was going to find a way to disable Fife's sub to keep him from sinking Drift.

She vanished without a splash.

Swimming closer, I eyed the spiraled point that looked as if it could drill through rock. At that moment, the moon appeared from behind the clouds and lit up the ocean.

The man on the deck spotted me in the waves just as I recognized him—Ratter. Of course, Fife would send his dog to do the dirty work.

His guffaws broke the silence. "Here to steal this salvage from me, too?" He put his booted foot on the circular railing and laid a harpoon gun across his thigh.

Drifting toward the skimmer, I saw Gemma inside the upside-down pod. Air was trapped inside, and she'd flipped back her helmet to give me a questioning look. "Don't you mean from Fife?" I yelled just to keep him talking while I assessed his sub. How was I going to damage it?

"Mayor Fife is busy getting himself arrested," Ratter said with a snort. "Broke down right off about selling stolen goods. Too bad he can't tell that Seaguard captain 'bout Drift, no matter how much she makes him cry."

"But Hadal said Fife was behind it."

"The stupid surfs will do anything if they think the order is coming from Fife—on account he might hold back their rations or something." Ratter smirked. "You think that showboat could come up with a *simple* way to make money? Not a chance."

"Simple?"

"Selling townships for salvage." Ratter waved at his sub with pride. "It's worked out real well for me."

Realization poured into me like molten metal. Killing hundreds of people at a time in order to lay claim to their township—no, that *wasn't* Fife's style. Cruel. Brutal. Senseless. It was pure Ratter. "Fife had to know what you were up to."

"Not a clue," Ratter bragged. "And he says I can't act."

Lack of oversight. The notion was so bitter in my brain, I could taste it. That was Fife's real crime—letting an evil thug do his dirty work unchecked. Fife could have found out easily enough that Ratter was issuing orders in his name—like the order to take Ma and Pa hostage. The memory of them being forced onto that very sub stabbed me with grief.

"Why did you have Hadal kidnap my parents?" I gripped the skimmer's bumper to keep from sinking since my limbs had grown too heavy to push through the water.

"Fife told me to bust up the deal." Ratter leaned back against the circular rail. "An' I figured snatching two settlers would save me having to bust up future deals. Didn't know it would bring the Seaguard down on Rip Tide." His eyes narrowed as if I were to blame.

"What did you do with them?" As much as I dreaded the answer, I *had* to know. "My parents—where are they?"

"How 'bout I give it to you straight, Dark Life?"

In the split second it took him to raise his gun, I splashed onto my back. A whoosh of air blew over my face as the harpoon whizzed past—one inch from my nose.

Ratter cursed loudly, which was followed by the double click of another harpoon being loaded. I dove and swam under the skimmer. Surfacing next to Gemma inside the pod, I flipped my helmet over my head, let the water spill out, and sealed it.

"Ty, he's coming!" She pointed past me at the green sub, which was now plowing backward. I could make out Ratter through the large viewport beneath the pointed drill.

"Dive!"

We dropped out of the pod and stroked deeper as fast as we could. I knew what was coming. Sure enough, the green sub switched to full speed ahead and rammed the front pod with its point, boring through the side.

The control panels in both pods were sealed—water wouldn't hurt them. But if the sub put a hole in both pods, the skimmer would sink. As it was, water poured into the first pod. Its weight would drag the back half down soon enough.

Ratter must have figured the same thing, because his sub dropped away from the skimmer and sped into the depths.

I gestured toward the surface, and we broke through the waves together. As soon as she caught her breath

Gemma said, "We have to stop him. He's going to sink Drift."

"Yeah," I said grimly. "But we have to save the skimmer first. Or we'll have no way to radio for help."

The front pod was nearly filled with water now and seconds from sinking. I entered the rear pod and flipped onto my back to study the upside-down control panel. As soon as I pressed the icon labeled 180, the back pod rolled over in the waves and sent me tumbling to the floor.

Gemma wiggled in while I righted myself and settled onto the pilot bench next to her. But before we could even exhale with relief, the weight of the flooded front pod dragged ours under. As the skimmer plummeted, we furiously searched for the button that would separate the two sections, finally flipping random switches until one of us smacked the right icon. With a hydraulic pop, the link between the pods snapped open. The front fell away, and we regained control over the rear.

We sped into the darkness, only to gasp simultaneously when the pod's head beams suddenly revealed Ratter's sub with its drill bit buried to the hilt in Drift. When the drill retracted, it left a gaping hole just above the township's bumper.

Fear clawed at the back of my throat. As soon as Drift filled with water, it would sink despite the upwelling, and everyone aboard would either drown or freeze.

"We have to cut the anchor chains," Gemma said, scanning the console. "Does this half of the skimmer have extendable clippers?"

"No." I watched Ratter's sub surge forward to drill yet another hole into the township. "It's got nothing that will stop him or free Drift."

"Then what can we do?" Panic sharpened her tone.

The only idea I had was a lousy one, but I'd try anything at this point. I climbed over the bench to the back port. "It's too late for Drift. Even if we cut the anchor chains, the township has taken on too much water. It won't float to the surface."

"So where are you going?"

"To trick Ratter into cutting a chain on one of the hatches so those people can escape."

"Escape to where? Ty, you don't even know if they can swim."

"Yeah, but trapped inside Drift with the ocean pouring in, they have no chance at all." I sealed my helmet. "While I'm out there, take the pod topside. See if you can reach anyone with a boat."

I didn't wait for her response, just filled my lungs with Liquigen and pushed through the port. As soon as I slipped into the water, Gemma tilted the pod upward and sped out of view.

I couldn't waste even one second on fear. I turned my crown lights on bright and swam down to Drift, fighting against the upwelling to reach one of the hatches. Ratter had looped a chain from the door's lever handle to a hand-grip, where a padlock held the chain tight. A metal cutter would do the job—not that I had one. But with luck, Ratter wouldn't be able to see that from the inside of his sub.

When the green sub circled Drift, I turned my back to it and made gestures, pretending to cut through the chain. At first I thought Ratter hadn't seen me, but then the sub flew backward like a retreating squid. I held my position, knowing the chances of this working were slim. More likely I'd get ground into tuna burger.

The green sub gunned for me, flying through the water with its drill bit churning. I didn't budge, even though every cell in my body was screaming, *"Move!"* I stayed in place until the last second, and then kicked up and out of the way.

The drill rammed the hatch, spewing metal as it dug in. I darted down, snatched the end of the chain, and tossed it onto the drill bit. Just as quickly, I got out of the way, swimming above the green sub for a good view of the action. As the spar rotated, the chain wound around the shaft until the links got caught in the base. The resulting clanks should have been enough of a warn-ing, but Ratter was either oblivious or, more likely, too stubborn to pay attention to the drill's ugly stutter.

Revving the sub's engine, he tried to drive the spar in farther. But he only ground the chain deeper into the drill's base until the links shattered and the chain fell away from the hatch.

I cheered silently, only to stop short when the drill gave out a metallic screech that fried my nerve endings. I peered down to see that the drill had stopped dead—its bit buried to the hilt in the hatch door. *Serves him right,* I thought, *since he bought the lethal contraption with blood money.*

Leaving Ratter grinding his gears, I swam around Drift and alighted on the bumper. Surfs crowded the window in front of me, gesturing desperately. In the glare from my crown lights, they looked blue lipped and colorless, bundled in blankets and wearing life vests. The boy on Nomad, frozen and silent, flashed through my mind.

I'd gotten a hatch unchained, but these people were already half frozen. How could they possibly muster the energy to swim to the surface? And that was assuming that they had Liquigen.

A dark-haired girl, not much older than me, moved to the front of the crowd. Even though she looked nothing like Hadal, the way the adults let her pass made me think she had to be his daughter. When she gestured to the floor, and I saw that the seawater had climbed past their knees, my guts twisted into a hard knot. If the township took on much more, it would drop like a rock into the depths. We were out of time.

Frantic, I pointed at the tube in the base of my helmet and then tapped my chest to indicate my lungs. She nodded and spoke to someone behind her. He passed her a Liquigen pack, which she held up. I gestured at the crowd around her to ask if there was enough for all. Again she nodded.

Suddenly the bumper tilted and the people inside tumbled past the window. Panic hummed in my ears as I swam downward, peering into each window, trying to find them again. They had to evacuate now. If Drift sank to the seafloor, even with Liquigen in their lungs they couldn't swim to the surface without diveskins to keep them warm. No one could.

Then I saw that it wasn't the climbing water that had caused Drift to roll to its side, but the added weight of Ratter's sub, which now hung off the township, bucking with his efforts to free the drill. If he wasn't careful, he was going to burn out the sub's engine. But Ratter was the least of my concerns. As I studied the situation, my doubts split off, multiplying like amoebas. Evacuating an entire township past a banging hatch with a lethally sharp drill bit poking through would be dangerous in the extreme. But at least the hatch was ideally situated — at the bottom of the township. There was no time to waste.

Catching hold of the now-vertical bumper, I climbed hand over hand until I faced the lowest window, where the girl waited for me. I pointed downward and mimed opening the door to the air lock, but none of the people inside understood what I was trying to say.

The girl turned and shouted at someone behind her. She held up a finger, telling me to wait. Did one of the surfs aboard know sign language? It was almost too much to hope for.

The group parted, allowing someone through. . . . Someone in a diveskin.

Pa!

I slammed against the viewport, forgetting for a second that it separated us. Pa shouted something over his shoulder, and the surfs backed away, letting Ma through. Like me, she threw herself at the window, and then settled for pressing her hands to it.

Despite their smiles, I realized that my parents were as blue lipped as the surfs and my joy at seeing them suddenly faltered. The situation was as dire as before. No, it was worse. The water inside Drift was higher than ever. We didn't have time for a reunion now, not if we wanted to have an actual one on the ocean's surface.

Signing to them rapid-fire, I warned them about Ratter's bucking sub, the drill bit, and the slamming hatch. Ma translated aloud for the surfs.

Pa decided that taking the hinges off the hatch from inside the air lock was the best option. Once Ma explained the plan to the girl, she had the others find him the tools he'd need.

"Ty," I heard Gemma say through my helmet's speaker. "Can you use this?"

Kicking away from Drift I shot my sonar into the dark water around me, searching for the pod. Before I could find it, I sensed something massive descending on me, twisting in the upwelling current. An old fishing net. I stroked out of the way, not wanting to get tangled up.

"I attached the top of the net to the skimmer," Gemma said through my helmet. "If any of the surfs can't swim, maybe they can use the net to climb up. Or, if they hang on, I could pull them to the surface."

Brilliant. I swam past the long net until I was caught in the skimmer's head beams. I shot her a quick thumbs-up and dove for Drift once more. Catching hold of the bottom, I dragged the net alongside the window to show the people inside. The girl made climbing gestures. When I nodded, she smiled faintly — as if I'd just given her a smidge of hope.

I swam down to where Ratter's sub hung beneath Drift. Just as I realized that the sub was suspiciously still, a harpoon tore through the water and missed me by a hair. I darted up again to take cover behind Drift. I scuttled farther along the rim, then peered over to see Ratter in an ill-fitting diveskin hovering outside the hatch, harpoon gun in hand, waiting for the surfs to show. A tether line attached him to his sub.

Beside me, Drift sank another foot. Without a weapon, how was I going to get Ratter away from the hatch so that my parents and the surfs could escape?

And then I knew. I did have a weapon. One that Representative Tupper had brought to my attention. Unease prickled my skin.

I'd promised myself I wouldn't try stunning a human with my Dark Gift, but what choice did I have? Too many people were depending on me to get them to the surface — to keep them from drowning.

The plan formed in my mind. I would stun Ratter just long enough to pry his harpoon gun from his immobilized fingers.

I swam along Drift until I was twenty feet from where Ratter last saw me. Once I left the cover of the township, he'd spot me quick enough and pull the trigger even quicker. I had to shoot first. Mustering my grit, I dropped past Drift, and with Ratter in sight, I blasted sonar more intensely than I'd ever shot before.

His body jerked as if he'd touched a stripped electric wire and then his hands sprang open. The harpoon gun rolled from his clutch and spiraled into the deep. Not knowing how long I had before he recovered, I kicked past Ratter, who seemed to be asleep, floating in place.

His face was slack, and behind the flexiglass of his helmet his lips were parted.

I caught the end of the net and swam for the hatch when suddenly, the sub's head beams went out. Probably Ratter had burned out the engine with his antics. The surroundings went dark, since there were no lights working on Drift except for the flashlights. Not that I was afraid. Between my helmet's crown lights and my Dark Gift, I could see just fine. The surfs were another story.

Without warning, the hatch dropped away, still impaled on the sub's drill. My helmet lights caught the metallic shimmer of Pa's diveskin inside the air lock. He'd managed to remove the last hinge. I looked back to see the sub slowly sinking—too heavy for the upwelling to keep afloat without an engine doing the majority of the work. Pa swam out of the hatch, signing for me to bring the net closer. It was only after I'd handed Pa one edge of the net and took up a position on the other corner that I remembered Ratter. In a sudden panic I shot clicks downward, into the depths where the green sub had fallen away.

When the echoes came back to me, I saw Ratter in my mind's eye. No longer stunned, his arms and legs were thrashing as he flew backward through the water. He was still attached to the sub by a tether line. But the weight of the sub was hauling him down so fast, he needed to react now—unfasten his dive belt and free himself.

But he didn't. Maybe his brain was still too dazed. Or maybe it had never worked well in high-pressure situations. And now that the surfs were evacuating Drift one after another, climbing up the fishing net, I needed to keep a tight grip on my corner. If the net whipped up in the current, someone could lose their hold. At this point, there was nothing I could do for Ratter even if I was of a mind to.

Despite the circumstances, the surfs stayed amazingly calm. Those that could swim hovered near the net, helping the climbers along.

Unable to stop myself, I sought out Ratter again with sonar. A mistake. Watching him trail after his sub as it crashed into the mountain of scrap below—it was awful. And it didn't end there. His sub kept going, sliding down the wreckage until it was teetering precariously atop a large derelict.

All Ratter had to do was unclip his dive belt and he'd be free. But no, he continued to flail at the end of the tether line, futilely trying to swim away even when the sub tipped off the derelict. Rolling as it fell, Ratter's prize submarine reeled him in, until finally he was crushed beneath its bulk. Poetic justice, maybe, but still horrifying to witness.

TWENTY-NINE

It was as if Drift had been waiting for all of its occupants to escape safely, because as soon as the last person dropped out of the hatch, the township sank into the depths.

Pa had headed for the surface some time ago, taking up two children, so I was alone when Drift crashed onto the mountain of derelict vessels. Not that Pa or anyone else could have seen what was happening in the darkness far below. Only I knew that the enormous township had settled squarely on top of Ratter's sub. Probably smashed the ill-gotten vehicle flat. In a grim sort of way, it seemed a fitting spot for Drift's final resting place.

Turning my attention upward, I let go of the fishing net and swam for the surface. An acre's worth of legs dangled above me — not treading water — just swaying in the current like tendrils of seaweed. An unsettling image for sure; they were so vulnerable.

The ocean's surface seemed strangely calm, considering that hundreds of people surrounded me. But they were all too weak to do more than bob in their life vests.

It took me a moment to locate Gemma among them. She was by the pod, hanging on to the bumper. But the two people tucked inside were old and frail — not my parents.

As I swam closer, Gemma said, "They're over there," anticipating my question. "They're trying to amplify the buoy's signal."

I spotted the crown lights of their helmets — the only illumination other than the moon. The cracked-open buoy floated between them. If anyone could amp up the buoy's signal, Pa could.

"Amp up." The phrase made me think of Ratter and how I'd amped up my Dark Gift. My heart fluttered in my chest, and suddenly I understood how Zoe felt about her ability to seriously hurt someone.

Suddenly it struck me as odd that only Gemma and I were clinging on to the pod. I asked her why. "Did Pa tell them not to?"

Gemma pressed the flexiglass bubble of her helmet against mine so that she could speak softly. "Ria ordered them to keep their distance. She didn't want the pod to sink under the extra weight. Not after we helped them escape."

"Ria?"

She nodded toward a girl a ways off, floating in a life vest that rode up on her shoulders.

"Your father had to talk her into letting them" — she tipped her head toward the two old surfs — "sit in the pod. Ria thought your parents should."

Though I could only see the girl in profile as she spoke to a clump of despondent-looking surfs, I knew she was the one I'd communicated with through Drift's window.

"Hadal's daughter?" I asked.

Gemma nodded.

"Did you tell her what happened to him?"

"She's been swimming around, trying to keep everyone's spirits up. It didn't feel like the right time to mention it." Irony might have tinged Gemma's words, but her expression was dead serious.

"Good call."

"Ty!" I heard my mother say, and closed my eyes to savor the sound. I'd never completely believed that they were gone. And yet, relief rushed through me now.

Hearing a splash, I turned to see them both cutting toward me. Together they swept me into a hug and then beckoned Gemma into the fold. She hesitated only a second and then threw her arms around all of us — at least, she tried to.

"Are you okay?" Ma asked, pressing a hand to my helmet as if she could stroke my cheek through the flexiglass.

"Me? I'm fine. You were the ones taken captive."

"The moment the sub met up with Drift, we were hustled aboard," Pa said. "The surfs didn't have any more choice than we did when Mayor Fife's man threatened to kill their sachem."

As we treaded water, the three of them filled me in on how Gemma had finally been able to reach Captain Revas's troopers on the other side of the gyre and that it would take them at least an hour to arrive. We looked at the people around us — so many of them shuddering. Even though the night was warm, the ocean was well below body temperature.

"And there's still nothing else in the area?" Pa asked. His voice was little more than a croak. "No trawler, no floaters? Someone has to hear that signal."

"I've tried every frequency on the pod's control panel," Gemma said. "There's no one out here."

"There's a flare gun in the toolbox behind the bench," I said as my sense of desperation grew. "Maybe if we —"

The radio inside the pod crackled to life and a man's voice said, "We've locked onto your signal. Tell the surfs to hold on, we're almost there."

Shocked, we exchanged looks.

"Who was that?" I asked.

Ma swung into the pod with an "Excuse me" to the elderly surfs on the pilot bench. She bent over the console.

"Can't be the troopers to the north." Straightening, she pointed west. "It came from over —" Her words ended in a gasp as in the distance, a small submarine zoomed out of the ocean. Then another sub surfaced beside it. Then more burst through the waves, all shining in the moonlight.

Within the span of a minute, a fleet of submarines had emerged — not a tight formation of Seaguard skimmers, but vehicles of many shapes and sizes, plowing through the water toward us. There were big cruisers like my family's, but more telling were the reapers, swathers, and combines — vessels that only subsea farmers owned. Lars had hoped to rouse a few settlers to join the search, but from what I could see, all of Benthic Territory had come to help.

The sounds of the approaching subs jolted the surfs out of their stupor and a shout of joy went up, growing louder as the vessels neared. But the cheer stopped short when the subs drew to a halt before reaching us.

I flipped back my helmet. "It's safer for us to swim to them," I shouted as best I could.

With numb limbs and teeth chattering, the surfs splashed forward — some actually swimming, others barely able to flutter-kick.

A hatch popped on the big cruiser in the front and a figure in a diveskin scrambled out. Lars. More hatches opened and I watched as my neighbors poured out of their subs and took up positions on running boards and bumpers with their hands outstretched to the surfs. Many plunged into the water to assist those who needed it. Gemma and I swam into the splashing throng to offer our help as well.

When the last surf was pulled from the ocean's icy grip, Gemma dog-paddled toward me, looking as done in as I felt — as if she couldn't lift her arm for even one more stroke.

After I tried and failed to hoist myself onto the bumper of the cruiser, Lars hauled me aboard and then did the same for Gemma.

Ria knelt on the bumper to my right. With her wet hair plastered to her cheeks, she peered into the waves as if she could see through them.

"Are you okay?" I asked, hunkering down next to her.

She looked up, her expression bleak. "Can we raise her?" she asked. "Tow her to the surface?"

"Her? You mean Drift?"

Ria nodded.

"Not a chance."

Gemma scooted behind me, popping me on the back of the head as she passed. I realized I shouldn't have put it so bluntly. Kneeling on Ria's other side, Gemma said, "Ty means the settlers can't do it. But surely there's another way," she added, directing the question to me.

"Nothing easy. Drift's filled with water at this point," I explained. "It'd take a rig the size of an ocean liner to hoist up that kind of weight."

Ria's composure crumbled. "What do I tell them?" She gestured at the departing subs — all heading back to the Trade Station. "There's no way to reclaim our home? Our fishing tools? That we have nothing?"

Gemma's eyes met mine and she gave me a silent nod in answer to the unspoken question between us.

"Actually," I told Ria. "You have Nomad." I pulled the metal square from the sealed pouch on my dive belt and held it out.

Confused, she didn't take it.

"The Seaguard fixed it up. The engines, everything," Gemma said.

Still, Ria didn't take the title card. "There were no survivors?"

I shook my head. "Gemma and I found it, so it's ours to give away."

"That means it's your salvage," she protested. "Yours to sell. Why would you give it to surfs?"

"You're our neighbors. And in Benthic Territory, when something terrible happens to a neighbor, we help out — doing what we can, giving all we can spare." I pressed the title card into her palm. "I wouldn't live any other way."

EPILOGUE

Torches circled the patch of high ground — the only part of the surfs' community garden that wasn't flooded. There, settlers and surfs worked together, dragging away chairs and tables to create an open dance area. Gemma and I took that as our cue to head for the water, even though I appreciated Ria having invited us in thanks for saving them — and for modifying the ordinance. Now the townships could fish anywhere on the continental shelf except inside the Benthic Territory boundaries.

I paused halfway across the torch-lit area to watch Lars and Raj clink tankards with several surfs and felt a rush of pride for all my neighbors. They'd come tonight bearing gifts of sea greens and had gamely eaten the surfs' halibut head stew. Although only Zoe had tried a seal eyeball.

When the music started up, Gemma touched my arm. "Looks like I won't be getting any more marriage proposals."

I followed her gaze and saw Jibby joining a circle dance even though he clearly didn't know the steps. But then, neither did his partner, Captain Revas, who had let her hair down for the evening and was laughing as the two of them tried to keep up with the other dancers. "Probably not," I agreed. "At dinner, she told him he could call her Selene."

Before anyone could wrangle us into dancing, we headed for the shadows on the far side. "You're sure you still want to?" I asked when we reached the water's edge.

At her nod, I climbed a ladder that took us into the skeletal remains of a building. Without hesitating, Gemma followed me onto a girder and out over the waves, where we sat, legs dangling. From this high up, I could make out Nomad floating at the garden's entrance.

"It's hard to believe these were ever buildings." Gemma's voice was tinged with awe.

I nodded, impressed as well. Each township had made the most of their assigned spot. Fruit-bearing plants climbed cable trellises throughout the ruins; stacked rain gutters held lettuce and carrots; and hundreds of glass bottles swung overhead, tinkling in the breeze — all part of the surfs' vast hydroponic garden.

When Ria had taken us on a tour, even Ma was amazed at all the ways the surfs had found to grow crops without soil. But even with such a bounty, Ria explained that their small section didn't provide enough to feed the whole township every month, which was true for all the townships. She wanted to keep the deal that

Hadal had struck with Pa — to buy our crops on an ongoing basis. And now that my neighbors had gotten to know these surfs, hopefully they'd consider selling their produce to other townships.

"Ready?" I asked Gemma.

"In a minute," she said, still gazing up at the bottles. "Who knew trash could be so beautiful?"

"And useful," I added, noting that the vines growing out of the bottles were heavy with tomatoes. The surfs were resourceful, no question. And inventive. They were surviving despite the odds and the hardships. I grinned, suddenly appreciating the irony.

"What?" Gemma asked.

"When I see garbage in the ocean, it makes me sad."

"Most people feel that way."

"Exactly. We see the *problem*. The surfs see possibilities. Know what that makes them?"

She shook her head.

"Pioneers."

Smiling, she nudged my foot with hers. "Now I'm ready."

I leaned in for a kiss, soft and swift. Then we flipped our helmets into place, took hands, and dropped from the girder into the moonlit waves below.